P9-CDU-160

Praise for *The Butterfly Sister*

"Heartfelt, suspenseful, and very, very satisfying!"
—Nancy Woodruff

THE BUTTERFLY SISTER

Amy Gail Hansen

WILLIAM MORROW

An Imprint of HarperCollinsPublishers

This book is a work of fiction. The characters, incidents, and dialogue are drawn from the author's imagination and are not to be construed as real. Any resemblance to actual events or persons, living or dead, is entirely coincidental.

P.S.™ is a trademark of HarperCollins Publishers.

THE BUTTERFLY SISTER. Copyright © 2013 by Amy Gail Hansen. All rights reserved. Printed in the United States of America. No part of this book may be used or reproduced in any manner whatsoever without written permission except in the case of brief quotations embodied in critical articles and reviews. For information address HarperCollins Publishers, 10 East 53rd Street, New York, NY 10022.

HarperCollins books may be purchased for educational, business, or sales promotional use. For information please write: Special Markets Department, HarperCollins Publishers, 10 East 53rd Street, New York, NY 10022.

FIRST EDITION

Designed by Diahann Sturge

Library of Congress Cataloging-in-Publication Data has been applied for.

ISBN 978-0-06-223462-9

13 14 15 16 17   OV/RRD   10 9 8 7 6 5 4 3 2 1

To my mother, Gail, for believing

Acknowledgments

First and foremost, I thank my mother, Gail Angell, for giving me the most valuable gift a parent can bestow on a child: confidence. Mom, you told me I could be anything I wanted to be, and you were right! You read countless drafts, answered a million questions, and listened to me vent and ponder and hope and dream. Most important, you resuscitated this book and restored my enthusiasm for it time and time again. I sincerely could not have done this without you, Mom! There is so much of you in this book; it's only fitting that your name (my middle name) is on the cover. I share this success with you!

I also thank my beautiful children, Andrew, Luke, and Amelia, for giving me a reason to be the best person I can be. I followed my dreams because I want you to do the same one day.

I am forever appreciative of my husband, Neil, for respecting my need to create and for putting up with my flair for drama, both on and off the page. Neil, you've been living with these characters our entire marriage! You believed in me, listened to me, and cheered me on every step of the way. I love you!

This book would not have made it into readers' hands without the keen eye of my amazing literary agent, Elisabeth Weed of Weed Literary, who made my New Year's resolution come true. Elisabeth, through our revision process, I felt like you truly absorbed this story and its characters, which surpassed my expectations. You go above and beyond the call of duty, and I am so happy to be working with you. I also thank Stephanie Sun for doing all the little things that made a big difference.

Another thank-you goes out to my foreign rights agent, Jenny Meyer of the Jenny Meyer Literary Agency, for selling Italian rights to Garzanti Libri in record time. You rock!

I am so grateful for my esteemed editor, Carrie Feron, at William Morrow/HarperCollins. Carrie, thank you for not letting my vivid imagination get the best of this story! You seem to know just when to let me go and when to rein me in, and your insightful suggestions brought this novel to its utmost potential. I also thank the hardworking team at HarperCollins, especially Nicole Fischer, Julia Meltzer, Mumtaz Mustafa, Shelly Perron, Diahann Sturge, and Tessa Woodward.

For believing in me with her perpetual you-can-do-it attitude and for reading an early draft, I thank my sister, Lisa Bauer. For her unique reader insights and constant encouragement, I thank my aunt, Jillian Schneider, who also made the act of writing on that basement typewriter look so cool. Thank you to my father, George Bauer, for bringing New Orleans into my life. For being an enthusiastic first publisher of sorts, I thank Mike Angell. I also thank my in-laws, Rick and Shahnaz Hansen, for proudly telling everyone they know.

For many late nights, literary discussions, and essential inspiration, I thank Heather Temple. Thanks to my forever friends and book club gals, Heather Arnold and Jill Tsuji, for reading this book twice and rooting for my success. For providing truly constructive feedback and heartfelt encouragement, I thank Melissa Citarelli, Lisa Damian Kidder, and Liz Hum.

For reading excerpts of this book and providing much needed camaraderie, I thank the members of the Algonquin Area Writer's Group and the Barrington Writers Workshop, especially Claire Beck, Toni Diol, Lisa Guidarini, Bev Ottaviano, and Shaku Rajagopal.

For helping me build my freelance writing career and for putting me in contact with some truly renowned authors, I thank my editors at Pioneer Press: Dorothy Andries, Michael Bonesteel, Andrea Brown, Robert Loerzel, Mike Martinez, and Jenny Thomas. A huge thank-you also goes out to Nancy Swanson, editorial assistant extraordinaire, for always being there.

I acknowledge the truly dedicated teachers who honed my writing skills, fostered my passion for literature, or otherwise inspired me: Sue Aavang, Sharon Barger, Tony Casalino, Sam Chell, Michael Craft, Caryl Dierksen, Annette Duncan, Travis DuPriest, Mary Kennelly, Micheline Lessard, Cris Mazza, and Pamela Smiley.

Thank you to the faculty and staff at Carthage College, for gifting me with four fabulous years of education. I am forever indebted.

I owe much to the brilliant women writers who paved the way before me and whose lives and works inspired aspects of this book: Charlotte Perkins Gilman, Sylvia Plath, Anne Sexton,

Sara Teasdale, and Virginia Woolf. I also note the books I referenced in understanding these women and reimagining them on the page: *Anne Sexton: A Biography* by Diane Middlebrook; *The Bell Jar*, Perennial Classics Edition, HarperCollins, foreword by Frances McCullough and biographical note by Lois Ames; *Charlotte Perkins Gilman: The Woman and Her Work*, edited by Sheryl L. Meyering; *The Norton Anthology of American Literature, Shorter Fourth Edition*, edited by Nina Baym; *The Norton Anthology of English Literature, Sixth Edition, Volume 2*, edited by M. H. Abrams; *Sara Teasdale: Woman & Poet* by William Drake; and *Virginia Woolf: An Inner Life* by Julia Briggs.

I also thank the following authors I interviewed for inspiring me and genuinely encouraging my writing goals: Elizabeth Berg, Jane Hamilton, Wally Lamb, Elizabeth Strout, and Nancy Woodruff. For sharing his insights on the Hero's Journey and critiquing my agent query letter, I also thank author Jay Bonansinga.

On the subject of fellow authors, I absolutely must thank Therese Walsh, whose novel *The Last Will of Moira Leahy*, prompted me to query Elisabeth Weed. Therese, the *for writers* section of your Web site educated, uplifted, and inspired me countless times while I was writing and revising this book.

For answering questions related to police work, I thank Detective Jay Tapia of the Waukegan Police Department.

I thank Liz Zona for borrowing my suitcase and leaving her luggage tag behind.

And last but never least, I thank my brother, the late Brian Bauer, for teaching me that life is too short not to follow your dreams.

What's past is prologue.

William Shakespeare, *The Tempest*

Chapter 1

Gwen could not have been more explicit at our first session: I was to cease reading books by or about women who killed themselves.

An unhealthy obsession, that's what my therapist called it, and I was inclined to agree with Gwen's diagnosis. There was, after all, no other logical explanation for the string of events that brought me to her office. Ghosts do not exist. I hadn't done mushrooms. No brain tumor. I resigned myself to the fact that what I'd seen and done was a consequence of a compromised mental state.

Like other women writers before me, I had simply gone mad.

I left Gwen's office that late December afternoon with a new-found interest in my bedroom bookcase. *A Room of One's Own* by Virginia Woolf went first, then *The Bell Jar* by Sylvia Plath, followed by Charlotte Perkins Gilman's *The Yellow Wallpaper* and Kate Chopin's *The Awakening*. Hemingway took a beating too. In fact, any title remotely relating to mental imbalance found its way into the donation box, even those seemingly innocuous stories like *Jane Eyre*.

Could I afford to leave the madwoman in the attic lurking on my bookshelf?

But it was all in vain—the books, the antidepressants, the therapy sessions with Gwen. Even time's wound-healing properties proved ineffective. Ten months later, my past was never more than one thought, one breath, one heartbeat away.

And then, on that particular October evening, it literally arrived at my doorstep.

Mom found me on the front porch swing that night, swaying with the initiative of a pendulum. Assessing my state of mind in a single glance from the driveway, she soon approached me, teacup in hand.

"How many today, Ruby?" she asked, handing me the mug.

I let the steam, the fruity tang of Earl Grey, tingle my nose. Bergamot, of course. A natural antidepressant.

"Twelve, but nothing tragic," I said. "Well, except for that sweetheart of a librarian Mrs. Talbot, the one who special ordered my books last summer?"

"She died? The one you said smelled like marshmallows?" Mom sat beside me. She was still wearing her nurse's scrubs, navy blue with periwinkle trim. "Do you want to talk about it?"

"She was eighty-nine years old." I shrugged. "I think it really was her time."

We sat silent for a beat, less the squeaking of the swing, while Mom churned her hands like a paddle through butter. I hoped she was just cold—still adjusting to Illinois's chilly autumn evenings—and not worried.

"I called in an order to Wu's," she finally said.

"You didn't have to."

"I wanted to."

Not cold, I thought. *Worried.* "But I'm fine. Really."

She shrugged. "Maybe I'm too tired to cook."

I wasn't convinced. Annette Rousseau, my New Orleans–born mother, had absorbed the Creole recipes for gumbo and shrimp étouffée in utero; they had crossed the placenta line along with the oxygen. She was proof that you can take the girl out of New Orleans, but you can't take the New Orleans out of the girl. Moving to the Midwest hadn't changed the fact that she could make a roux the color of caramel, even at 3:00 A.M., even after a double shift at the hospital. And yet she'd ordered Mongolian beef and crab rangoon from Wu's on Seventh Street—my comfort food.

"You know, the hospital gift shop is hiring," she went on. "A floral assistant. You like flowers."

"But I love my job." It came out too emphatic, too defensive.

Mom raised an eyebrow, an arc so perfectly curved, so accusatory. We locked eyes, each of us trying to read the other's thoughts. Looking at my mother was like looking at a computer-generated police sketch, an age-progressed version

of myself. Our hair was not red, but auburn—a color reminiscent of autumn, football games, and hayrides. Where my curls
held tight, though, hers hung loosely. Over time, her eyes had
turned more of a hunter green than emerald.

"I'm worried about you, Ruby," she said. "When do you see
Gwen again?"

I smiled at her rhyme, then let the grin fade. There was no
joking when it came to my therapy sessions with Gwen.

"This week," I told her, trying to look serious but not sad.
"On Thursday."

"Well, she's the professional. See what she says."

"About?"

"About whether this obituary job is right for you." She patted
my knee. "All things considered."

I nodded, as if to say I would do just that. Truth was, I'd let
the opportunity to tell Gwen about my new job pass two times
already. Writing for a local newspaper had been Gwen's brain-
child. I needed to put my "skill set" back to use, she'd stressed.
So I applied for the obit gig, the port of entry for budding journalists and the only position open at the *Cook County Chronicle*.
My official title, obituary coordinator, meant that while journalists composed witty leads before deadline, I typed information into a template, modified errors in Associated Press style,
and occasionally changed the euphemism *passed away* to *died*.

Perhaps Gwen would have applauded the fact that I got hired,
but I feared she would psychoanalyze my choice. Was I punish-
ing myself? Was writing about dead people some sort of self-
imposed penance for my past sins, like one of the rings of Hell
in *Dante's Inferno*?

I didn't want to answer that question.

Fortunately, Mom dropped the subject. And while I finished my tea we chatted about less pressing matters—like the new Toulouse-Lautrec exhibit opening at Chicago's Art Institute—until a white van rounded the street corner not fifteen minutes later.

"That's got to be a new record," Mom said, rushing inside to get cash.

I approached the van, expecting to see Mr. Wu's son—a seventeen-year-old with a toothy grin and the work ethic of someone who'd survived the Depression. I expected an olfactory delight, the unmistakable smell of grease and soy sauce when he opened the door. Instead, a woman in a khaki uniform stepped out; her ponytail, the color of a cardboard box, slipped through the back hole of an equally brown cap that shadowed her eyes. In lieu of slacks, she had feminized her look with culottes.

"You Ruby Rousseau?" Her accent—Boston or Brooklyn—made my name sound foreign to my own ears.

Before I could answer, she slid open the van door and lifted a suitcase from inside. "Betcha glad to see me. Or rather, *this*," she said, before setting the luggage before me with a thump, like a cat bringing its owner a dead mouse.

I rested my eyes on paisley print, swirls of red and gold and blue. I choked on the crisp fall air, my own saliva. "That's not mine."

"Your name's awnit."

I crouched beside the suitcase then and stroked the fabric, rigid like a heavily starched shirt. As if reading Braille, I ran a fingertip over the American Tourister emblem. And then I reached for the luggage tag and stared at my name and address in curvy script.

I soon felt my mother's breath on my cheek. She was crouched beside me, thirty bucks in hand. Our eyes locked once more.

"But it's your handwriting," she whispered.

I let the tag fall and stood, even stepped back, as if to disown the suitcase through mere distance. "This is a mistake. I borrowed this suitcase from a friend in college last year. She must have forgotten to take my tag off."

"What's ya friend's name?"

"Beth. Elizabeth, rather. Elizabeth Richards."

"She lives round here? In the Chicago suburbs?"

"Wisconsin," I corrected. "At least, she did."

The woman told us to wait while she made a call from her van.

My mother made a *tsk* sound then, as if she'd been trying to solve a puzzle only to discover the answer blatantly simple. "This is the suitcase you were supposed to take on our trip to Paris," she said. "The one I returned to that girl in your dorm."

I nodded but kept my eyes on the van.

"Okay, here's the deal," the delivery woman finally said. "Ya friend—this Elizabeth Richards—it seems she hasn't filed a lost luggage claim yet. Now, I can take the bag back, but it's gonna sit in storage 'til she claims it." She lowered her voice. "Look, between you and me, it's gonna get back to her a heck of a lot faster and without a whole lotta red tape if you'd just, you know, contact her directly."

"Me? But isn't she tied to the bag somehow?" I tried to remember how it all worked. Mom and I never flew to Paris after all, but I was certain the sticky tag, the one the attendant puts through the bag handle, displayed the owner's name and flight information.

"If all goes right, yeah. But that tag's destroyed." The woman lifted the mangled piece of black-and-white paper hanging from the suitcase. "The bar code's unreadable. Probably got caught in one of the machines and missed the flight. Seen it happen a dozen times. Airline figured it was their fault, so they sent it to the person on the personal tag. And that's *you*." She cleared her throat. "Didn't the airline call?"

I looked to my mother. She said no.

"Your dad probably took the message and forgot to tell you," the woman prompted. "My hubby does it all the time."

I shook my head no. My father died almost two years prior.

"Look, it's not my bag," I argued, avoiding my mother's gaze, evading any pain that might have flashed through them at the mention of Dad. "So it's not my problem."

Mom curled her fingers over my shoulder then. "Call the girl, Ruby," she said. "You'd want someone to do the same for you."

It was a valid point, but I knew Mom was picking up where Gwen had left off. If I called Beth Richards, I'd be forced to reconnect with someone from Tarble, a private women's college in Kenosha just over the Illinois-Wisconsin state border. I'd dropped out of Tarble my senior year, one semester short of graduation.

"But I don't have her phone number," I spat back. "We didn't stay in touch."

"You could call the college," Mom suggested. "The alumnae office, perhaps."

"I didn't graduate."

"Who cares?" She waved her hand through the air, as if batting a fly. "If you ever went to a school, you're an alumnus."

The delivery woman impatiently tapped her clipboard with a pen, as if keeping time.

"People sometimes keep important information *inside* their suitcase," she said. "Maybe there's anotha tag somewhere. You can look. I can't. I just deliver. And speakin' of deliveries, I gotta get goin.' What do ya want me to do?"

Mom seized the suitcase handle. "We'll take care of it," she announced, and I forced a scribble on the clipboard.

When the delivery woman began to drive away, though, I stopped her. The van lurched when she hit the brakes.

"What if I can't find her?" I shouted through the window glass.

The window came down, and she handed me a business card. "Just call," she said.

And then I watched the van disappear into the setting sun.

Mom pulled the suitcase into the house then. "You're sure you don't have Beth's phone number?" she asked, as if she'd done nothing wrong, as if we'd been in on the whole thing together.

"We weren't exactly friends," I explained. "More like acquaintances."

My relationship with Beth Richards had been one of supply and demand. I'd needed a larger suitcase for a trip to Paris with my mom. And Beth, who lived three doors down from me in North Hall, had offered her bag. I recalled Beth Richards then, her golden hair and almost six-foot stature.

"The alumnae office would be happy to help you," Mom offered again.

"You know I can't call there."

"You have no reason to hide."

"It's Sunday night," I noted. "The alumnae office won't open until tomorrow morning."

"Couldn't you call Heidi?"

Heidi Callahan was my former roommate at Tarble and subsequently, former best friend. We'd met at freshman orientation. Over weak coffee and Maurice Lenell cookies, we discovered a mutual passion for hazelnut creamer. One morning of talking turned into a friendship, and by the next semester, we were roommates. Boyfriends came and boyfriends went, but most weekends, it was always the two of us watching romantic comedies, eating pepperoni and green pepper pizza, sipping cheap boxed wine out of plastic tumblers. But all of that changed senior year. She moved out at the end of first semester, and I hadn't talked to her since.

"Can't we just look inside?" I begged.

We handled Beth's things gingerly, spreading them on the foyer floor like jigsaw puzzle pieces, so we'd be able to put everything back the way we'd found it. It all added up to the inside of a woman's suitcase. A pair of Gap jeans. A gray hooded zip-up sweatshirt. Socks and underwear. A cosmetic case full of Redken, MAC, and Colgate. A travel sewing kit. None of it told me how to find Beth Richards.

And then Mom discovered a thin book in the folds of a T-shirt and held it out at arm's length, like she does when she isn't wearing her reading glasses. I read the title then, small black letters on a white binding. Trying to control a visceral reaction, I barely made out the words.

"Virginia Woolf," I said. "*A Room of One's Own.*"

"Isn't that the book? The one you wrote your senior thesis on?"

I nodded and paused to recall Woolf's lengthy essay, based on lectures she'd given at two women's colleges. In the book, the modernist writer asserts "a woman must have money and a room of her own if she is to write fiction."

Mom handed me the book without sensing consequence, like handing a bottle of Nyquil to a recovering alcoholic. Per Gwen's instructions back in December, I'd donated my own copy. And yet, somehow, temptation had found its way back to me.

Like failing at a game of hot potato, I dropped the book, let it fall to the ceramic floor with a plop. A postcard stuck out from the pages then and I pulled it, instantly recognizing the blue expanse of water, ornate streetlights, mounds of yellow and orange mums, and the name *Tarble* etched in stone. It was a postcard announcing Tarble's Reunion—the women's college equivalent of Homecoming—set to take place the following weekend.

Mom retrieved the book from the floor and opened it. "You're in luck," she said, attempting to hand it to me once more. "She wrote something inside."

I looked down then to see Beth's name neatly printed in blue ink at the top of the inside flap, and below that, a phone number with a recognizable area code for southern Wisconsin.

"With all the sickos out there, that's a dangerous thing to do," Mom said. "It must mean an awful lot to her."

It means a lot to me, I thought.

Mom suggested I wait until after dinner to make the call, but I knew the sooner I called, the sooner the suitcase—and the book and the temptation to read it—would leave my hands. So I took the cordless phone to the porch swing. I'd left my empty tea mug there, and I held it as I listened to the rings, running my finger along the inside groove of the handle. Finally, a woman answered; a paper-thin voice prickled my skin.

"This is Ruby Rousseau," I said. "I'm trying to reach Beth Richards."

I endured an awkward silence. All I heard was breathing. "Hello?" I tried again.

"I'm Beth's mother," the woman said.

"Oh. Good. Look, I went to Tarble College with Beth, and I actually have her suitcase. They just delivered it to me by mistake. Is she back from her trip?"

A gasp. "This is a miracle."

"Yes, very strange. For some reason, she left my name on the tag."

I heard the woman begin to cry, what sounded like a weeping elation, tears of sadness mixed with joy. "I've been praying for this. For something. Anything. A sign. She's going to come back to me."

"Back? Back from *where*?"

"Beth has been . . ." The woman started but stopped. She got the rest out in fragments:

"Missing. Since. Friday."

The mug slipped from my hand then and shattered on the floorboards at my feet, the remaining drops of tea seeping into the porch cracks. "Mrs. Richards, I'm so sorry. I had no idea. I mean, Beth and I weren't close. I mean, we just kind of knew each other," I rambled. I wanted to pick up the mess, wanted to say something more appropriate but couldn't formulate words.

"The police say they have no leads," Mrs. Richards continued, as if she hadn't heard me. "They said 'Hope for the best and prepare for the worst.'"

Prepare for the worst. Beth Richards was missing but hopefully not dead, hopefully not like the hundreds of people I'd written about at the *Chronicle.* I told Mrs. Richards I was sorry once more.

"No, Ruby, don't you see? They were wrong. Because this is a lead. This could be how we end up finding her."

I recalled the mundane items Mom and I sorted in Beth's suitcase. There was nothing there to suggest Beth's whereabouts or foul play. But I wasn't about to trounce on a distraught mother's hopes.

"Tell me where you live," Mrs. Richards asserted. "I'll come right now to get it."

I asked Mrs. Richards exactly where she lived, then told her it was a two-hour drive to Oak Park from Milwaukee, but she said she didn't care. She'd drive to Canada if she had to. I fumbled in my pocket then for the business card the delivery woman had given me.

"It's better, don't you think, if you just stayed home?" My words came out like hers had, in bits and pieces, interrupted by thoughts and breaths. I felt guilty for not offering to bring the suitcase myself, for allowing Beth's mother to drive at night in her condition. "Let the delivery service bring it to you. That's their job."

"But I have to *do something,* Ruby. I can't just sit around waiting for a phone call, waiting for the police. Waiting for Beth to walk through the door. I have to get my daughter back."

"I know. I know," I said, though I didn't know at all. I could only imagine, and the guilt tripled. "But what if the police call while you're gone? What if Beth does come walking through the door? You need to be there."

"But the suitcase . . ."

"—I'll bring it to you." The promise slipped from my mouth. I couldn't take it back. "Tomorrow. After work."

This appeased Mrs. Richards enough to give me her address, and I went inside for scratch paper on which to jot it down before we said our good-byes.

When I returned to the porch, I noticed that *A Room of One's Own* still lay open on the swing, and despite the promise I'd made Gwen back in December, I started reading it. I read only a sentence before I felt the stitches in my heart—the ones I'd sewn up daily since I left Tarble—unravel.

I came undone at a handful of words.

Chapter 2

One year earlier

Before knocking, I studied the nameplate on the half open door, the words MARK SUTER, ASSISTANT PROFESSOR OF ENGLISH. Then, with fingers curled around the frame, I peeked inside.

From the first day of senior seminar, I had thought my teacher attractive, counting it a blessing that Professor Margaret Preston, who usually taught the course, had taken a sabbatical that semester to research Victorian literature in London. Mark Suter, though untenured, having taught at the college only three years, was a welcome replacement. All of my classmates thought the same. Perhaps it was his hair, the color of wet sand, just long enough to curl behind his ears. Or maybe his eyes, a true baby blue, playful but sedative. Or was it his smile, a grin exposing not only flawless, pearl white teeth but less perfect—and thus, irresistibly endearing—creases around his eyes? Whatever it was—I don't think there was a single way to quantify it—Mark Suter was that disarming, paradoxical blend of rugged and refined. A cowboy in a blazer. A bad boy with a Ph.D. During class, I often had to glance out the window to allow my eyes a rest, to drain the red from my cheeks, to settle the flutter in my stomach.

Though I'd long been a straight-A student, no other teacher had treated me with as much esteemed regard as Professor Suter. In fact, on the second day of class, he'd referred to my analysis of a John Donne poem as a "sheer stroke of brilliance," much to my classmates' chagrin. And ever since, I'd found myself milking opportunities to be in his presence. I was the first student to enter his classroom and the last to leave. And he always seemed to notice.

"Professor, do you have a minute?" I asked that October afternoon, rapping the door with my knuckle. It was only then, with the door fully open, that I saw a student slouched in the chair opposite his desk, a backpack in her lap. Her short, black hair—chopped at odd, pointy angles—reminded me of a raven, and subsequently, of Edgar Allan Poe.

Professor Suter stood from his chair then, and his six-foot-three frame commanded the attention of the entire room, even the inanimate objects—the corner ficus tree, the framed Modigliani print above his head, the second hand on the college-issued wall clock. Each seemed to accommodate his stature with a subtle shift, a minute modification. His eyes darted to mine with respectful anticipation, as if I were one of his colleagues at the door, not a student. It was the reaction I expected, but the gesture still made me blush. As usual, I took respite by looking away.

"Sorry," I blurted. "I'll come back."

"Nonsense. We're done here," he said, without allowing his student time to disagree. "Just add a few more transitions, a few more examples from the text," he told the girl, escorting her by the elbow to the door, "and I'll take another look."

The girl fixed her eyes on the toes of her tattered Converse high-tops, on which she had drawn a checkerboard pattern with what looked like black Sharpie.

"Madeline," he said, quick and sharp, like a doctor trying to snap a woozy patient back to consciousness.

"Can I bring it back in an hour?" she asked.

"I'll be here."

Passing me in the doorway, the girl finally made eye contact. Although she flashed me a smile, her red-rimmed eyes defied her. She'd been crying.

With Madeline gone, I stepped fully into the office, a corner room with a corner window, one pane facing Lake Michigan and the other, a forest rich with autumn. It seemed larger, longer than my other teachers' offices, perhaps due to two oversize bookcases stocked with what looked like a game of Tetris, hundreds of geometric book spines at perpendicular angles. The room also boasted an eggplant purple love seat, the cushions housing more books, plus piles of magazines—back issues of *The New Yorker* and *Ploughshares*—that seemed permanent, as if the couch were a storage unit all its own. I smiled at my professor's disorganized organization, his obvious obsession with print media, his zealous promise to read everything, cover to cover, in due time.

When I heard the door click shut, I turned to find Professor Suter watching me, his feet planted squarely on the floor, his arms crossed. Under the wrinkled, rolled-up sleeves of his otherwise starched button-up shirt, I admired his biceps, just large enough to indicate masculinity without appearing forced, the kind of muscles you get from chopping wood not pumping iron. His jeans, dark but faded at the meaty part of his thigh, also hinted at his athletic physique.

My professor stepped closer; the subtle scent of musk—his cologne, shower gel, or deodorant, I couldn't say—was reminiscent of my father's aftershave and tickled my nose with familiarity.

"The first year's the hardest," he said, his voice as steady as his stance. "When they discover this isn't high school English."

I nodded understanding. "You're really good. I mean, you were really good with her just now." I gestured at the hallway beyond the now closed door, into which Madeline had vanished, my movement exaggerated and overdone. "I mean, the way you handled that. You could have said tough luck."

"True, but tough luck won't teach her how to craft a cohesive essay."

"And speaking of cohesive essay," I started, "I want to talk about my thesis." I eyed the slew of papers on his desk, a half-eaten peanut butter and jelly on rustic whole wheat. "You're sure you have a minute?"

He seemed to size me up then, down to my boots and up to my breasts, but not in the way that earns most men a slap. "For you, Ms. Rousseau, I have all afternoon."

He waited for me to slip into the chair opposite his desk, where Madeline had sat only minutes earlier—the cracked, faux leather cushion still so warm, I wondered how long she'd cried in his office about her essay—before seating himself.

"Your thesis." He rubbed his hands together fanatically, as if preparing to throw down a triple-word score in Scrabble. "You've had me wondering for weeks. I have a knack for guessing which texts my students will choose. But you . . ."

"—Me?"

His eyes narrowed, like a detective spotting an overlooked clue. "You're my wild card."

My cheeks tinted scarlet. I wasn't sure which word I relished more, *wild* or *my*.

"I'm happy to hear I'm unpredictable," I said. "But wouldn't that make guessing correctly more rewarding?"

I hardly believed my own ears; the playful, casual tone I took with my teacher, how easy it was to banter with him, alone in his office with the door closed, despite the professional nature of our relationship.

He smiled, and those characteristic eye wrinkles curled in unison with his lips; it was a grin that made my heart stop and start again. "It would."

"So guess."

"Kate Chopin."

"Virginia Woolf," I corrected.

His sapphire eyes gleamed with thought. "Woolf, huh? I knew you'd go with a feminist. I take it you like stream of consciousness?"

I nodded. "When I read *Mrs. Dalloway* in sixth grade—"

"Sixth grade?"

"I was precocious," I explained. "But even at eleven, I didn't know it was called stream of consciousness. I just remember thinking Woolf wrote how I thought, lots of tangents and asides, weaving in and out of the past and present."

He studied me for a moment, as if conjuring me as a pubescent, nose in book on a quiet playground bench while my classmates played kickball in the distance.

"Precocious, indeed," he finally said. "So it's *Mrs. Dalloway* then? You'll critique Woolf's use of flashback as a literary device to define her characters' pasts? Or maybe explore the themes of homosexuality through Clarissa Dalloway's affection for Sally Seton?"

I admired his ability to spout off character names so effortlessly. I shook my head no. "Those are excellent topics, if I was going to write about *Mrs. Dalloway*. But I'm not."

He cocked his head with intrigue.

"*A Room of One's Own*," I said.

"Ah, yes. What is it Woolf said?" He cleared his throat. " 'A woman must have money and a room of her own if she is to write fiction.' Something to that effect?"

"Word for word," I said, before launching into the monologue I'd practiced an hour earlier in the bathroom mirror. "I plan to use Woolf's essay as a springboard for a larger umbrella question, which is: Why did so many women writers, Woolf included, succumb to depression and ultimately, suicide?"

He cocked his head again, and this time, in the acute angle

of the tilt, I saw he was preparing to play devil's advocate. "But suicide knows no gender boundaries," he argued. "What about Hemingway?"

"What about him?" I countered. "He shot himself. Easy. Quick. Decisive. But Woolf? She drowned herself by loading the pockets of her overcoat with stones and wading out into the depths of the River Ouse. Sylvia Plath stuck her head in an oven full of gas. Charlotte Perkins Gilman overdosed on chloroform. And Anne Sexton? Carbon monoxide poisoning. She donned her mother's fur coat and swigged a glass of vodka before heading to the garage to sit inside her car while it was running." I paused only to breathe. "These women were complicated and conflicted, right down to the intricate, muddled, haunting ways they chose to leave the world. And yes, they were artists—mad artists, plagued by mental illness and creativity complexes—but they were also female, women trying to infiltrate a historically patriarchal tradition. And so they crafted literary female characters not unlike themselves—mothers, sisters, wives—who were equally distressed by their own creativity and intelligence. And why? I think the explanation lies with Woolf's essay. Without the opportunity to fully express herself and her creativity—without money and a room of one's own—a woman can simply go mad."

I let out an exhaustive breath, both exhilarated and frightened to hear my professor's response. And while I waited, I studied his forehead wrinkles. Tarble girls often speculated about his age. The consensus was forty-two.

"It's fresh," he finally said. "It crosses curriculum with psychology and history. I'd expect that from a grad student or faculty member, not an undergrad. Tell me, other than an appreciation for Woolf's writing, what was your inspiration?" His fingers curled and waved, as if he was literally, physically trying to pull information from me. "Did you read about this somewhere? Say, in a literary journal?"

The idea had come to me over the summer, when I found myself rereading most of Woolf's books before gravitating toward the works of Plath and Gilman. I was well into a book of Anne Sexton's poetry when I realized the common thread of suicide. Were my summer reading choices indicative of something macabre? I'd wondered. An obsession with death since my father's passing? An attraction to melancholy?

"My inspiration was originality," I said instead. "I didn't want to choose something domestic like Austen or something pretentious like *The Wasteland*. I didn't want to be like the other girls in your class."

His eyes shot to mine. "You could never be like the other girls."

I looked down at my feet, where my toes curled inside my boots. I sensed him studying me long and hard, like a fire he wanted to contain.

"You're not from the Midwest, are you?" he asked.

I looked up. "What makes you say that?"

"There's something 'otherworldly' about you. Your attitude, the way you think. It's refreshing. And your accent . . . I noticed you don't always pronounce the *r* at the end of certain words. And with a last name like Rousseau, well, I'm thinking French Canadian?"

I smiled. It wasn't the first time someone up north had tried to pinpoint my accent and failed. Because that singsong twang—how folks from Mississippi or Alabama talk—was absent from my dialect, people never guessed I was from the South.

"I'm from Louisiana," I said. "New Orleans to be exact."

"That's it." He tapped the desktop in defeat. "Of course, it's New Orleans. I should have known. I got my bachelor's at Tulane, you know. Best four years of my life."

"Really? My parents went to UNO."

He nodded, then looked past me, as if recalling his own coed memories. "New Orleans," he mused. "What a sultry, sinful city."

"Have you been back? Since you graduated?"

"No, but I'm actually flying down there in a few weeks for a symposium at Tulane. That's the kind of thing you have to do to get tenure around here," he added as an aside. "Attend symposiums, serve on panels, publish papers. And interestingly, this symposium pertains to your thesis. Gender and Creativity is the topic. Any chance you're visiting Mom and Dad at that time? You could be my guest."

I gushed at the idea, that I attend a real symposium—something I'd heard of but never experienced—at Professor Suter's side. But I hadn't been to New Orleans in almost a year, since we buried my father two days after Christmas, and my mother relocated to the Midwest to assure I'd finish school. I didn't think I could go back. New Orleans—once the magical setting of my charmed childhood—had morphed into a fractured backdrop for nightmares.

"We don't live there anymore," I said. "Home for me now is Oak Park, Illinois."

"That's too bad." He flashed his killer grin once more. "For you and for me."

He's flirting, I thought. *Is he? Isn't he?*

"So you approve?" I asked, trying to keep my blushing at bay. "Of my thesis?"

"Absolutely." He raised a finger. "But I do have one caveat. It sounds like you'll be analyzing several sources. Not only Woolf's essay, but also Plath's *The Bell Jar* and Gilman's *The Yellow Wallpaper*?"

I nodded.

"It may prove to be too much, even for a student of your caliber."

"I can handle it."

"No doubt you can. But still, you're young. It's your last year at Tarble. You don't want to give up your social life, do you? Leave your boyfriend up to his own devices on Friday nights?"

I swallowed. "I don't have a boyfriend."

"Good. Because you'll be busy reading and researching. Bouncing ideas off of me. In fact . . ." He eyed his watch. "Let's say we get out of here. Grab a coffee. Discuss this more in depth."

I pointed to the hall lobby. "You mean at the bookstore?"

He scrounged his lips. "I don't drink that stuff. I was thinking that quaint coffee shop in downtown Racine."

He held my gaze a moment, intently, as if assessing my very character.

"Shall we?"

He insisted on two things, that I call him Mark and that I ride in his Jeep to Racine. From Kenosha, it was a scenic drive north on Sheridan Drive, during which we swapped vignettes about New Orleans, from roast beef po'boys—the blessed union of hot gravy beef and cold lettuce and tomato on crusty French bread—to Tennessee Williams and Truman Capote and William Faulkner, authors who once called the Crescent City home.

Inside the coffee shop, I tried ordering a regular drip coffee but he objected, saying I had to have a latte. I didn't object to his suggestion or the fact he paid. It was the courteous thing to do, even if he was my teacher.

"Tell me," he said, once we were seated at a table near the back. It was more like a TV tray pretending to be a table and so cozy, I felt his pant leg skim mine underneath. "What happens to Ruby Rousseau after she graduates from Tarble?"

I wiped my lips of vanilla-infused foam and grinned at his playful use of the third person. "Graduate School. I already applied to Iowa."

"Ah, yes, the infamous Writers' Workshop," he said. "A solid choice. If you want to stay a bit closer to home, though, I could pull some strings for you at Northwestern. I did my graduate work there."

"I'd appreciate that."

"Consider it done." He sipped his latte. "And after graduate school, where do you want to teach?"

"Oh, I'm not going to teach. I'm going to write." I watched him smirk with skepticism. "I know, I know. I'm breaking the circle of literary life: you study English or literature or creative writing and then you teach it to some poor soul who studies it only to teach it to someone else. No offense."

"None taken. Poor soul," he mused. "I like that." He leaned

into me then, his voice soft and secretive. "You know why I do this?"

His question was hypothetical, but I shook my head no all the same, adamantly, as if he'd asked me whether I knew about carburetors. It was a sudden, nervous reaction. I had never seen my teacher so close, had never been under the trance of his blue eyes for so long,

"Because I love words. Always have, ever since I was a kid."

"You knew you wanted to be an English teacher, even then?"

"No, like every other boy my age I wanted to play Major League Baseball. But I broke my hand pitching in the All-Star game and spent the remainder of the summer reading *Lord of the Flies* and *The Other Side of the Mountain,* and I got hooked." His words came out soft and warm, like flannel sheets fresh from the dryer. "I'm a teacher because I want to infect others with that passion, foster an appreciation for syntax and metaphor and poetic prose. It's often a thankless job, but I think it's worth the sacrifice."

"Sacrifice? But you're Mark Suter." I raised my voice over the loud, sudden shushing of the espresso machine. "We sacrifice for *you.* We stay up all hours taking notes on Milton or Yeats, so that if you happen to call our name during class, we'll have the answer you want, an answer that will please you."

"What I meant is, I'm not always writing as much as I should, publishing as much as the college would like. My time goes first to shaping the brilliant minds of tomorrow." He paused then and frowned, checking his watch with a sigh.

"What?" I asked.

"My student. Madeline. I was supposed to look at her essay again."

Disappointment crept up my throat. "Should we go back?"

He seemed to consider this option, then shook his head. "I can look at it later, right?" he asked, as if trying to convince even himself of the fact.

"Right."

"Right," he repeated. "See, Ruby? Teaching is a sacrifice at times." He downed the rest of his latte like a shot of gin. "And between you and me, it's practically destroyed my marriage."

Marriage. My classmates often debated Mark Suter's status. It was something my best friend and roommate, Heidi Callahan, and I had discussed in the dark at 2:00 A.M. when we couldn't fall asleep. He never wore a wedding ring.

I stole a peek at his left hand then and saw only a bare, manly knuckle; thick skin dusted with fine hair.

"Meryl, my wife, teaches math at Georgetown," he went on. "I'm right brain, and she's left. I'm the gas, and she's the brakes. We're proof that opposites attract, but don't endure."

"Are you separated?" I asked.

"We see each other once a month. She comes here one month. I go to D.C. the next. It's an arrangement of sorts."

"I've heard of those." I straightened my back so as not to slouch. "Couples who live and work in different cities."

"Meryl hates the Midwest. But it's home for me. I didn't fully understand that until my mom died."

"Your mom died?"

He nodded. "Cancer."

"I'm so sorry." I swallowed the small lump forming in my throat, hoping to relieve the sudden stinging in the corners of my eyes. But it remained, and I dabbed my eyes with my coffee-stained napkin, trying to control a full-fledged outburst.

Mark laid his hand on top of mine then, his meaty and warm fingers curled slightly over the edges, blanketing my skin. "You okay?"

I shook my head yes, and then no, when more tears—fat droplets of salty sorrow—fell down my cheeks. "My dad died too," I divulged. "Last year."

"Was he sick?"

"No, nothing like that. It was an accident. A car accident," I lied.

Mark sighed through his nose, the kind of empathetic breath that connotes sadness and anger and frustration all at once. "What was his name?"

His question took me off guard, because my friends—back home in New Orleans or at Tarble—never asked follow-up questions when I mentioned my father's passing. They either stared at me as if I had crawfish crawling out of my ears or changed the subject. I knew it wasn't because they didn't care; they just didn't know what to say, how to navigate the rocky terrain of death. But here was Professor Suter—Mark—asking the most intimate of follow-up questions. He wanted to know my father's name; he wanted to know what people called him.

"Julian," I said.

"Julian," he repeated slowly, like the final sip of wine from a centuries old bottle. "And what was he like?"

"Passionate. Strong-willed. A history buff. He was an antiques dealer. He was the one who introduced me to writers like

Woolf and Thoreau and the Brontës. He'd bring home musty, yellowed copies of books from his store, the bindings always ornate and gold etched. He cared more about the past than the future. Tradition and history and family—those are the things he valued. So he couldn't fathom why I wanted to go to Tarble, in Wisconsin of all places. Where it snows. Where they eat brats and beer and cheese. Where Mardi Gras isn't a real holiday, a day you get off school and work."

"I gather he didn't approve of your choice?"

"People who were born and raised in New Orleans don't leave," I explained. "They just don't. The only time we ever left for longer than a week's vacation was when Katrina hit, and only because they mandated the evacuation. When I told my dad I wanted to go to Tarble, he said we had good schools in New Orleans. Tulane and Loyola and UNO. The only thing he liked about Tarble was that it was all-girl."

"He was protective, huh? Gave your boyfriends the third degree?"

I laughed. "The third degree? Try the tenth. If he'd owned a shotgun, he would have sat out on the porch with it cocked and loaded at curfew."

Mark finally lifted his hand from mine, and my fingers immediately sensed the absence.

"You're smiling now," he said.

And I was. With just a few, simple questions, Mark had made me remember my father—who he was down to his very core—and not his death.

"What about your mom?" I asked in turn. "What was her name? What was she like?"

"Cassandra, but everyone called her Cassie. She was a writer. A lover of literature and books, like us. She was a single mom but saved enough money from working two jobs to buy herself this little cabin in the woods. She would go there, sometimes all day, and write."

"A cabin in the woods?" I hugged my coffee mug. "How idyllic."

"Yes, it's very Henry David Thoreau. But my brother and I didn't see it that way at the time. We were jealous of it, as much as you can be jealous of a place. We used to call it Cassie's Cabin. We'd ride our bikes there and play games to see who could come the closest without getting caught. Funny, it always looked brown from far away, but close up, you could see it used to be white. The paint had chipped. Anyway . . ."

I saw pain cross his eyes, and I reached for his hand just as he had mine, then immediately retracted it. There were boundaries I dared not cross, however enticing, however magnetic.

"Looking back, I was just a kid," he went on. "I didn't get it then. I didn't understand she needed to have a place to think, to write. If she didn't, she probably would have gone crazy. Resented us. It's like Virginia Woolf said, isn't it? She needed a room of her own."

I admired Mark's sensitivity toward his mom, a woman conflicted with both a mother's heart and a writer's mind.

"So what happened?" I asked. "To the cabin?"

"She sold it. I guess once my brother and I moved out of the house, she didn't need it anymore. But in a crazy case of good timing, it was for sale when I moved back. So I bought it. I live there now."

I imagined Mark scraping old paint and rolling out a fresh coat of white. I saw him hammering floorboards and sweeping cobwebs from corners. I saw him eating dinner alone.

"Meryl didn't come with you?" I asked.

"She'd just gotten department chair. How could I ask her to give that up?"

It was clear he hadn't asked, nor had his wife offered. Instinctually, I reached again to pat the top of his hand, but he flipped his wrist, and soon my palm fell inside of his. He brought my hand toward him an inch or two. My heart thumped in my ear.

He's married, I reminded myself. *No. Separated.*

"Ruby." He stared back at me with intense eyes; his mouth parted in a half-smile. "Is that your birthstone?"

"No, my dad came up with it," I said. "My hair was bright red when I was born."

He studied me. "Doesn't Rousseau mean . . ."

"—A red-haired person."

"Then you're a real redundancy, Ruby Rousseau." His tongue seemed to revel in the alliteration. "Tell me more. Tell me more about you."

My breath tangled in my chest. "What do you want to know?"

"Right now? This minute?" He strengthened his grip on my hand. "Are you hungry?"

It was close to midnight when Mark pulled his Jeep onto the red bridge at the edge of campus and parked under tree branch shadows. Tipsy from three glasses of wine, despite the filet mignon and au gratin potatoes I ate during our three-hour dinner, I didn't care where he dropped me off. But Mark said the bridge was the safest place. And it would be the safest place next time.

Next time.

His fingers soon went to my hair; he combed through it several times to expose my neck fully. A prickling thrill swept down the backs of my arms at the drunken thought he had fangs, and I might succumb to his paranormal powers right there in his car. But he didn't bite me. Instead, he tucked his hand into the crook of my inner thigh, and leaned in to press his lips to mine. And in that moment, kissing him, every muscle in my body simultaneously contracted and relaxed. It was like bungee jumping and meditating at the same time. I felt something I hadn't felt since my father died.

I felt alive.

He pulled back from my mouth but still kept his face close to mine. "I don't know how to do this," he whispered.

"I think you're doing just fine."

He laughed. "Thanks. But I meant us. I've never been in this situation before, wanting something so badly, so powerfully, something other people won't understand. I know I should walk away. But I can't. Because you're *it*. Beautiful. Intelligent. Creative. But if anyone were to find out . . ."

"—No one will find out."

"We need to be discreet."

"I won't tell a soul," I vowed.

He kissed me again, this time harder and deeper. A promise.

We said good-bye, and I walked back to my dorm room numb to the autumn evening chill, my mind floating, my thigh still warm from his touch, my lips fat and tingling. Heidi was still awake when I opened the door.

"Finally," she said, leaping from her bed. "I was about to put out an APB. Where the hell were you?"

I immediately stood behind my dresser and began changing. "Oh . . . I was studying. My thesis." I winced when I realized I'd left my backpack in Mark's Jeep. Would she notice I didn't have it?

"The library closes at ten," she said, peeking around the corner of my dresser, oblivious that I was standing in my bra. We always undressed in front of each other.

I finally made eye contact. "I went to the diner."

"I was starving," she cried. "I would have gone with you."

"Sorry, but I thought it would be fun to go by myself." I grabbed my pajamas from the dresser drawer. "You know, be that mysterious woman alone in the corner booth."

Heidi shook her head at me in jest. "You are *such* a nerdy English major."

"Are you still working on something?" I asked.

"Unfortunately." She sighed. "Are you going to stay up too?"

I knew I would be awake most of the night, energized by the ball of frenzy in my chest, recounting every moment of the evening, every look, every touch, every confession, but I told Heidi I was beat, hoping she wouldn't notice the change in my bedtime ritual. I couldn't bear to wash my face or brush my teeth, for fear of losing Mark's scent, the tang on my lips.

I kissed Mark Suter, I imagined telling my best friend as I got into bed.

And he tasted like a man.

December

Sometimes I wonder about Mark's parents, if I should blame them for what happened. Not his father for abandonment, and not his mother for neglect, but both of them, equally, for the mere genetic timing of his conception. Had they conceived him on a different day, in a different hour, at a different minute, perhaps his eyes would not have been so blue. Perhaps they would have been a murky brown, or a mossy green, and not that gleaming magnetic sapphire.

I fell in love with Mark with a childlike innocence, as if I saw a buoyant red balloon and followed it, grasping for the string, farther and farther beyond home, until at last I held it in my hand a moment before I plummeted into the depths of a neighbor's backyard swimming pool. And even as I thrashed and choked, I held on to that balloon, believing it would lift me out of the water and into the sky, into the promise of the horizon.

At what point was there no turning back? Was it when he first touched me, the electric sensation of his skin on my skin? Or when we first kissed, the smell of his breath that lingered long after we embraced?

No. No.

It was earlier, the first time I looked into his eyes.

Those blue eyes were the end of me.

Chapter 3

The night I found out Beth Richards was missing, nothing—not even my mother's warm honey almond milk—coaxed me to sleep. I lay awake brainstorming scenarios in which Beth Richards could be missing but still alive.

She had amnesia.

She was trapped at the bottom of a well.

She ran away to marry her first cousin.

What bothered me most was that I could not conjure Beth, not vividly. I couldn't recall details other than her blond hair and striking height, and her face remained a blur in my mind, like that of a fabric doll whose eyes, nose, and mouth were removed by a puppy appropriately named Chewy. If I had kept any memorabilia from Tarble, like my yearbooks, I could have looked her up.

It was only natural to belabor Beth's whereabouts—she was a missing person, a girl I knew, a girl my age—but there was another reason for my incessant thoughts. Pondering Beth's disappearance provided a respite from things I didn't want to think about, the memories that had flooded my mind upon reading the first sentence of *A Room of One's Own*:

Tarble. My father. My thesis. New Orleans.

Mark.

The biggest consequence of my insomnia, not counting a migraine headache, was that I arrived forty-five minutes late to work Monday morning. Unlike the staff reporters at the *Chronicle*—who came and went at odd hours to attend school board meetings or chase after incidents announced via police scanner—I actually kept a regular schedule as obituary coordinator. Technically, I was supposed to be at work by 8:00 A.M., but I'd been able to manipulate my start time by a good half hour. Georgene, the editorial assistant, was guardian of the office door, and I'd soon learned to bribe her with Starbucks—a white-lidded, seasonal coffee concoction with foam spilling out of the drink hole, set on the edge of her desk with a smile. Georgene usually kept her eyes on the treat, not the clock. But that morning, the morning after Beth's suitcase arrived, she hardly looked at her pumpkin spice latte or the slice of pumpkin loaf I'd added to sweeten the deal.

"What's going on, Ruby?" Georgene barely opened her mouth. I saw only her bottom teeth, speckled fuchsia from her lipstick.

"I overslept." I nudged the wax paper pastry bag toward her. "Why are you whispering?"

"The police are here to see you."

It was not so much what she said, but how she said it. *The police.* I imagined an entire squad of black uniforms around the corner, guns cocked, ready to fire at my next erratic move.

"Me?"

A solemn nod and a *follow me* gesture later, Georgene darted down the hall toward the break room. Obviously, this was what she'd been ordered to do: deliver me to the police at once.

Through the break room doorway, I saw a man of Cro-Magnon size, with dark eyes and a matching three-piece set of bushy black: hair, mustache, and eyebrows. He wore a black trench coat, and under that, a white shirt and red-and-gray-striped tie. With mammoth, broad shoulders, he stood motion-less. His face was equally still; it conveyed nothing.

"Here she is," Georgene said, shoving me through the door-way. My brown boots, and drips of coffee from my to-go cup, both spilled onto the shiny linoleum.

His dark eyes narrowed at the sight of me. "Ruby Rousseau?"

I looked to Georgene for moral support, but she was already halfway back to her desk. I willed that slice of pumpkin loaf to turn dry and stale.

"Who are you?" I asked.

"Detective Steve Pickens of the Milwaukee Police Depart-ment." He put just enough space between his words to convey authority. He flapped open a black wallet before me, revealing a gold badge. "Are you Ruby Rousseau?"

"What is this about?" I could see the detective's upper lip twitch at the corner. He was annoyed. "Beth's suitcase," I said after a moment, answering my own question.

He seemed to study me, perhaps taking in my greasy hair. I had chosen coffee over a shower that morning.

"You realize that suitcase, belonging to Ms. Richards, is evidence in a missing persons case?" he asked.

"No. I mean, yes, I thought . . ." I swallowed saliva mixed with air. "Beth's mom insisted she come get it, and so I offered . . ."

"—Take a deep breath, Ms. Rousseau."

I followed his orders, but paranoia took over, and I wondered if the man was an imposter, if he was simply pretending to be a cop, with a stereotypical mustache and trench coat he'd copied from reruns of *Murder, She Wrote*. Perhaps he was the same man who had abducted Beth. He had already murdered her mother, and now he was coming for me.

"Can I see your badge again?" I asked.

He handed me the black leather wallet, and I inspected the shiny gold inside. It looked real. I noticed a thin, silver band on his ring finger. I wanted to ask him how he knew where I worked, until I remembered what he did for a living.

"Where's the suitcase?" he asked.

"In my trunk. I was going to drive to Milwaukee after work."

"I'll be taking it with me." He eyed my Starbucks cup and the spill on the floor. "For the record, I did go to your home first. You weren't there."

I wiped the coffee spill up with a paper towel. "I needed the caffeine," I explained. "I was up half the night."

"What disturbed your sleep?"

"I just found out a girl I knew is missing, Detective. Does that not warrant insomnia?"

"You said *knew* instead of *know*, Ms. Rousseau. Does that

mean you haven't been in contact with Ms. Richards as of late?" He adjusted his massive body into one of the break room's plastic bucket chairs and invited me to do the same with a wave of his hand. "Phone calls? E-mails? Texts?"

Because journalists like reading the competition, picked-apart sections of the *Tribune* and *Sun-Times* littered our break room table. I started sorting them to steady my nerves, but the detective placed a fat hand on top of mine and shook his head in disapproval.

"I haven't talked to Beth since I borrowed the suitcase," I clarified. "That was in December of last year. Almost ten months ago."

He scribbled something in his notepad.

"What happened to her, Detective?"

"That's what we're trying to figure out."

"No, I mean, when was the last time anyone saw her? Because I tried looking it up online in the Milwaukee newspapers. I didn't find anything. I was surprised. A young, beautiful girl goes missing, and it isn't splattered all over the news?"

"The details of Ms. Richards's case are being withheld at this time." He stared at me, long and hard like Superman using X-ray vision, then said, "You're sure you haven't spoken to Ms. Richards recently? Chatted with her on Facebook? Twitter? FaceTime?"

I nodded. I was sure. I had wanted nothing to do with Tarble College or its affiliates.

"Mrs. Richards said you graduated from Tarble with her daughter," he said.

"We were in the same graduating class," I corrected.

"And what was the nature of your relationship?"

"We were acquaintances."

"And yet you borrowed her suitcase?"

"It's a small school, Detective. We lived on the same floor," I explained.

Just then, I caught sight of my boss, managing editor Craig Hewitt, as he walked past the half-open break room door. I checked the wall clock. It was past nine. I was going to get fired.

"We had mutual friends," I added. "But we didn't hang out or anything."

"How would you describe Beth Richards?"

"Pretty. Nice. I think she majored in some sort of science?"

"Have you been in contact with any other classmates from Tarble?"

"No."

"Why not?"

Mark's face came into focus then—his discerning blue eyes, chiseled jawline—so vivid compared to my halfhearted memory of Beth. I started playing with the plastic lid of my coffee cup, but when it squeaked, I stopped.

"I don't know," I said. "Life goes on, I guess."

"Have you been back to campus since you graduated?"

"No."

"Why not?"

"No reason," I said. "Work. Life. Stuff."

"Stuff?"

"I don't know," I snapped. "Why do I feel like I'm a suspect here?"

"Are you a suspect?"

"You tell me, Detective."

"Look at it from my point of view, Ms. Rousseau. I get a call from Mrs. Richards saying some girl in Illinois has Beth's suitcase, a suitcase she took on a trip during which she disappeared. It's suspicious. Can you give me that?"

"But it was the tag. See, I wrote my name on the tag. And I guess Beth didn't notice and didn't change it. The airline thought it was mine and sent it to me."

"I believe you."

"You do?"

"But I still have to do my job."

"But I don't . . ." My voice cracked. "I don't know anything else."

We played a game of stare down and I lost, my eyes diverting to my lap. I looked up in time to see the wrinkles around his eyes soften.

"Here's what I can tell you," he said. "Ms. Richards flew to Pittsburgh Friday evening to attend a weekend photography workshop. The airline confirmed she was on the plane. However, no one has had contact with her since before she boarded. No cell phone calls. No credit card purchases. No trace of her."

I let the information sink in. "Did you track her cell phone?"

The detective let out a grunt. "Let me guess, you watch *CSI*? Yes, we can track a cell phone, but only if the phone is turned on. Any call to Ms. Richards goes straight to voice mail. The phone's dead, has been turned off or was discarded. Do you have any other investigation suggestions for me?"

I shook my head no.

Detective Pickens stood then, reached into the pocket of his coat, and handed me a business card. "If you think of anything else, please give me a call," he said. "I'm on the case in cooperation with the Pittsburgh PD."

I stood too. "What about the suitcase?"

"Of course," he said. "The suitcase."

He escorted me past the front desk, past Georgene's perked ears and peripheral stare, and through the parking lot to my Corolla. I noticed a black sedan with tinted windows parked a few cars down from mine and realized it was his. I hadn't noticed it on my way in. I opened my trunk, and he hoisted the suitcase with an out-of-shape huff. Immediately, he inspected the tags, just as my mother and I had.

"The delivery service brought it yesterday?" he asked.

"Around six o'clock," I said, fishing the business card from the delivery woman out of my pocket and handing it to him.

"Did you look inside?"

I cringed. "Yes, but we put everything back the way it was." I shut the trunk to avoid his stare. "I hope there's something in there that helps."

He unzipped the bag, looked inside, and zipped it again.

"Do you think Beth is alive?" I asked.

His eyes went dead. Cold. Apathetic. "Do you know how many active missing persons cases exist in this country? Close to one hundred thousand."

"What does that mean?"

"Ms. Rousseau, I've been working missing persons for twenty years now, okay? We never find some of the people we're looking for. And the ones we do find are . . ."

"—Are what?"

He paused. "Do I really need to spell it out for you? You write obituaries, after all."

I had just booted up my computer when I felt a warmth behind me, heard a man clear his throat. I swiveled my chair to see Craig Hewitt standing at the entrance of my cubicle, resting an elbow on the partition. I diverted my eyes to the stack of faxes in his hand, willing my boss not to fire me.

"Busy day for the dead," he said, handing me the papers, still warm from the fax.

I flipped through the info sheets the funeral directors had sent. Georgene usually brought them to me, not Craig.

"Did you know I started out in obits?" he asked, twirling a black Bic between his fingers like a baton. "They say it's the best way to learn newspaper style."

I nodded but kept my eyes on the faxes.

"Here's a fun fact," he continued. "Did you know that more people die in the month of January than in any other month?"

I shook my head no.

"And the least number of deaths occur in August," he went on. "Murders generally happen on Sundays and suicides on Wednesdays, not Mondays as previously thought."

I thought back to that cold, December evening. Yes, it had been a Wednesday.

"That's all very interesting," I said.

"Useless knowledge." He paused. "Ruby? Can I see you in my office?"

"Is this about the police?" *The police.* I said it just as Georgene had.

He took inventory of the newsroom with his eyes before sitting on the edge of my desk, balancing his weight by spreading one hand out before him on the desktop. I stared at his wrist, where his silver watch broke up the density of light brown hair on his forearm. He had manly hands, sexy wrists.

"Is there something I should know, Ruby?"

I raised my hands in defense, waving my palms back and forth in protestation. "That wasn't about *me*. I mean, I'm not in trouble or anything. With the law. It's just that a girl I know, a girl I *knew* rather, she's missing. She disappeared a few days ago. The detective was just, you know, asking questions."

"Missing?" Craig raised his eyebrows. "Is she local?"

"Milwaukee. I went to college with her."

"Where at?"

I hesitated, because I'd lied about my degree on my application. They never asked for a copy of my diploma or anything. "Tarble," I finally said before adding, "you've probably never heard of it."

"I know Tarble. Funny, I wouldn't have pegged you as the women's college type."

"What does that mean?" I asked, although I knew exactly what he meant.

"Never mind." He smiled. "Anyway, this missing girl. She's a friend of yours?"

"Acquaintance," I said for what felt like the hundredth time. I told Craig then about the suitcase mix-up, and he listened intently, asking questions, making me clarify specifics.

"Do you want to write this up for news?" he asked once I finished my spiel.

"Oh. No. I don't write."

"What do you mean? You write every day."

But writing obituaries isn't really writing, I wanted to say. It requires no creativity, no imagination, and therefore, no risk. "I don't write *articles*."

"But you could. I see it in your eyes. You're an observer, Ruby Rousseau."

I finally allowed a long look into his brown eyes—a creamy light brown, like the Werther's Originals I used to scavenge from my father's coat pockets—and felt my chest flutter before landing in my belly.

"This could be your opportunity to break in to writing copy," he continued. "That's how I got my start, you know. It was third grade, and the class's pet hamster went missing. And whom did Mrs. Clark choose to cover the case for the monthly newsletter? Yours truly."

His story was adorable, but I refused to give in to his charm. I kept my expression deadpan. "Are you *seriously* equating a missing girl to a missing rodent?"

"You're missing the point."

"Which is?"

He smiled wholeheartedly. "Don't let a great opportunity pass you by."

Unable to resist smiling back, I allowed my lips to curl. "Okay," I said. "So what happened to the hamster?"

"The janitor found him in his toolbox."

"Dead?"

"Just sleeping."

I sighed. "Let's hope Beth is just sleeping."

We sat in abrupt, solemn silence until I finally gestured to the faxes he'd delivered. "I guess I better type these up now," I said.

Craig stood but still didn't walk away. "Hey, a bunch of us are doing deep dish for lunch today," he said suddenly.

"What's the occasion?"

"No occasion," he said, shifting his gaze to the gray carpet. He dug the toe of his shoe into the Berber weave. "Why do you ask?"

"Because nobody ever goes out to lunch, unless it's somebody's birthday or something."

"It's nobody's birthday."

I pointed to the brown bag beside me. "I brought my lunch today."

"Eat it tomorrow."

"I don't have any cash on me."

"My treat."

I thought of Mark that afternoon at the café, when he'd insisted on buying me a latte. "Thanks anyway," I said, pretending to read the faxes. Really, I was just letting the black words grow fuzzy into the blinding white paper.

Craig finally walked away, and I looked up in time to see his shoulders slump.

"Hey, Craig?" I called after him, a knee-jerk reaction at the thought I'd hurt his feelings.

He doubled back to my cubicle with earnest eyes. "Yeah, Ruby?"

"You left your pen," was all I could say.

That night, Mom worked the evening shift at the hospital and left a sticky note on the kitchen table instructing me to eat the leftovers from Wu's. I microwaved a serving on a paper plate and ate it standing up next to the garbage can. Ten minutes later, I was sick enough to go searching for stomach antacid. Our medicine cabinet left something to be desired: an empty bottle of Tums and a bottle of Pepto-Bismol so expired, it was orange not pink. Sad, really, considering my mom's occupation, but she had cleared out all of the other meds like pain reliever and cold and flu remedies back in December, per my doctor's recommendation.

Just in case, he'd said.

I eventually found Rolaids in the top drawer of the foyer console table, which was crammed with pens, coupons, receipts, playing cards, keys that open nothing, and scratch paper. I opened the drawer wide enough for me to grab the antacids and chewed two of the chalky calcium tablets as quickly as a toddler does candy. But when I tried to close the drawer, it wouldn't budge. I fought with it a good minute, even slammed it with my hip, until I decided I needed to take everything out just to put it all back in again.

And that's when I found the culprit, under the pad of scratch paper I'd used to write down Mrs. Richards's address the day before. Beth's copy of *A Room of One's Own* stared back at me from inside the drawer, like a flask of vodka I'd stowed away in case I fell off the wagon.

I could have sworn I returned the book to the suitcase, and yet, there it was. How had I forgotten to put it back? I thought then of Detective Pickens, imagined him arresting me for harboring evidence.

"It was an accident," I imagined saying in turn. "I didn't *mean* to keep it."

And yet, I wondered if that was really true. Because instead of calling the detective immediately, I took the book to the front porch swing and began reading it, despite the memories it induced the day before.

Masochistic, I heard Gwen say.

Flipping through the book, I realized that if Beth was in fact dead—like the detective implied—the book had preserved her in one very real way. It had maintained her consciousness. In the margins, Beth had taken notes in a rich, blue ink. She had starred a passage here and there. She had written things like "Aha!" and "So true!" On some pages, she had simply drawn an arrow to the margin, where she wrote an exclamation mark. It was enough to make me shiver. It seemed a reason to believe Beth was still alive. The words she scribbled there still had a pulse.

At first, I thought turning the pages would prove a treasure hunt for me, anticipating more words or symbols to appear. But when I turned the second page of chapter one, all I could do was stare. There, next to the paragraph where Woolf states the importance of having a room of one's own, Beth had written the words *Like Cassie's Cabin.*

How had Beth Richards known about Mark's mother's writing retreat?

It was possible, I reasoned, that Beth had taken one of Mark's English courses at Tarble, one where the students read *A Room of One's Own* as part of the curriculum. It was probable too that

Mark had gotten chatty with his students one day and told his entire class, including Beth, about his mother's cabin in the woods, the place he and his brother deemed Cassie's Cabin. It pained me to think he would divulge so personal a story—the story he told me intimately at the café—to his students. But even more distressing was that Beth had scribbled a note down about it in her book. Why would Mark's story mean so much to her?

The realization hit me hard, a sucker punch to the stomach. It was a question best answered by a question.

Why did it mean so much to me?

Chapter 4

One Year Earlier

After our kiss in his Jeep, I spent all of my free time with Mark, and my not-so-free time too, even ditching class twice to see him. It was two weeks of hand-holding, cheek-stroking, and kissing, over lattes and cabernets and late dinners, until he invited me back to his cabin one Tuesday night.

I had no idea such secluded parts of Kenosha existed. I'd driven down only the outskirt country roads, past barns and cornfields, in the stretch between Lake Michigan and the Interstate. But off the main thoroughfare, just a few miles north of Tarble, a small gravel road beckoned us into an oak forest, where I heard only crickets and leaves rustling through the open window of Mark's Jeep. No people. No cars, less the sound of wheels crunching the gravel.

"It's so quiet," I said as he parked in front of what used to be his mother's cabin. Size-wise, it reminded me of a concession stand at a Little League field. "You're right. It's like Walden Pond back here. I love it."

"I thought you would. Not everyone appreciates its . . . simplicity."

And by *not everyone,* I knew he meant Meryl.

We stood in silence at the doorstep as he slid the key into the lock and jiggled the doorknob with just the right amount of pressure, the right sequence of turns.

"Persnickety," he explained, once the doorknob turned.

When we stepped into the darkness, I smelled wood—a tangy, sweet odor emanating from the pine walls and floor. The air at first smelled dry, like the inside of a sawmill, but a waft of humidity suddenly hit my nose like an aftertaste. Mildew.

"Home sweet home," he said after he flipped a switch beside the door. A lamp flickered, shedding a dim light, equivalent in glow to a jar of captive fireflies. "One step up from camping, actually."

"But you have a kitchen," I argued, pointing at his minimal cooking quarters. "A deep sink. Two burners. A good-size fridge. I camped a lot as a kid, in the bayou with my dad. This is at least three steps up from camping, maybe four."

"It's tiny and needs to be gutted."

"It's cozy," I corrected, "and needs a little TLC."

He pulled me to him then, holding my wrists behind my back,

my arms removed from the equation so he could press his body fully against mine. And then he kissed me, softly at first like he sipped wine and then more deeply, as if deciding to gulp the whole glass.

"What was that for?" I asked when our lips parted.

"Your optimism. I'm a grown man living in . . . this is a shed, let's call a spade a spade, and here you are trying to sell me on it."

"Show me the rest of your shed," I said.

Another lamp and a few floor creaks later, and I'd seen the whole place. A table with two mismatched chairs, one vinyl and one wood. A full-size bed with no frame or headboard and unmade, the sheets twisted with a wool blanket in a striped pattern, a candy cane effect. A stone fireplace. A bulky, lopsided sofa. No television, but a radio. It had all come with the place when he bought it. Rustic Bachelor Pad—that's what the real estate agent called it in the MLS listing.

"Do you want something to drink?" he asked.

"What do you have?"

"Water." He cringed. "Well water. Or . . . I think I have orange juice?"

I realized then why we'd gone out for coffee and drinks and dinner so often in the past weeks, why Mark seemed to live at his office. I was sure a peek into his fridge would reveal a lonely colony of ketchup packets. *This cabin needs a woman's touch*, I thought. *He needs a woman's touch.*

"I love orange juice," I said, making myself comfortable on the couch.

He brought me water. No juice after all. To make up for this, though, he put on a fire. I watched him heft several massive logs onto the hearth and understood why his biceps were so defined. He probably split the wood himself, using nothing but an ax.

"I can see why your mom liked it here," I said, once more scanning the room, now soft and hazy under the orange glow of fire light. "No distractions. That's what you need to write."

"It's quiet and sentimental, yes. But it isn't romantic." He sighed. "But we can't go to your dorm, can we? And my office is too visible."

I knew then that a platonic tour of Mark's home was not the extent of our agenda that evening. I'd probably spend the night; drink coffee with him in the morning. The thought made me giddy.

"You don't need to impress me," I said. To prove this fact, I sipped the water. It tasted like sulfur, but I didn't dare purse my lips. "I like it here. Because I'm with you."

He sat beside me on the couch and kissed me again, hard but sweet; it shot through me like an electric shock, down to my feet and back again. And then he stared into my eyes and brushed his knuckles across my cheek.

"Come with me this weekend," he blurted.

"Really?"

"Really. I don't think I can go three whole days without you."

My heart melted. Mark's impending trip to New Orleans, for the symposium at his alma mater, had been hovering above me like a rain cloud. We hadn't been apart for more than half a day in the past weeks.

"I can't imagine how expensive a flight would be on such short notice," I said.

"Ruby, I'll take care of *everything*. Flight, hotel, meals. Let me do this, let me whisk you away to somewhere picturesque and charming." He gestured at his unkempt surroundings, as if they were the antithesis of both these things. "I can book us a room in the Quarter. Somewhere historic," he added. "The Hotel Monteleone, perhaps. They say it's haunted. If we're lucky, we can throw back a few pints with Faulkner's ghost at the bar."

I had never stayed at the hotel before—you never stay at the hotels in your own town—but I knew it had been a literary haunt for famous authors like William Faulkner and Truman Capote and served as the setting for short stories by Ernest Hemingway and Eudora Welty. And I wanted to go with him, more than anything. I was romanced by his determination to romance me. But I didn't know if I could do it, if I could go back home. While a student at Tarble, I had flown into New Orleans twice a year—for Christmas and Mardi Gras, per an agreement with my father. But the very last time I'd flown there was the morning after he died. I'd taken a red-eye flight, and Mom had waited for me past the security checkpoint with churning hands, flattened curls, pale lips, and a vacant stare. She'd embraced me as if I were an emergency floatation device. "I'm so sorry," she'd whispered selflessly, as if, for a moment, it was my loss not hers. And then we'd driven home in unusual silence, cognizant that we, just the two of us, were now the extent of our family. One of us had been removed from the equation, not from our hearts—never from our hearts—but from the physical realm in which we lived and breathed. We would survive, of course we would, but we had known, even on that very first day without my father, that the wound would never fully heal. It would bleed, and it would scab. But it would scar.

Could I walk through the French Quarter now, knowing my father's antiques store was no longer there, probably leased to a touristy patchouli-scented voodoo shop? Would the guilt I harbored about his death overcome me, overshadow my time there with Mark? And what if I ran into someone I knew—which seemed inevitable after living there so long—how would I explain what I was doing there, and who Mark was? And perhaps most important, how quickly would the news of my sordid affair travel a thousand miles north to my mother?

"You're making it very hard for me to say no," I said.

"So don't."

I exhaled. My reservations came out with my breath. I said yes.

And then it was settled, and we relocated our conversation—a discussion suddenly made up of actions not words—to the ruffled sheets of his unmade bed.

By the time we checked into the Hotel Monteleone that Friday night, it was dusk, my favorite hour in the Crescent City, when waves of violet streak the horizon, when day succumbs to night and you know there is no turning back.

We stood aimless for a moment in front of the hotel doors, and I watched Mark look up and down the street, then take in a big whiff of city air. "It's exactly how I remembered," he said.

My eyes moved down the street. We were on Royal—Rue Royal—and my father's storefront was just a block away. But New Orleans was not exactly how I remembered. The hues were all wrong. The pink facades appeared more coral than salmon;

the green ferns looked more emerald than kelly; the ironwork more espresso than black. Being back in New Orleans was like kissing an ex-boyfriend, simultaneously familiar and foreign. I knew this place by heart, and yet time had passed.

We had changed.

"You're my tour guide," Mark said. "Where to?"

I pointed down Rue Royal in the direction of my father's store.

As Mark and I walked arm in arm into the Vieux Carré, my heart began to pound, mimicking the sound of my black high heels *click-clacking* against the sidewalk, a rhythmic cacophony, like horseshoes hitting pavement. By that time, most of Royal's antique and jewelry shops had closed for the day, but the street remained busy with tourists savoring the afterglow of daylight. To settle my nerves, I watched our reflection in the glass of the shop windows. I saw my black silk dress, my red shawl swept over one shoulder, my curly auburn hair pulled up girlishly on one side. I saw Mark's black blazer and white shirt tucked into tan trousers. Each window was its own frame, and the distance between shop windows made the frames appear and reappear, flicker like an 8 mm film, as if we were actors in a silent movie.

The movie played until we reached what used to be my father's store. It was still an antiques shop, not a voodoo tourist trap as I'd feared, but the gold-framed mirror on display in the front window catapulted me back in time. And suddenly, I was seven years old again.

It was late summer, and school had just resumed. Dad had taken me to his shop after school. If I behaved, if I didn't break anything, he'd promised to buy me a naval orange in the French Market, and I'd earned my treat. I was already peeling it as we made our way back to the streetcar, dropping orange rind behind me like Hansel and Gretel's bread. When we came to an intersection, he'd reached for my hand but pulled back in surprise at my wet, sticky palm.

"You're a mess," he'd said, rubbing the drips of orange juice staining my white button-up shirt, one of two I wore every day to parochial school.

"I want to see," I'd said, even though I'd just placed a new orange segment in my mouth.

He'd lifted me, his hands deep in my armpits, and walked me up to the window of his antiques store, where I saw myself in a bejeweled display mirror. Orange bits dotted both my cheeks, and the juice dripped off my chin. I'd smiled at my reflection. Then, I'd stuffed the last crescent moon segment of orange into my father's mouth, and the juice came pouring down his chin too.

"We're twins now," I'd said.

"No telling where you start and I begin," he'd added. And then my father had lowered me to the ground and held my hand tightly as we crossed the street. He'd never let go, not until we reached the streetcar. And by the time he'd fished for fare in his pocket, our hands were literally glued together by dried juice.

Mark interjected my thoughts. "Is something wrong, Ruby?" he asked, because I'd stopped walking. "You look so sad."

My eyes blurred with impending tears. "I don't think I can do this."

He swallowed. I watched his Adam's apple bob up and down in a gulp. "Are you having second thoughts, about us?"

I shook my head no and kissed him then, a soft brushing of lips, because he looked so vulnerable, like a little boy hugging his piggy bank, waiting for the ice cream truck to drive by his house on a humid August afternoon.

"This used to be my father's shop," I divulged. "I thought I could do this. Come back here. But the last time I was here was for his funeral and it's all . . . it's like it all just happened."

"Oh, sweetheart, why didn't you tell me?" He gripped both of my arms, crouching down so he could look up at me from under downcast eyes. "We could have gone to Vegas or New York, somewhere else, another weekend."

"But I wanted to. And I'm fine. It's fine. I'm fine."

He studied my face; he didn't believe me. "I just wish you would have told me."

Why hadn't I told him? Why hadn't I shared my anxieties about the trip, the impact I feared it would have on my psyche? Because I didn't want to be that girl anymore, the girl whose father died. I didn't want to have an emotional handicap. Learning to live without my father had been like learning to live without a leg, and I didn't want to limp anymore. Mark had become my prosthetic so quickly, so effortlessly—he'd filled that aching, empty space, ever since the night we kissed in his Jeep. And I wanted to indulge in the euphoria of feeling whole again.

"Do you want to go home?" he asked.

More than anything, I thought. *I want to go home, to a New Orleans that no longer exists, the one where Dad is alive.*

"Don't be silly," I said. "We flew all the way here. We checked into the hotel already. And we have the symposium tomorrow."

"None of that matters if you're not happy, if you're not comfortable. Say the word, and I'll book us on the next flight back."

"You'd do that?"

"Of course." His expression was solemn, determined, earnest—the countenance of a knight in shining armor the moment before he rescues the princess.

I wrapped my arms around the meaty part of his waist and rested my head on his chest as I weighed the decision. "Let's stay," I finally said.

He took my hand then and led me past my father's shop, our palms bonded by a love as strong, as adhesive as orange juice.

Mark and I created an alternate New Orleans that night—a city once again built on hope, on dreams, on the promise of tomorrow.

We ate dinner at a courtyard table for two, under antique lamps and strings of white lights swirled through a canopy of branches and vines. Our mouths were romanced by a roux done just right, by the perfect balance of garlic and onion and celery, and later, the buttery warmth of Bananas Foster. And then, with bellies full and senses heightened, we strolled down Pirates Alley, pausing to pay William Faulkner homage outside his 1920s apartment, before stepping into a hauntingly darkened Jackson Square, lit by streetlamps and the glimmering candlewicks of fortune-tellers. We watched the fog settle on the Mississippi River and listened to the moans of cargo ships— late-night calls that echoed the bliss beating in our chests— before hitching a ride on a horse-drawn carriage.

"But that's for tourists," I argued, when Mark pulled out a wad of cash for the driver.

He sported an irresistible smile. "Isn't that what we are?"

And then, as if we hadn't been up and down almost every street in the Quarter, we walked them all again, sometimes in silence and other times, in unadulterated conversation. With every sight and sound, Mark's memories from his college days seemed to sharpen—they were mostly related to being drunk on Bourbon Street— and it was almost midnight when we found ourselves back where we'd started the evening, in front of our hotel.

I slipped off my heels and stood barefoot on the cool sidewalk, my shoes dangling by their backs from my index finger. Mark embraced me, his mouth going to the tender spot behind my ear. His warm breath sent a chill down my spine. And then he slid a dress strap off my shoulder so he could kiss the skin above my collarbone.

"Are you going to invite me up to your room?" he whispered.

"You know what I could go for?" Mark asked an hour later, his body pressed against mine under the sheets like a spoon. "One of those powdered sugar doughnuts."

I loved his phrasing *I could go for*; it sounded familiar, like we had always been like this, had always been together.

"You mean beignets." I placed a reprimanding finger to his lips. "Never call them doughnuts. Cardinal sin."

"Sorry. Beignets." He eyed the nightstand clock. "Do you think that café is still open?"

"Café Du Monde? It's always open."

"Let's go."

"Now?"

"Why not now?"

And so we threw on the clothes we'd strewn across the hotel room floor and headed to Café Du Monde. This time, though, I wore flip-flops and Mark opted out of his suit jacket for the plain white shirt, unbuttoned at the collar. We grabbed a table on the periphery of the café overlooking the sidewalk, where a saxophonist had left his instrument case open to collect spare change for playing "Dream a Little Dream of Me." Mark kept an eye out for the waiter while I took in the sights and sounds of the café.

Two tables over, I saw a group of college students who looked like they'd just stepped off Bourbon Street. Beads adorned the girls' necks. Red kiss marks covered the guys' cheeks. One girl still carried a tall souvenir glass, a few sips of pink daiquiri remaining. Her bright eyes and pink cheeks revealed she had finished most of it. I studied each student in the group, and not one looked familiar. I breathed a sigh of relief. There would be no awkward "Didn't I sit next to you in Mr. Harrison's biology class?" conversations.

Next to the students sat a woman, perhaps midthirties with brown, wiry hair and dark-rimmed glasses, more New York than New Orleans. She seemed to be writing in a notebook. Something about the tilt of her head and her smooth, relaxed jaw made me believe she truly had nowhere else to go and nothing else to do.

And then there was the man folding napkins into origami, the transvestite, and the amorous couple, who French kissed between slurps of coffee. I smiled, happy to see the café as I often had in the past—filled with artists, eccentrics, and lovers. The waiter, a young Vietnamese man wearing the uniform white paper cap, approached us then with a stone face. Mark asked for two café au laits and an order of beignets.

"So tomorrow," he said once the waiter left. "We'll ride the trolley out to Tulane?"

"Streetcar," I corrected.

"Streetcar. Beignets." He rolled his eyes. "For people who chant *Who Dat,* you sure are particular about semantics."

I laughed. "What time do we need to be at the symposium?"

He grimaced. "I wish you could tag along, Ruby. Truly. But I think it's too risky. I still know quite a few people at Tulane—my former professors, colleagues in the field. If anyone would see us, put two and two together . . . Besides, I don't think I could concentrate with your pretty face in the crowd." He stroked my cheek. "You can keep yourself busy, right? Nose around campus and the bookstore until I'm done?"

My heart sank. I'd simply assumed I was going to the symposium with him, since he'd asked me to attend that afternoon in his office, even before our relationship began. I hid my disappointment with an exaggerated head nod. "I'll go to the library. I need to work anyway."

"I knew you'd understand." He squeezed my hand. "And how is your thesis shaping up?"

"Really well. Right now, I'm working on the connotations of the word *room.* When Woolf said a woman should have a room of her own, did she mean only a physical space? I think *room* could be something more abstract, a corner of the mind perhaps, a place free of judgment and guilt and expectation."

He said nothing but looked back at me with warm eyes and a soft smile.

"What?"

He shook his head. "Nothing. I just love the way your mind works."

Love. He loves me. Does he love me?

"Anyway, I'm still in the note-taking stage," I went on. "I have fifteen pages so far, but there's still so much information to sift through. So actually, it's a good thing I'm not going to the symposium. I can hole myself up in one of those study cubicles."

"Well, don't work *too* hard," he cautioned. "I wanted this weekend to be about pleasure not business."

I placed my hand on his upper thigh. "Well, I'm certainly enjoying myself."

"Me too. But . . ." He studied me like a crossword puzzle clue, as if both confused and challenged by me. "I think we should talk about what happened earlier. On Royal Street. I'm beginning to think you haven't told me the whole story."

"Story?"

"About your father. What happened when he died."

Mark must have seen my eyes water then, because he tucked one of my errant auburn curls behind my ear, then cupped my cheek with his hand. And the warmth of his hand caused the first tear to fall, and the rest followed suit. I pushed my fingers into the corners of my eyes to stop the weeping, but like a Band-Aid on a gushing cut, it didn't work. In a matter of seconds, I was blubbering—a sudden, snotty-nosed, ugly cry. I covered my face with my hands.

"I'm so sorry," I blurted.

"There's nothing to be sorry about." Mark made a shushing noise. "Ruby, I want to know the whole you, not just the parts you want to show me. I like it when you're happy, but that doesn't mean I don't want to know when you're sad. So don't leave me in the dark, okay?"

I blew my nose first into a napkin plucked from the metal holder on the table.

"It was my fault," I said.

"You said it was a car accident. Were you driving?"

I shook my head no. "It was a hit-and-run. He was just crossing the street."

"How could that be your fault?"

"It wouldn't have happened if I had come home like I was supposed to."

I continued to tell Mark the details, how every year, on the night before Christmas Eve, my father and I went to the Celebration in the Oaks, the annual holiday light display in City Park. It was traditionally just the two of us, ever since I was a toddler, because my mother always took extra shifts at the hospital to assure she'd be off Christmas Day. And with each passing year, the holiday outing became as sacrosanct as Mardi Gras.

"But last year, Heidi invited me to go home with her to Minnesota. And I said yes," I explained. "I wanted to experience a real 'White Christmas.' But more than that, I think I was testing my autonomy. Maybe I wouldn't move back home after graduation; maybe I would stay in the Midwest. And I needed to prove to myself that I could do it, that I could cut that tie—to New Orleans, to my family, to my father. Of course, I had no idea what would happen. He would still be here if I hadn't been so selfish."

"If you had been here, you would have been hit too," Mark rationalized.

"No, because the timing would have been off. Dad and I always went out for cheeseburgers and fries first. It was our little indulgence, our little secret. We'd load up on fat and carbs and then walk the food off in the park, walk the stench of it off our clothes, so Mom wouldn't smell it on us when she got home. But I didn't come home for holiday break, and my father went alone. Not for the cheeseburgers, just the light show. And so if I had been here, we would have been crossing the street at least an hour later. It wouldn't have happened."

"You can't blame yourself, Ruby. You can't play the 'what if' game."

"But I play it all the time, ever since it happened. Even in my sleep. Right after, I started having these recurring nightmares, where my father is walking alone in the park, and people—moms with snot-nosed kids wearing reindeer antler headbands—are glaring at him as he passes because, what forty-five-year-old man goes all by himself to a holiday light show? A pedophile?"

"You're being too hard on yourself," he said.

"Do you know it snowed here last year?" I went on. "The first time in a very long time. It snowed that night, just a few inches, but people here don't know how to drive in snow, not like people up north. They close school here for a dusting of snow. They close roads. And that night, it snowed. And whoever was driving the car that hit him—the police never caught the person—

probably didn't know how to handle driving in that kind of weather."

"This is an awful amount of guilt for you to bear, Ruby." Mark sighed. "Have you seen someone?"

"When it first happened, yes, especially when the nightmares kept me up all night. I was an insomniac. I was diagnosed with post-traumatic stress disorder and prescribed sleeping pills. But I've been fine lately. I've been sleeping well. I haven't been feeling guilty. Until now and . . ."

"—Come here," Mark said, wrapping his arms around me so tightly, his hands clasped at the small of my back. We sat like that—my face buried in his chest, my tears dotting our laps below us—until I gained control of my breathing.

It was then, after we pulled back from the embrace, that I noticed the woman with the notebook—the one who'd looked like she had nowhere to go and nothing to do—watching us. She stared at me as if she knew me, as if trying to place me in her memory, and my mind raced through faces: women my mother used to work with at the hospital, the mothers of my grammar school friends, our old neighbors. Do I know her? I wondered. Does she know me? Had she known my mother and saw a resemblance? No, her expression did not suggest recognition but rather disgust. It seemed she'd seen our exchange. Or had she overheard our conversation? Either way, it was clear she didn't approve.

The waiter provided me a respite from her damnation when he appeared with two mugs filled with a liquid the color of a good summer tan, and a small plate of fried dough coated in powdered sugar. Mark paid while I gave the woman one more glance, and sighed relief when I saw her reabsorbed in her notebook. Maybe she hadn't been looking at me after all, but someone or something past me. I turned to look behind me but saw only an empty table.

I sipped my coffee then—the rising steam a comfort to my red eyes—and delighted in that unmistakably earthy taste of chicory. Meanwhile, Mark's mouth was already full of dough. White powder coated his lips and fingertips after only one bite. He looked adorable.

"Have one," he said, pushing the plate toward me. "Nothing has the power to cheer you up like a big dose of fat and sugar."

Unfortunately, there is no ladylike way to eat a beignet, so I held the mass of warm dough and watched the powdered sugar dangle at the edge, preparing to sprinkle my black dress with Café Du Monde fairy dust. The napkins were so small, I would have had to use twenty of them to protect my lap. With my head positioned above the plate, I brought the beignet to my lips, and I ate the whole thing that way, shoulders curved, chin up. But the powder, miraculously, still sprinkled the front of my dress. I dabbed the spots with water, but the sugar seemed imbedded in the black silk. My rubbing had turned the smudges into splotches.

"I think my dress is ruined," I said after exhausting all efforts.

Mark tossed me a playful wink. "So you'll take it off."

We didn't say more about my father. I think Mark sensed I was emotionally drained from the conversation. Instead, we ate and we drank, listened to the saxophonist, enjoyed the ambiance of the café, the high ceiling and twirling fans, the cup and saucer clinks, the noisy chatter of people out in the wee hours of the morning.

When we finally left the café, we had to pass the college students and the transvestite and the origami artist but first, the woman and her notebook. She lifted her eyes as we went by, but I could not look into them. I feared they'd remind me too much of my mother's, of the guilt I'd somehow escaped in my affection for Mark. I saw only the corners of her mouth turn down, her head shaking.

"Tsk, tsk," I thought I heard her say under the café murmurs and clanking dishes.

Or had she said *mistress*?

Once on Decatur Street, I tried to concentrate on the night sky, on the spires of St. Louis Cathedral aiming for the stars. But I lost the image. The woman's disgust was all I could see. I rubbed the front of my dress once more.

"There's no use." Mark reached around my waist. "What's done is done."

I knew it would wash out. I knew no one would see it that time of night. But until we reached the hotel room, I kept my hands before me, hiding the powdered sugar stains on the front of my dress: the letter *A* the woman from the café had placed there with one hard look.

I opened my eyes to a dark hotel room. The heavy curtains worked so well, I didn't know if it was morning or the afternoon of the following day. But soon, I saw a thin stream of hazy early light where the curtain met the wall.

Mark was still asleep on his stomach, his arm curled over the pillow. The position revealed his muscular arms and toned obliques. I wanted to slide my arm around his waist and kiss him softly on the shoulder, not only for how handsome he looked in slumber, but also for breaking the ice about my father. How could I repay him for his kindness at the café? He'd been so sweet, so strong. He'd seen through my facade. He'd asked the hard questions. He'd listened. How could I wonder if he loved me? Was that not evident in his actions?

I decided not to wake him and instead, slipped out of bed. I'd fallen asleep reading Virginia Woolf's *A Room of One's Own*. The book, my alternative to sleeping pills, was still in bed with me, and I placed it on the nightstand. And that's when I thought of Leonard Woolf.

From my research, I knew Virginia Woolf's husband had been equally as kind, caring for her during the bouts of depression and nervous breakdowns that inevitably followed her completion of a novel. Leonard had given his wife so much time, so much understanding, that she'd come to feel like a burden, that she was ruining his life. In addition to hearing voices and the sensation she was going mad, it was one of the reasons Woolf took her own life in 1941.

"You have been entirely patient with me and incredibly good," Virginia had written to Leonard in the suicide note she penned just before she drowned herself in the River Ouse. "I can't go on spoiling your life any longer. I don't think two people could have been happier than we have been."

I didn't want Mark to see me as a burden. I didn't want to

take advantage of his compassion. And I vowed then not to cry about my father the rest of the weekend, not to appear weak, injured, needy, or emotional. I would prove to him that I was strong. Stoic. I would be fun and easy and carefree, the kind of woman he deserved.

I approached the window then to witness the dawn of a new day. Pushing the curtains aside, I saw the foggy courtyard below. Fog, especially first thing in the morning, is as characteristic to New Orleans as jazz or seafood, and I watched the hazy cloud of white as it revealed tables, chairs, and a chaise lounge, all enjoying the tranquil aftermath of a light morning rain. I reached for Mark's watch—he had set it on the writing table near the window—and found it was quarter to six. I had slept a mere three hours. We'd made love again after the café au lait and beignets and powdered sugar spill. But somehow I felt refreshed enough to venture out for a coffee from the hotel lobby and a courtyard stroll. I would bring Mark back a fresh cup, fixed just the way he liked it. We would start the day off right.

Sunlight slowly penetrated the veil of fog and continued to lift it as I walked through the courtyard that morning. After only a few minutes, the humidity cooled my coffee and it became chalky, but it was a nostalgic taste, actually, like chicken soup. It reminded me of the many Saturday mornings I'd sat with my mom at the kitchen table talking about everything and nothing. I longed to call her, to burden her instead of Mark, but she had no idea I was in New Orleans with him, with my professor, a married man. She would certainly disapprove of my relationship with him, but somehow that seemed a secondary issue to a more unpardonable sin: I went back to New Orleans without her.

I decided to return to the hotel room then, and I was on my way to the lobby to fix Mark's coffee, when I stopped abruptly at the sight of a woman standing just below our hotel room window. Even in the haze of fog, her profile struck me immediately. I recognized her, but in a vague way, like seeing a childhood friend all grown up. Her hair, the color of muddy water, was pinned at the nape of her neck and appeared unkempt and yet refined. Perhaps it was her blouse, white with a frilly lace neck, which suggested reservation. Or her brown ankle-length skirt. Or the narrow, pointy nose of a nun.

I closed my eyes, then reopened them, but still she was there. I stared at her in the silent courtyard, watched her hands fiddle inside the pocket of her cardigan, and tried to place her. She did not look well; her skin was pale, or was it the whiteness of the fog still lifting?

"Hello," I said.

She did not startle, but guided her eyes toward mine with a languid turn of her neck. Her lips parted, but not into a smile. More like a smirk; an all-knowing smirk, almost condescending, as if she knew things I could only read about. And then she simply sauntered away, vanished into the hallway leading to the hotel lobby.

I stood there a moment, numbed by her expression and the ease with which she'd left. I had not heard footsteps. But I soon followed into the hotel's marble-floored lobby. No one was there, except a hotel desk clerk.

"Did someone just come through here?" I asked him. "A woman?"

He twisted his lips and eyebrows together in puzzlement.

"I just saw her. She went this way." I looked back into the courtyard. How could the woman have disappeared so quickly? "She was . . . I think she was wearing a costume?"

The clerk nodded. "This hotel is haunted. We have many resident ghosts," he said rather coolly, as if he'd said the hotel had many available suites.

Ghosts are a part of New Orleans culture as much as parades and pralines; there are ghost tours, cemetery tours, and voodoo tours. But there was something so striking about the woman I'd seen. Her hair, her nose, her outfit. Why had she looked so familiar and yet unable to place? And then the realization exploded in my mind, and I rushed upstairs.

I opened the hotel room door with stealth, but Mark stirred anyway. After looking next to him in bed, he craned his neck to find me. "I thought I heard you leave," he said. His voice was scratchy, as if he'd been in and out of the bars on Bourbon Street all night.

I went straight to the bedside table, where I'd set the copy of *A Room of One's Own* I'd been reading, and flipped to the back cover to study Virginia Woolf's picture. In it, she is young; her hair dark and pulled back at the nape; her skin smooth and white like porcelain; the collar of her blouse feminine and lacy. It is a profile shot, so her nose is prominent and pointy. In contrast, the woman I saw in the courtyard was not so young. She was wrinkled. No, weathered. But the similarity of the two profiles—the Woolf in the photo and the woman in the courtyard—was so striking, a wave of pinpricks swept down the backs of my arms.

"What is it? What are you looking at?" Mark asked.

I didn't answer. My mind was still replaying everything I'd seen and hadn't seen. The woman had looked so real, and yet she'd vanished faster than humanly possible.

"Ruby?" he almost shouted. His voice was forceful, authoritative. It reminded me of that first afternoon in his office, how he'd addressed that girl Madeline and snapped her out of her sadness.

"I saw a woman in the courtyard," I finally divulged. "She looked just like her," I added, pointing to the picture of Virginia Woolf on the back of my book.

Mark rubbed his eyes of sleep, then studied the photo. "If memory serves me right, this city is crawling with characters," he offered. "Lots of people dressing up in costume for no good reason. You probably saw one of those street performers who stands perfectly still for hours, just to get a few quarters."

"But she didn't look like a real person," I argued. "She was pale and white and muted. And she disappeared so quickly. The front desk clerk didn't even see her, and there's no other way out than through the lobby." I paused. "Do you believe in ghosts, Mark?"

"Ghosts. God. I see a lot of gray." He narrowed his eyes. "You think you saw a ghost?"

"No," I said, and then: "I don't know."

"Weren't you reading this last night?" He tapped the book I still held in my hands. "Before you went to bed?"

I nodded.

"You didn't get much sleep," he added.

He was right; I was sleep-deprived.

"You probably saw a woman, someone staying here, who kind of looked like Virginia Woolf," he offered. "And it was foggy, and you were tired, and you only imagined the woman was Woolf."

"It was foggy," I said.

"Well, see. There you go."

His tone was casual, but I noticed the wrinkles of concern forming beside his eyes.

Don't burden him, I thought.

And so I let it go, chalked it up to fatigue and fog. Looking back, I should have known foreshadowing when I saw it. The repercussions of seeing Virginia Woolf in the courtyard did not fully occur to me then.

I had no indication of the dark, twisted path I was about to follow.

Chapter 5

I knocked softly—an apprehensive bumping of my knuckle to the metal screen door—and waited for Mrs. Richards to answer, waited for my courage to emerge.

This is a stupid idea, I thought, staring at the peephole, imagining a discerning eye on the other end. *What possessed you to drive to Milwaukee—during rush hour no less—to see someone who may or may not be home, who may or may not welcome your visit?*

Mark.

Well, Beth and Mark.

I'd finished reading Beth's copy of *A Room of One's Own* Monday night, hunting for more notes in the margin, more clues as to Beth's possible relationship with Mark, and found nothing as incriminating as *Like Cassie's Cabin*. And yet, I couldn't shake the notion that Beth Richards had been in love with Mark. I admit, it was illogical thinking. Three words—a simple reference to his mother's writing retreat—was not proof of her affection. And yet those words, the deep indigo hue of the ink, the whimsical, curly tips of the letter *C*, connoted an emotion I understood at my core, a sick-to-your-stomach aching to love and be loved. I had to know.

And that is why I stood outside Beth Richards's home at dusk on Tuesday evening, despite logic.

Curiosity trumped logic.

I rapped on the door again, this time more deliberately, but my knocking was met with silence, less the flutter of a light breeze. I waited another minute before walking back to my car in defeat.

I was putting my car into reverse when I saw the front door of the brick bungalow swing open, and a woman—her shoulder-length blond hair a shade darker because it was wet—dash down the porch steps toward my car, so quickly, she skipped a step and almost slipped. She waved a yellow towel at me, then mimicked a crossing guard by raising her hand in an effort to get me to stop. She was mouthing something too, but I couldn't hear her over the car radio.

By the time I put the car into park and rolled down my window, she was beside my driver-side door.

"I was in the shower," she blurted between huffs of breath.

"I'm sorry."

She shook her head so adamantly, drips of water fell from her hair to the men's flannel shirt she was wearing; it was two sizes too big, more like a nightshirt, and something I imagined she threw on just to answer the door.

"No, *I'm* sorry. I was in there all of about three minutes." She spoke feverishly, still coming off the adrenaline rush from her Olympic feat of answering the door. "Of all the times for you to come . . . Is this . . . Are you here about Beth?"

The woman needed no introduction—she was Beth Richards's mom. I knew that the moment our eyes met. She looked exactly like her daughter, only older, in the uncanny way my mother and I looked alike, and I immediately recalled Beth Richards, something I had up to that point been unable to do without access to my college yearbooks. My memory of her sharpened—the long blond hair, the calm blue eyes, the lean and athletic build of a runner, and a natural beauty, one that did not depend on lipstick or eyeliner but rather a healthy glow similar to the pink-cheeked aftermath of exercise.

But Mrs. Richards did not have that glow. Her eyes—rimmed by puffy, dark circles from a combination of sleep deprivation and tears—danced wide and focused with desperate anticipation. A bead of water ran down the side of her face, but she didn't seem to notice. The towel remained in her grip.

I opened the car door to address her more directly. "I'm Ruby Rousseau," I said before adding, "I had Beth's suitcase."

"Yes. Yes. Ruby." She nodded too many times, reminding me of a bobble head, before furrowing her brow. "Didn't the detective get it from you yesterday?"

"He did. You haven't seen it?"

"I can't, not until they 'process' it." She used air quotes to illustrate her frustration.

I was about to explain what I was doing there, but she continued her rant.

"And the Pittsburgh Police don't seem to be doing anything either. You know, I wanted to go out there, to Pennsylvania, and they told me not to. I offered to call Beth's friends or people she knows, and Detective Pickens told me to let the police do their job. I told them I wanted Beth's picture on the news, and they said we needed to wait. Wait for what? We don't have time to wait."

After looking into Mrs. Richards's desperate eyes, hearing the anxiety in her voice, I chastised myself for even being there. This woman's daughter was *missing,* presumably dead, and I had the audacity to bother her, drag her out of the only shower she'd probably taken in days—the only three minutes in which she'd thought of herself—just to snoop into Beth's private life, just to find out whether something I "sensed" from reading the margin of a book was true. Mrs. Richards wanted information, clues to her daughter's whereabouts. That's why she'd rushed out the door with sopping wet hair, almost breaking her neck on the steps. *What a disappointment,* I thought, *when she discovers I have nothing concrete to offer.*

I swallowed the lump of guilt in my throat. "I can't imagine how hard this is for you, Mrs. Richards," I said, preparing to leave. "I'm so sorry to have bothered you."

She stopped me.

"I want to be bothered." Her voice boomed. "The police

haven't bothered me enough. I'm going crazy, Ruby, just waiting for things to 'process' or 'solidify' or 'come to fruition' or whatever police jargon the detective is using today." She looked back at me, her eyes suddenly soft and tearful. "I need to talk. To a human being, someone other than myself. Can you . . . can you come inside?"

Stepping into the foyer of the house, I took in the smell of burnt coffee and stale air, a home in desperate need of a cracked window. A volcano of unopened mail had erupted on the console. Several newspapers, still in plastic sleeves muddy from a recent rain, sat on the yellowed linoleum just inside the door.

Mrs. Richards threw her wet towel on top of the pile of newspapers. "There's all this shit in this house," she blurted. "And yet without Beth, it feels so empty."

I found her vernacular both startling and endearing, yet I didn't know what to say, or whether I should say anything. Suddenly I felt the need to lie, to give a solid reason for my impromptu visit. But just as I was about to speak, Mrs. Richards let out a sigh, took my hands in hers, and patted them hard several times, as if to absolve me of a lifetime of sins.

"Should we have something warm to drink?" she asked.

I was about to say "I don't want to bother you" but remembered she wanted to be bothered. Instead I followed her to the kitchen.

Mrs. Richards cleared space for me at the table, and I stole a glance at the plethora of sticky notes and maps and papers and photos that had not only overtaken the tabletop, but also grown like a vine up the adjoining wall. It seemed Mrs. Richards was running her own investigation on Beth's disappearance, and the table served as headquarters.

"I keep going over it, every detail, thinking I'll see something different than last time," she explained as she pulled her damp locks up into a ponytail before moving to the stove to put on a teakettle.

A Room of One's Own—Beth's notes in the margin—could be the *something different* she is looking for, I thought, but I decided to take the book out of my purse later, when the time was right. We would baby step our way there; we would meet her needs before mine.

I eyed her collection of sticky notes and maps again and imagined my own mother doing the same if I were the missing girl, that she would not rest—physically or mentally—until she found me. My curiosity mounted.

"I don't know much about what happened," I said. "The detective was pretty tight-lipped about Beth's case."

Mrs. Richards pulled a canister of tea bags from the countertop and set it on the table. "I'm Beth's *mother*, and I can't get information out of him."

"It wasn't in the newspaper either," I added.

"Thank you." She plopped down in the chair across from me then, as if I'd finally given her permission to do so. "I just don't understand why Beth's face isn't all over the television. I mean, how can people find her if they don't know she's missing? How will they spot her if they don't know what she looks like?"

I remembered asking Detective Pickens a similar question, and his answer had been elusive. Like Mrs. Richards, I couldn't fathom why Beth's story had not made it to the national news stations.

Beth's mother reached past me for a manila folder, pulled a photo from it, and handed it to me. "This is the one I picked out for the news broadcasts," she said.

It was Beth's senior picture from Tarble. "She was beautiful," I said.

"*Was.*" Mrs. Richards's lips trembled as she stared at her daughter's picture over my shoulder. "I can't get myself to use that word."

"*Is,*" I blurted, damning the obituaries for conditioning me to use the past tense. "She *is* beautiful."

She gave me a forgiving smile, not big but perhaps the most she could manage.

"Do you want to go over it again?" I offered, trying to repair the damage of my earlier word choice. "I actually work for a newspaper in Chicago."

"You're a journalist?"

I nodded, then shrugged, then nodded again. Given the circumstances, it would be inappropriate, I thought, to tell her what I really did for a living.

"I've got a fresh pair of eyes and ears," I added.

Mrs. Richards let out a long breath, as if she'd been holding it under water for weeks.

"It was Friday. Just this past Friday," she finally said. "I dropped Beth off at Mitchell—that's the airport here in Milwaukee—just past three o'clock. She was going to Pittsburgh for the weekend for a photography workshop. Did you know Beth was an amateur photographer?"

I shook my head. "I thought she majored in science."

"She did. Biology. She's in medical school now, here in Milwaukee. But her dad bought her a thirty-five millimeter when she was five, and I guess you could say photography has been her artistic outlet ever since."

Beth's mom went on to tell me that the workshop, the one Beth was going to in Pittsburgh, was on wedding photography. Beth thought she could shoot ceremonies on weekends and during the summer to help pay her steep tuition.

"I didn't understand why she had to go to Pittsburgh of all places," her mother noted. "But I know better than to question Beth when she sets her mind to something, though I am the one who convinced her to fly. She wanted to drive, and I told her it wasn't safe. A woman alone driving on the Interstate for ten hours." She rested her chin on her hand. "It's my fault."

I recognized the guilt contracting the muscles of her face. "But how could you have known? My mom would have said the same thing," I offered.

She nodded, but unconvincingly. "I made Beth promise to call when she got there," she continued. "Her flight was at five, and it's an hour-and-twenty-minute trip, give or take, so I expected a call no later than seven. But hours went by, and she never called. So I started calling her, a dozen or so times, and it just kept going to voice mail. I thought maybe her flight had been delayed, and she couldn't answer her phone because she was still in the air. But then I checked the status of her flight on the computer—Beth showed me how to do that once—and that's when I found out her plane had landed on time, many hours before. And so I called the hotel, it was nearing midnight

by then in Pittsburgh, and they said she hadn't checked in yet."
She paused only to take a breath. I didn't interrupt.

"I knew something was wrong. I just did. It wasn't like Beth,
but I told myself to be rational. You know, I didn't want to over-
react. I started thinking she had missed her flight and took another one, a later one. And maybe she hadn't charged her phone
and that's why she hadn't answered it. But I watched the sun
come up, and I *still* hadn't heard from her. I didn't know who to
call. So I dialed 911 and they connected me to Detective Pickens."

I recalled my conversation with the detective the day before.
"And he found out she was on the plane, after all?"

"Her ticket had been processed, and the flight attendant
remembered her." Mrs. Richards's eyes teared then, and she
pulled a crumpled tissue from the pocket of her jeans. When
the tissue gave out, she used the back of her hand. She crossed
her arms then, as if warding off a chill, the remnants of what
no longer looked like a tissue dangling from her hand. "So Beth
is somewhere in Pittsburgh. But where? What happened to my
daughter?"

As if on cue, the stove flame singed the wet bottom of the teakettle and let out a startling hiss. Mrs. Richards hurried to the
stove. Silence filled the room while she tended the teapot and
I looked through the assorted tea bags in the canister on the
table. I selected something herbal, cinnamon apple, and set the
bag down in front of me as soon as she started talking again.

"And the police . . . I don't understand. Have they checked the
hospitals? Beth wasn't feeling well before she left. She'd been
fatigued and lethargic. She didn't have much of an appetite.

Maybe she fainted in the airport bathroom and hit her head and has amnesia. And she's just sitting in some hospital bed in Pittsburgh, staring out the window, not knowing who she is."

As Mrs. Richards poured hot water into two mugs on the counter, I looked at the contents of the table and wall once more. There was a timeline, including exact times for every Internet search Mrs. Richards had conducted over the course of four days, and every phone call. I found my name there under Sunday @ 6:15 P.M. It was misspelled "Ruby Russo," with the added detail, "Friend from Tarble, has Beth's suitcase," in black pen and another note in red pen, perhaps an afterthought, "Sounded genuine. Not a suspect."

I turned my eyes from the wall when Mrs. Richards approached the table with our mugs. Each boasted its own silver stirring spoon.

"What do *you* think?" she asked, selecting the same herbal tea I did from the jar. "How did my daughter vanish into thin air?"

I stalled by dipping my tea bag into the mug several times; it was piping hot, and I burned my finger. "Mrs. Richards . . ."

"—You can call me Janice," she said.

"Okay. Janice. I don't think it's my place to hypothesize."

"You can be honest."

I shrugged and wondered if Detective Pickens had shared his missing persons statistics with Beth's mother, if she knew the odds were against her.

"A mother should know, shouldn't she?" Janice went on. "If her own child is dead? I would know. And I just don't believe . . . I feel her, Ruby. Here." She placed her palm flat on her chest.

I remembered how I'd felt the evening prior, reading Beth's book in its entirety, looking for more clues about Mark. I'd felt Beth, even heard her voice, as if she was speaking to me not beyond the grave but perhaps just before it.

"Then trust your instincts," I told Janice.

Beth's mother clutched her mug like a teddy bear and stared into her tea. She looked so lonely.

"Do you have other children?" I asked.

She shook her head. "It's just Beth and me. Ken—my husband, Beth's father—passed a long time ago. Beth was seven. She was devastated. You know how little girls are with their daddies."

I did know, and yet I would have said I knew better how little girls were *without* their daddies. I told Janice then about my own father's unexpected death, and that I too was an only child.

"I never knew we had so much in common," I said, suddenly reminded of why I'd come to visit Janice in the first place. Did Beth and I have more in common than family dynamics? I wondered. Had we both been in love with the same man?

"Did Beth keep in touch with many girls from Tarble over the summer?" I asked, playing with the tea bag in my cup. I sensed Janice had met an emotional threshold on the subject of her daughter's disappearance and would be up to changing the subject, a subject I so desperately wanted to indulge.

"Sure. She went there to visit some friends taking summer session."

I dropped the tea bag. "Do you remember any of these girls' names?"

"One of them works for the college. Heidi. She was in your class."

Heidi Callahan. I'd thought my former best friend—the only Heidi in our class—was back home in Minneapolis. And yet all summer, she'd apparently been at Tarble, working for the college after graduation. But Heidi and Beth had never been friends; they were acquaintances, just like Beth and me. Was it possible they'd become friends after I dropped out?

"How often did Beth go?" I asked.

"Almost every weekend."

"She went for the day?"

"Sometimes she stayed overnight, even though we live so close. It was fun for her, I think, staying in the dorms. Like she never graduated." Janice set her mug down on the table then with a thud, as if she'd reached a conclusion. "Ruby, I see where you're going with this. And I think you're right."

I stared back at her in confusion. There was no way she knew my ulterior motive. "I am?"

"We need to tell people at Tarble about Beth."

"Oh. Right. We do."

"The detective talked to some students and professors at the med school, but I don't think he has talked to anyone from Tarble. Except you. And there might be someone who knows something."

Could it be Mark? I wondered. Was he the *someone* who knew *something*? Had Beth really been visiting Heidi Callahan all summer? Or was that just the excuse Beth gave her mother so she could spend weekends with Mark?

"When was the last time she went to Tarble?" I asked.

"I think it was the beginning of September. She's been home every weekend since."

"Why did she stop going?"

"School started. Too busy, I guess. Plus, like I told you, she wasn't feeling her best." Janice set her mug down again. "You know, I've been meaning to call Sarah to tell her. But I don't have her phone number."

"You mean Beth's roommate? Sarah Iverson?"

Janice nodded.

"She doesn't know Beth is missing?"

"I wanted to call her, see if she'd heard from Beth, but the detective told me to wait. Like I said before, wait for what?"

I didn't understand why Detective Pickens was keeping a tight lid on Beth's disappearance, why he wasn't interested in Beth's past friends or relationships at Tarble. He had a hidden motive, perhaps. And I had mine. By that point, Beth's book was burning a hole through my purse, and I needed to find a nonchalant way of introducing the topic to Janice.

I remembered the postcard tucked inside the book.

"Did you know Tarble's Reunion is this weekend?" I asked, finally removing the bag from my tea. It had grown bitter from being steeped too long. "Did Beth mention it?"

Just then, the phone rang, and Janice ran out of the room to answer it. "I don't let any call go to the answering machine," she explained.

I finished my last sip of tea before picking up a stack of photos from the table. I saw Beth at age six, wearing a pink tutu. Beth at age twelve, in a ski parka and glasses. Beth at sixteen in an aquamarine evening dress, posed in front of a fireplace beside a boy with a matching cumberbund and bow tie. Janice must have collected the snapshots in the past few days, trying to scrounge up the memory of her daughter, physical evidence that she existed, and still exists. I started thinking that if Beth was dead—I wanted to believe she was alive—but if she was dead, if she never came home, these photos would be all she had left. And it was then I decided not to show *A Room of One's Own* to Janice. I would not dare introduce the idea that Beth might have had an affair with a married man. I wasn't going to be the one to destroy Beth's reputation with her mother. It wouldn't be fair. After all, my own mother did not know about Mark.

I peeked around the corner of the kitchen then and saw Janice had taken the phone to a four-season room at the rear of the house, perhaps for privacy. I figured it was the only chance I'd get to return Beth's book to its rightful place, and I took it.

I found Beth's bedroom door partially ajar at the end of the hall and pushed it open, forcefully, because it stuck on the thick carpet. Once inside, I felt the urge to snoop, to peek into the life of this girl I had not truly known. But I feared Janice would somehow know I'd intruded. Instead, I let my eyes examine the space. Beyond the neatly made twin bed, recently dusted dresser, and clutter-free desk, the room served as an exhibit of sorts for this budding photographer. Pictures—some portraits, some landscapes, some abstract—covered every available inch of wall space. Some were displayed in formal frames behind glass; others hung nonchalantly off metal clips resembling wooden clothes hangers.

Along the far wall, a collection of photographs caught my eye, each an artistic-angled snapshot of the Tarble College campus. Beth's subject choice startled me. Far from being commercial or brochure worthy, the pictures captured the day-to-day happenings of campus life with the keen eye of a student. A sunlit staircase in Langley Hall. The sun rising over Lake Michigan. A tree losing its leaves in front of the student center. The little red bridge over the creek at the edge of campus.

The red bridge. It had been Mark's favorite spot to meet up, conveniently on campus but private. I'd walk there and wait for him—sometimes feeding bread to the ducks swimming below, sometimes just taking in the tree-lined view of Frieburg Chapel. Coincidentally, Beth's picture, taken in late fall, captured my exact perspective the very last time I'd stood on that bridge waiting for Mark. Bare tree branches. A muddy gray sky.

I released the photo from the metal-and-wire hanger to get a closer look, disregarding my earlier decision not to touch anything. Immediately, I heard a *whoosh* sound echo off the wall, followed by a crisp tap on the baseboard. It was another picture, one Beth had concealed behind the photo of the bridge. Two faces stared back at me as I reached to pick it up. Beth and Mark. Together. Smiling. His arm around her. Her head resting slightly on his shoulder. It was a close-up, the background fuzzy. But I guessed the photo had been taken at some sort of play or musical performance. In the distance, I made out a few men in suits and a woman wearing an old-fashioned wide-brimmed hat and draped scarf, obviously one of the performers interacting with the audience in the lobby after the show.

"You know the problem with photographs," Mark had said to me once, when I tried to take our picture, my arm extended as far away as possible to snap a good shot. "They're like diaries. Incriminating."

As my cheeks flushed with jealousy, I heard footsteps in the hallway and instinctually tucked the photo into my purse, between the pages of *A Room of One's Own,* to keep it from being bent. It was officially the second personal belonging I'd stolen from Beth Richards.

I turned in time to see Janice in the doorway and prepared to explain why I was in Beth's bedroom without her. Janice did not look angry, though. All the color in her cheeks had faded to gray. Her eyes had turned glassy.

Palms open, she held the cordless phone out to me, as if it were covered in blood.

"The detective said Beth fits a profile," was all she said.

"A profile?" I asked. "Of what?"

Janice dropped the phone. "The victim of a serial killer."

Waiting to talk to Detective Pickens, I sat in the Milwaukee Police Department corridor and tried to erase the images from my mind—of Beth's hands bound with rope, her mouth gagged, her pale white body floating facedown in a river, a dirty fingernailed man approaching her from behind—but they replayed like scenes from *Law & Order.* And the words came: *Beth Richards, 22, of Milwaukee, died October 8—*

Fortunately, Detective Pickens maneuvered through the heavy steel door and interrupted Beth's obituary middraft. "Ms. Rousseau?"

I jumped to my feet. "You startled me."

"You've succeeded in surprising me as well. What can I do for you? Or did you drive two hours just to say hello?"

"I was at Janice's house when you called," I explained.

Truth was, I hadn't had time to return Beth's book to its

proper place in her room. And I certainly wasn't going to bring it up to Janice after she told me about the serial killer. My only option—once Janice's sister, Susan, arrived to relieve me of my *sitting with Janice* duties—was to deliver the book to a more objective party.

Detective Pickens, unfortunately, was that person.

He lurched his head toward the door. "To my office," he said.

I followed him into a white hallway that seemed brighter than the midday sun. We walked in silence, down one hallway and then another, passing black steel doors fitted with square heavy paned glass windows. In one room, a man sat with his head in his hands. Was he a witness or a suspect? I wondered.

In his office, Detective Pickens offered me a chair covered in soiled, orange pleather. I sat, but only on the front half of the seat, not wanting to get too comfortable, if that was even possible. Meanwhile, he crammed his body into his desk chair and moved a stack of manila folders to another spot on his messy desk. I watched him rub the rolls of fat on the back of his neck.

"How much do you know?" he asked.

"Beth fits a profile?"

Another sigh. "The Pittsburgh PD is staking out a suspect this very moment. Beth is his type. He likes them young, tall, and pretty, okay? Blond hair. The others also went missing from PIT. One a year ago, another about six months ago. In other words, he was due to strike again. We have him profiled. Everything fits, even the time frame."

I conjured images of the Boston Strangler, Son of Sam, and Ted Bundy. "What happened to the other girls?" I asked. "The ones who went missing from the Pittsburgh airport?"

"Found them dead. Raped, stabbed, dumped in a body of water."

Raped. Stabbed. Dumped. I imagined Beth's white arm, a gold bracelet dangling from her delicate wrist, buried in a clump of muddy weeds.

"Without a body or an arrest at the moment, we're refraining from breaking this to the news." He shook his fat finger in my face. "So no talking to your colleagues at the *Chronicle,* okay?"

I nodded my agreement. It made sense to me then, why Beth's disappearance had not been splattered all over the national news like stories of other missing girls. In a tactical move, the police were withholding information from the suspect.

The detective licked his lips. "You're a far cry from Oak Park, Ms. Rousseau. What brought you to Milwaukee this evening?"

"I went to visit Janice."

His eyes burned through mine. I looked away.

"And?" he probed.

"It's probably nothing."

"Uh-huh. Then why are you here?"

I hugged my purse. "It's probably moot now, considering this new development, but there's something I think you should know." I swallowed hard and searched for the right words. "Beth was, or I think there's a chance she might have been, romantically involved with one of her professors at Tarble." My hands spun in a circle before me, my best mime for what *romantically involved* meant.

Detective Pickens seemed unmoved.

"He's married," I added.

Still, his face was stone. "How do you think you know this?"

"I don't, not for *certain,* but . . . it was in the book." I felt small—physically and mentally—in the detective's presence and suddenly lost all dexterity in my fingertips. To get to the book, I had to remove almost everything from my purse—cell phone, wallet, a tampon, my receipt from Starbucks, a Ziploc bag of almonds, my vitamin tin. The detective eyed the guts of my handbag as I handed *A Room of One's Own* to him, open to the page in question. "Beth took notes in the margin, and from what she wrote, I think . . ." I stopped talking because I sounded ridiculous. How would I be able to convince the detective of this fact without showing him the picture I stole from Beth's room, a picture that I had safely zipped into the inside pocket of my purse with the Reunion postcard? How would I do it without sharing my own sordid past?

Detective Pickens merely glanced at the page. Instead, he fixed his eyes on me. "Did you take this from the Richards's home today?" His voice was harsh, accusatory.

"Actually, it was in Beth's suitcase."

"You mean the suitcase I retrieved from you yesterday? The one I have locked up right now in evidence?"

"It was a mistake. I took the book out when I looked through it. See, that's how I got Beth's phone number in the first place. From the inside front cover."

As I watched the detective examine the inside flap, I added, "And I could have sworn I put it back in there. But somehow I didn't, and—"

"And you decided to have yourself a little read."

"I fully intended to return it."

The detective sighed, revealing a bottom row of crooked, yellowed teeth. He turned the book over in his sausagelike fingers and hung it upside down, letting the pages sway back and forth, waiting for something to fall out. Nothing did. Then he flipped back to the original page. Looking down the bridge of his nose, he read with wide eyes, "'Like Cassie's Cabin.'" He paused, scratched his mustache. "What does *that* mean?"

"It's a reference to this professor's cabin; it belonged to his mother first."

"Oh, of course that's what it means." The corners of his lips curled downward, making the distinction between the end of his chin and the beginning of his neck impossible to find. His sarcasm was thick. "Obviously."

"Her name was Cassandra," I explained. "But she went by Cassie."

"And *his* name?"

"Mark Suter."

Detective Pickens seemed to swipe the inside of his cheek with his tongue. He jotted something down on a scratch sheet of paper. "And how does this mean Beth had an affair with Mark Suter?"

"He told Beth about his mother's cabin, and that's something . . . I guess you would call it intimate? Not something he would tell just *any* student. Unless, you know." I made that romantically involved circle again with my hands.

"But *you* know about it." He mimicked my gesture. "So, you know."

I shifted in my chair and the orange pleather squeaked under my jeans, mimicking the sound of passing gas. I watched a smile form at the detective's lips for a half second then disappear.

"I just thought it was a clue," I said into the sudden silence.

"A clue? That's cute. Like Harriet the Spy. But every clue has an implication, Ms. Rousseau. Are you suggesting this Suter kidnapped Beth? Killed her?"

"I never said that." My chest tightened, realizing I hadn't thought the conversation all the way through. What *was* I implying? *Who* was I implicating? Was this about finding Beth or satiating my own curiosity?

I reached into my purse then and grabbed the Tarble postcard. "I also found this in the book. Maybe Beth was still seeing him. She went to Tarble a lot over the summer, Janice said." I pointed to the dates listed on the card. "Maybe she was planning to see him this weekend."

The detective barely looked at the card; he stared instead at my purse. "Is there a bottom to that bag?" he asked. "What else you got in there?"

The photo. If I showed it to him, he'd see the proof, that Beth and Mark were in love with each other. Then, he'd confiscate it—just like the book and the postcard—and call it *evidence.* And he'd probably arrest me for petty theft.

"Nothing," I said.

"Okay, look, you did the right thing by bringing this to my attention," he said brusquely, his patience deflated. "But right now, the chance that Beth *might* have had an affair with her married professor is, as you so eloquently said earlier, moot. Because I know the Pittsburgh PD is about to arrest the man responsible for Beth's murder. A man who was, verified by airport surveillance, at PIT when Beth's plane landed."

I said nothing. He coughed.

"Besides, I'll have you know, I did my job here," he continued. "I scoured Beth's credit card statements, her cell phone calls, her med school e-mail, and personal e-mail. We searched her car and her bedroom. And I uncovered nothing to suggest Beth Richards was having an affair with a married man or anyone else for that matter. There were no patterns or frequent phone calls." He licked his lips. "Okay?"

"Okay."

As I stood to leave, I watched the detective toss the book and postcard to the end of his desk, where an empty potato chip bag also sat, as if it meant nothing to his investigation. As if it meant nothing to Beth Richards.

As if it meant nothing to me.

December

   If there's one image of Mark that haunts me, it's this: he's walking through campus, amid the chaos of academia, seemingly oblivious to the world around him. He strolls, actually. And that requires confidence, faith, and clarity.

   I envied that.

   His world was his own creation. Mine was too, until I fell in love with him. And then my world became a mere collection of the places we went to together: the coffee shop off campus, Royal Street, the banks of the Mississippi River, Café Du Monde. If he wasn't with me, I wasn't alive. I could not drift into foreign lands beyond the pages of our love story.

   Does Mark love me? I think so, at least he did at first, when we were happy, when the future was ours. And if he loved me then, he could love me again.

   They say time heals all wounds, but I beg to differ. It seems time only deepens the scars.

Chapter 6

One Year Earlier

By midmorning on Saturday, the fog had long dissolved, but the image of Virginia Woolf did not dissipate from my mind. Her pointy nose and pale skin shadowed me like a restless night's sleep. She was there, ever present while Mark and I had coffee and eggs, and there still, as we rode the streetcar down St. Charles to Tulane University. I wasn't able to shirk her until we were walking through the quad near Gibson Hall toward the symposium.

"I used to play football there," Mark said, pointing to the large grassy area beside us.

I imagined a nineteen-year-old Mark tossing the old pigskin in the open space with his college buddies, his hair lighter, sun kissed. At that time, my parents, only three years older than Mark, lived in an apartment above a store on Toulouse Street. That meant Mark and I had lived in proximity for several years. Had we passed each other one afternoon in Audubon Park? I wondered. Me in a stroller and he, a twentysomething college student, out for a jog? I wanted to believe it was possible, that our paths had crossed all those years ago, proof we were destined to be together.

I also wanted to coil my arm through his but didn't. Someone might see.

"Do you miss it?" I asked instead. "Your college days?"

"I didn't think so. It's been decades. But being here . . . yeah, it makes me a little nostalgic."

I had visited Tulane a few times in high school at my father's suggestion—he'd urged me to attend a college close to home—and I remembered the campus was beautiful, a haven for trees. I stared up now at the thick, moss-covered trunks giving birth to litters of twisted branches.

"Tell me something about you," I said. "From when you went to school here, something that would surprise me."

"Like what?"

"I don't know . . . Did you throw wild parties? Or teepee the president's house? Maybe you streaked through this quad on a dare?"

"Teepee and streaking? Nope, not me."

"Did you ever do anything crazy?" I prodded. "Unexpected?"

Mark studied the corridor of buildings for a moment. "Okay. You see that bench there? In front of that stone building with circular windows in the eves?"

I nodded eagerly.

"I once sat on that bench for six hours straight."

My mind went first to academics. "Were you conducting some kind of sociology experiment?"

"Nope. I was stupid and in love."

The space between my breasts ached suddenly, as if my lungs had deflated. Had Mark met his wife, Meryl, in college? Here, where we now walked?

"Her name was Jenny," he continued.

The aching subsided. Meryl was, once again, miles away.

"Jenny?" I repeated.

"She was a freshman. Brunette. A theater major. I saw her one day in the student union." He let out a small laugh, as if embarrassed. "And I so admired this girl from afar that I waited outside her class all day, just to strike up a conversation. Unfortunately, she was sick that day of all days. But two days later, she saw me in the union and approached me, saying she'd heard about my heroic feat and was flattered. We dated a few months until . . ." A shadow crossed his face then. "She dumped me for some football player. Henry something or other. All brawn and no brains. Such is life."

"Poor baby."

"Probably a blessing in disguise. She was . . . a troubled girl. I guess that's what I would call it now. Emotionally unstable. She was a very talented actress—even got the lead in *The Mikado,* if I remember correctly—but like a lot of creative people, she had her emotional demons."

After my crying spells the night before, what I'd divulged to Mark in the café—about my guilt and nightmares and sleeping pills—not to mention the Woolf sighting that morning, I worried if Mark would describe me as *emotionally unstable*. Did he think I was the creative type with emotional baggage?

"Did she marry the football player?" I asked.

"Doubtful. I heard she dropped out of school to . . . I don't know, go into the Peace Corps or something." He shrugged the memory away then stopped suddenly on the path. "The symposium is just down this way. I think we should part ways here. Just in case."

"Fine," I said, trying not to look sad.

"For the record, I want to kiss you right now. More than anything."

I smiled and gave him a firm handshake instead. "Good-bye, Professor Suter."

"Good-bye, Miss Rousseau," he said, holding my hand longer than necessary.

I walked a mere three steps before he called after me. "Are you going to be okay?"

"I'll find my way around."

"No, I was talking about . . . what happened this morning. You're okay, right?"

"Oh, I was just tired," I explained. "Like you said, I didn't get much sleep."

He nodded, his lips pursed with worry, and I turned before he could say more. I'm not sure if he watched me walk away, because I never looked back, afraid to see if his concern had traveled from his lips to his eyes, to those creases in his forehead.

Maybe his concern was valid, after all. Because when I got to the library and pulled my thesis materials from my messenger bag, my notes—all fifteen handwritten pages of quotes and comments and details—were missing. Gone.

I'm losing my mind, I thought as I scoured every pocket and zippered compartment of my bag, sorted every item, flipped through the pages of every book.

Again.

And again.

And again.

Later that day, as we rode the streetcar back to the Quarter, I asked Mark if he'd seen my thesis notes in the hotel room before we left. He couldn't remember.

"I'm sure they'll turn up," he said. "Speaking of your thesis, I hope you don't mind, but I shared some of your ideas at the symposium today."

My cheeks flushed with flattery. "You did? What?"

"Your contemplations on the word *room.* What you said last night in the café was brilliant. I had to share it. I gave you credit, of course. Not by name. I just called you my star pupil."

I punched his arm. "You did not."

"Okay, I didn't. I referred to you as a *colleague.*"

"Colleague." I smiled. "I like the sound of that."

"Well, you have a real gift—a complex and intricate mind."

He thinks I'm brilliant, I thought. *Not emotionally unstable, but complex. Intricate.*

When I turned to say more I found Mark's eyes closed, lulled by the white noise and rhythmic motion of the streetcar, his head resting on the back of the bench seat. It had been a long day. So I took the opportunity to check the contents of my bag a final time, convinced the passage of hours would merit different results. They didn't, and I passed the time instead by rereading Charlotte Perkins Gilman's *The Yellow Wallpaper*.

In the story, a woman suffering from postpartum depression is forced by her doctor husband to spend a summer on "rest cure" therapy in a room with a "repellent, almost revolting" yellow wallpaper. Diagnosed with "a slight hysterical tendency" and denied the opportunity to write, the woman becomes obsessed with the wallpaper's pattern and what she sees beyond it: a creeping woman. The main character begins to believe the creeping woman is being held captive by the wallpaper's maddening twists and turns and is disturbed to the point of ripping the paper off the wall, peeling it back piece by piece.

I had just gotten to the description of the infamous yellow wallpaper when Mark stirred.

"Sorry," he said, shaking off sleep. "I don't know what came over me."

"It's okay," I said, slipping the story back into my purse. And then, the words crawled up my throat without permission. "I want to go to the cemetery."

His eyes shot wide open. "Did you say what I think you said?"

I nodded. "I want to go to my dad's grave."

He rolled his neck from side to side and sighed. "Okay, confession time: cemeteries freak me out. Especially the ones here. Dead bodies should not be aboveground."

"Don't you ever visit your mom?" I asked.

"Only in my mind."

I looked outside the streetcar window and saw the sun was

already dipping below the horizon. It would be dark soon. "Can you make an exception?" I kissed his neck. "For me?"

He let out a low growl, as if I'd targeted some sort of G-spot on his neck. "Of course. I can't in good conscience let you wander around a cemetery at night by yourself. Where is it?"

"He's in Lafayette," I said, already pulling the cord above my head to alert the driver of our stop. "We can get off on Washington Ave."

While we walked a block to the cemetery, I told Mark I wanted him to wait for me at the front gate. "This is just something I have to do alone," I explained.

"I'm not letting you out of my sight," he argued.

So we struck a compromise: he would walk me to the row of graves and wait while I made the rest of the journey alone. He would be able to see me, but not hear me. That would suffice.

Unlike Mark, I had never been afraid of cemeteries, thanks to my father. When Mom started working second shift at the hospital, he used to bring me to Lafayette Cemetery as a girl to see his family's tomb. We'd picnic there—fried chicken and biscuits with butter and honey—on the two steps leading up to the vault door. I grew to appreciate the tombs' ornate architecture and features as we strolled the aisles of graves. I likened the cemetery to a small village, outfitted with houses all the perfect size for a six-year-old girl.

"I want to live here someday," I had told my father on one occasion.

"Someday, you might," he'd said. "But a long, long, long time from now." He had brushed the curls from my forehead, pushing my bangs in the direction of my cowlick. "A long time," he repeated.

"Why a long time? I want to live here now. I could live in the little house with Grandma and Grandpa."

"But they don't live here."

"But this is where we visit them."

"Their bodies are here, but their spirits aren't. Grandma and Grandpa only come when we're here."

"But if I lived there, they would be here all the time."

"You can't live here, Ruby. You need a special ticket; you know, like the ones we get at the movie theater? You need one to get in, and you don't have one."

"How do I get one?"

He'd paused, as if considering his choice of words. "You get one when you die."

"Then I'd like to die."

"Don't say that," he'd scolded.

"I'm sorry. Did I say something bad?"

"No, sweetie." Again, he'd pressed my bangs to my forehead. "Dying isn't bad. It's just that you have a long, beautiful life to live."

"But can I die later? After my beautiful life?"

"Yes," he'd said. "You may."

"Will you die with me?"

"I suppose. You, me, and Mommy, we can all die together. As a family."

"And Fat Tuesday?"

My father had considered our obese housecat. "Sure. He can come too."

I'd thought it over and agreed. "And then we can all live with Grandma and Grandpa in the little white house?"

He'd tapped my button nose with his index finger. "All of us."

All of this came back to me as I traversed the stretch of grass leading to the rear section of the cemetery. I knew the way to my father's grave, even in the dark, as if my brain had been programmed like a GPS to find it.

It was smaller than I remembered as a girl. The tomb, which had once seemed big enough to house my entire family, was only the size of a large pantry or bathroom. And I walked the perimeter to ascertain that fact. One side was sunken a half foot and the white plaster exterior had been weathered by the elements. It had seemed more pristine to me as a child.

"Hi, Daddy," I said, sitting on the stoop. "I should have brought you some chicken."

And then a sudden pain stabbed my eyes, and tears fell through my closed lids.

"Oh, Daddy," I said. "I'm so sorry."

I sat beside the tomb then and sobbed, and I knew I wasn't only apologizing for the sequence of events, the guilt I bore, that led to my father's death. I knew I was saying sorry for something else. Something I hoped I didn't have to say out loud, something I hoped he could understand from his side. Something I had tried to rationalize since I first kissed Mark in his Jeep. Something I realized the night before, after the woman in the café and the stain on my dress.

I was a bad girl.

The wind picked up just then and brought a chill past the tomb. I heard a thump and looked up through blurry eyes, wondering if Mark had decided to follow me after all. And that's when I saw the shoes—girlish, black lace-up boots with a sharp toe—sticking out from behind a nearby mausoleum. I shot up from the stoop to see a woman wearing a long black skirt and a matching black jacket that came to a ruffled V at the top, exposing a high-neck lacy collar. I blinked, rubbed my eyes, even repeated the word *no* in my mind, willing her to disappear from my view. But she didn't. In the dark of night, I squinted to discern her black hair, parted down the middle then braided on each side of her head and pinned up in the back.

I knew who she was, and she was not Virginia Woolf.

I squeezed my eyes shut, my fists also clenched at my sides, and counted five long seconds. When I opened them again, she was no longer there. But I caught a flash of something—black, flowy, the corner of her skirt perhaps?—from behind the edge of the nearby tomb. Had I made the woman disappear, or had she simply walked away?

I ran in the direction I'd seen her, behind the tomb and others, zigzagging between them so forcibly I tripped on one and slammed against the white cement, scraping my hand. Even though my palm burned—a thin layer of skin lost during the fall—I kept running until I came to the exit. When I felt a hand on my shoulder, I jerked away, screaming into the night.

But it was only Mark.

"It's me. It's me," he cried. "Jesus, Ruby. What happened?"

Catching my breath, I looked left and right for her, as if expecting the woman to reappear and prove my sanity to Mark.

"She was right here," I panted.

"Who?" And then I saw it, the worry of wrinkles around his eyes. "Virginia Woolf?"

I shook my head no and looked again for her.

But Charlotte Perkins Gilman—who had looked real enough to touch only a moment ago—had, like Virginia Woolf that morning, vanished.

I caught my breath once we were on the streetcar again, but my heart still pounded in my chest. *Crazy, Crazy, Crazy,* I heard with every beat.

"There's a logical explanation for this," Mark said.

"There is?"

"Stress. It wreaks havoc on the psyche, Ruby. Trust me, I've written enough term papers and crammed for enough tests in my life to know. You overworked yourself today, that's all, and you saw something that wasn't there."

"Are you saying I hallucinated?"

He shook his head. "I'm sure there was someone walking in the cemetery tonight. A woman in a long skirt. And you imagined it was Gilman. Because you still haven't had a good night's sleep. You were upset, being at your father's grave." He overannunciated his words, I thought, as if talking to someone still learning English. "I think we should head back to the hotel. We can order room service."

"I thought we were going out."

"We were but . . . this is the second time you . . . I just think we should relax. We can order a bottle of wine. We can take it easy."

It was kind of Mark to say *we,* even though it was me.

He put his arm around me. "I'll draw you a bubble bath."

"Okay," I said, resting my head on his shoulder.

We sat in silence the rest of the trip. Even though my body lay perfectly still under Mark's arm, my mind moved at a record pace as I attempted to make sense of the day. Was Mark right? Could something as common as stress be the culprit? I wanted to believe that, wanted to accept Mark's reasoning, because it was the most rational explanation, preferable to hallucinations or ghosts. And it boasted the least consequences. After some rest, some relaxation, I would theoretically be cured, just like the woman in *The Yellow Wallpaper.*

I wondered then about the boundaries of fiction and memoir. How autobiographical was Gilman's short story? I knew she suffered from depression all of her life and wrote *The Yellow Wallpaper* after seeing a doctor who prescribed rest therapy as a cure. The physician told her to "live as domestic a life as possible" and to limit her hours of mental stimulation. Essentially, he told her to stop writing. What effect did this treatment have on Gilman's mind? I wondered. Had she ever seen women creeping behind wallpaper? Had she seen things that weren't there? In the end, she overdosed on chloroform in 1935. Afflicted with breast cancer, she chose "chloroform over cancer," per her suicide note. She didn't want cancer to dictate her death, so she did.

When we returned to the hotel, Mark filled the bathtub like he'd promised. He laid the hotel-issued white robe out for me on the bathroom vanity, dimmed the lights, and even held my hand as I stepped into the bath, before kneeling beside me to tuck a rolled-up towel behind my neck.

"Are you sure you didn't have sisters?" I asked.

He laughed, then gave me a soft but sensual kiss. "Take your time," he said.

The pillow, warm water, and lavender aroma of the bubbles relaxed me so much, I fell asleep. When I woke, my fingers and toes were pruned, and I was light-headed when I finally stood, but my body and mind felt numb in a good way. I felt sane. Wearing the robe, I stepped out into the cool bedroom to find Mark fussing with a corkscrew.

"I was just about to get you," he said. "Are you hungry?"

"Starving."

"Good. I ordered a few things because I wasn't sure what mood you were in." He rushed to lift the silver lids and reveal his selections. "Oh, and I bought you a present," he added, handing me a small brown paper bag, with gold tissue paper brimming at the top.

Inside, I found a journal. The brown leather cover—worn, cracked, and soft from years of use—boasted a gold fleur-de-lis. The pages inside, all edged in gold, were unblemished but flecked with hues of black and gray and blue.

"It's all recycled materials," he explained. "The cover, the paper. Even that silk ribbon bookmark. The clerk at the antiques store said it came from the hem of a vintage dress. I thought you could write about your dad. Your memories. It might help you."

"It's beautiful," I said, running my fingers along the fresh, crisp pages. It was the sweetest gift a man had ever given me, the kind of gift that told me exactly how he felt about me. He loved me. He cared about my feelings, my thoughts, my most cherished memories.

Then again, he also thought I needed *help*.

I threw my arms around his neck then, realizing there was only one woman obstructing our future. And it wasn't Meryl.

It was me.

Chapter 7

For the third time Wednesday morning, I hung up before the phone call went through, before I even heard it ring. I wanted to call. I did. I was beyond curious, and nearing being obsessed. I'd been at work a whole hour and I'd barely touched the quarter-inch stack of obits on my desk. If I could just let the call to Tarble go through, just let Heidi pick up, just break the ice somehow, maybe I could stop obsessing. Maybe.

Janice Richards was right about Heidi working at the college. She was now the alumnae coordinator for Tarble according to the school's Web site, which I'd perused that morning in lieu of writing obits. Heidi's major had been public relations, so she was the opposite of me: bubbly, diplomatic, and great at bullshitting, albeit genuine. Still, I was surprised she'd stayed on to work at the college. A third-generation Tarble girl, Heidi had been told—not asked—where she wanted to go to school, and she had always made that fact known to anyone who would listen. Of course, I'd listened. While other girls found her obnoxious, I'd found her refreshing. I'd admired her outspoken manner and in-your-face attitude.

I should have stopped exploring the Web site then, but I clicked the faculty link, regretting the action even before the new page loaded. And then, there Mark was, in blue hyperlink. He was an associate professor now, no longer an assistant. The tenure committee must have found him fit for a long-term position at Tarble after all. His head shot, however, had not been updated. It was the same photo I'd stared at a year ago when I missed him. I used to love its urban feel; black-and-white, with Mark looking away from the camera, off into the distance.

But now, I saw he was simply looking past me.

I tried typing up an obit but got only the deceased's name down before I picked up the phone a fourth time. Holding my breath, I waited out the initial silence after I dialed and endured several shrill rings. And then someone answered, and it was too late to hang up.

"Alumnae office." The girl's voice was perky like espresso.

"Can I speak to Heidi Callahan?" I said.

"Is she expecting your call?"

"I'm an old friend of hers."

"Whom should I say is calling?"

"Tell her it's . . . tell her it's Holly Golightly."

While I waited, my stomach did somersaults, but I glued the receiver to my ear until I heard a click on the other end.

"Hello?" Heidi said, her voice full of air and hesitant.

"Hi." I paused. "It's me." I paused again. "Ruby."

"Oh, it *is* you," she gushed, her voice as loud and cacophonous as I remembered. "I wanted it to be you, but I didn't want to get my hopes up. But who else in the world would call and say they were Holly Golightly? No one but you, Ruby. I just love that you said that."

Tears blurred my vision and stung my throat. Whatever tension I'd imagined, whatever loathing I feared, did not exist. Everything had changed between us, and yet everything was exactly the same.

"I wasn't sure you'd remember," I said.

"Breakfast at Tiffany's? Are you kidding me?"

We shared a laugh, perhaps to conceal the deep emotive significance of the movie we watched over and over again the semester after my father died. Despite its glamorous exterior— Audrey Hepburn standing in front of the Tiffany's jewelry window in that telltale black dress and oversize sunglasses— the film, based on Truman Capote's short story, is at its core a journey through depression. I understood the difference between the blues and the mean reds.

"I can't believe you work at Tarble," I said.

"I know. Me of all people. My mom is, of course, thrilled, but I keep thinking I'm going to get the boot one day when some video of me turns up on the Internet, one of my many rants about pixie-haircut lesbians who wear Birkenstocks and peasant skirts and don't shave their armpits."

"Now that sounds more like you."

"But I've changed. Well, sort of. Doesn't matter. I won't have to keep a positive attitude about single-sex education for long.

Did you hear Tarble is going coed next year? The board of trustees isn't set to vote on it until next week, but it's practically a done deal."

"But President Monroe always opposed coeducation," I argued.

"Even she had to face the truth. It's either go coed or close our doors for good. Our enrollment is at an all-time low, not to mention so are donations from alumnae. We just can't compete for applicants if we don't admit men."

A sudden bitterness filled my mouth. It could have been the aftertaste from my morning coffee, but more likely, it was a sour reaction to the news. Since I'd dropped out, I had tried to forget Tarble, push it to the recesses of my mind, but now I suddenly longed for the school, a gnawing ache for ivy-covered brick.

"That's sad. It won't be the same," I said. "I guess I should have finished my degree when I had the chance."

Heidi was quiet for a moment. "Ruby, I am so, so sorry," she finally said. She let out a heavy sigh, as if she'd carried those six words up six flights of steps.

"I'm the one who should be saying sorry."

"Absolutely not. I feel so guilty for moving out. You needed me, and I wasn't there for you. What kind of friend is that?"

"It's okay."

"It's not," she argued. "Did you know? That I came to see you at the hospital?"

"You came?"

"The nurse said you'd already been discharged."

"But you came."

"We're best friends." Her voice cracked. "Did you think I was mad at you all this time?"

"You didn't come to the hospital; well, that's what I thought. And then you never called."

"I wanted to call, but I thought you'd hang up on me," she divulged.

"I thought *you* would hang up on *me*."

We laughed again; we sounded like seventh grade girls.

"I'm so glad you called, Ruby. Today is so the best day."

And then the image of Beth, tied up in the back of a dirty van, returned, and I prepared for how to ruin Heidi's good mood.

"I did want to talk to you, Heidi," I started. "About everything. But I also called for a specific reason. You know Beth Richards?"

"Sure."

"She's missing . . ."

"She's missing what?"

"Missing. As in, she disappeared several days ago."

"What?"

It was a hypothetical question. I didn't respond.

"God, Ruby, I feel like I'm gonna throw up. How did you hear about this?"

This was Heidi's polite way of asking how I'd found out about Beth before she had. And I gauged from her reaction to the news—sad, confused, but not devastated—that she hadn't been having slumber parties with Beth all summer long.

I told Heidi the story then, about Beth's suitcase and the tag with my name on it, everything from Janice Richards to Detective Pickens to the Pittsburgh PD. I left out the other details, though: the serial killer, *A Room of One's Own,* and Mark.

"I just can't believe it," she said after I'd finished. "I'm not sure of protocol, but we may need to bring in therapists or something. I mean, we just graduated. There are still a lot of students on campus who knew Beth."

Two words caught my attention: *we*—as in when *we* graduated. It was sweet of Heidi not to mention the fact I'd dropped out and never actually gotten my diploma. And, of course, *knew*—as in *knew* her. Heidi, like me, was already talking about Beth in the past tense.

"Plus, Beth spent so much time at the college over summer," I added.

"Did she?"

"You didn't see her on campus?"

"Beth Richards? I haven't seen her since graduation."

I told Heidi about Beth's summer visits to Tarble, per my conversation with Janice, not mentioning how Beth had used Heidi as an alibi. "You're sure you didn't see her around?"

"You know how small this campus is, Ruby. Believe me, I'd remember seeing her."

It was Mark, I thought. It had to have been Mark. Beth hadn't spent summer nights on campus hanging out with Heidi; she'd spent them with Mark, no doubt at his cabin, in his bed, the same bed in which he'd made love to me.

"I must have misunderstood," I covered. "At any rate, Beth's mom thought the college should know about this. Plus, she wanted someone to tell Sarah Iverson."

"I can do that," Heidi said. "But I'd feel better telling her in person, not over the phone. I'll see her this weekend."

I recalled the postcard I'd found inside Beth's book. "You mean at Reunion?"

"A lot of the girls from our class are coming, probably because it's the last one. So I'm not sure how to handle this Beth Richards thing." I recognized stress in the waver of Heidi's voice and could hear paper shuffling in the background. "I need to talk to President Monroe right away."

"Sounds like I should let you go—"

"No, you will not *let me go*. Yes, we can get off the phone, but we are not even close to being done talking, Ruby. I want to know how you are and what you've been doing all this time, and I just want to pick up where we left off."

Her insistence made my eyes water. "Me too."

"Well, Miss Golightly," she quipped. "What the heck are you doing this weekend?"

Craig had left his office door ajar, so I knocked and waited politely in the corridor.

"Yeah," he shouted, as if I'd knocked not once but four times.

"You're busy." I chickened out. "I'll come back."

"Ruby, wait," I heard him say after I'd turned away. He was at the door immediately, tugging my sweater sleeve to stop me. "It's just Georgene has been in here seriously twenty times today. I thought you were her. Again."

"But still, you're busy so I'll just . . ."

Craig pulled at my sleeve once more. "Please, come in. Sit down."

I followed his instructions. "I was wondering if your offer still stands," I said.

"Of course. We can go tonight. That is, if you're free." He attempted to make eye contact. "Are you free tonight, Ruby?"

We stared back at each other a moment. I took in his brown eyes and his chestnut hair neatly parted to the side. His arms were crossed, the cuffs of his plaid shirt had shifted to reveal those beautiful wrists.

He's a nice-looking boy, I heard my mom say.

But he's my boss, I argued back to her in my mind.

"Actually, I wasn't talking about pizza." I looked at my lap to avoid any disappointment on his face.

"Oh. Sorry. I just thought . . . What were you talking about?"

"The article? About the missing girl from Milwaukee? The girl I went to college with?"

"You want to write a story?"

"Well, you said I could, if I wanted to . . ."

"I'm just surprised, that's all." His words came out slowly, professionally. He was all business now. "You didn't sound interested before."

I finally looked him in the eye, and if disappointment had been there, it left no trace. And oddly, I felt disappointed he didn't look more upset. "There have been some new developments in the case." I matched his businesslike tone. "And I have a few leads. But I can't tell you anything. Yet. It's all hush-hush right now. The detective made me swear to secrecy."

"If the police are keeping a lid on the case, why tell you?" he asked.

"Because I was playing Nancy Drew."

"I was a Hardy Boys kid myself, but I always wondered about that Nancy."

"Well, I'm no Nancy. Actually, the detective referred to me as Harriet the Spy."

"Ouch." Craig feigned a shot to the heart. "Well, I guess I'll just have to wait to read your story, Harriet." He eyed his desk calendar, where he'd written and crossed out so many things in blue ink, it looked like a pen had exploded. "Can you get it in to me first thing Monday morning?"

"First thing," I promised. "But it's going to require travel."

I told him then about the Tarble College Reunion festivities that weekend. "A lot of Beth's former classmates will be there, not to mention professors. Lots of possible interviews, good sound bites. They might have some sort of vigil for Beth. I just spoke to a representative from the college."

"A campus in sorrow, but grasping for hope?"

"Precisely."

He fanned his hands out, as if to say ta-dah. "Looks like you got yourself an assignment."

I smiled; it had been so easy to earn his trust as a reporter. But could I trust him? What if he didn't like my writing? Then again, was I actually going to write this article? I had agreed to Heidi's invitation to Reunion—after she begged me three times—not because I wanted to make amends with my alma mater, and not because I wanted to write a story for the *Chronicle,* but because of my obsession with Beth and Mark. Was it curiosity or jealousy? Both. Someone at Tarble had to know something about the nature of their relationship—perhaps Beth's former roommate, Sarah Iverson, or another student who took summer session. The possibility of finding out any salacious details was enough incentive for me to swallow my pride and show my face at Reunion, even if former classmates whispered behind my back, even if that meant being within an uncomfortable radius of Mark.

"There is one more thing," I added. "I need Friday off, to get an early start."

"I'll have Georgene fill in for you," he said.

I stood then and offered my hand, but before we could solidify the agreement with a handshake, his desk phone rang. He raised a finger and motioned for me to stay.

"Hewitt," he said.

I watched his face muscles melt, his chiseled cheekbones flatten. And then, he turned his back to me. "It's not a good time," he said in a muted tone. "We can talk about this tonight." A pause. "Because I'm *at work,* Victoria."

I could tell he was about to slam the phone receiver down, but he looked at me and refrained; instead, he set it lightly in its cradle.

"Sorry about that," he said.

"We were done anyway." I took a few steps toward the door.

He sighed, as if the phone call had depleted all of his energy. "I guess I can't keep this a secret from you any longer."

I swallowed, caught on the words *this secret from you.*

"I'm recently divorced," he went on.

"That's none of my business," I blurted. And then, I surprised myself by adding, "I didn't even know you were married."

"Five years. But it all came down to kids. I wanted them, and she didn't. We separated six months ago. The divorce was final last Friday."

I connected the dots. "Is that why you went out for pizza on Monday?"

"It was my divorce party."

"Why didn't you just tell me that?"

He shrugged. "I didn't want you to judge me."

I shook my head in protestation. "But it's none of my business," I repeated. "I'm just one of your employees. I mean, I'm nobody."

He stood then but looked weakened, as if I'd just delivered the final blow of a fight.

"But you're not," he said. "You're not nobody to me."

He neared me then at the door. I took another step back, my defenses heightened. But he only held out his hand. "I believe we were about to shake on that agreement?"

I let out a breath and nodded, offering my best, most professional handshake.

The movement released an auburn curl from behind my ear, and Craig reflexively tucked it back into place. And that's when I began to wonder whether I was destined to repeat my past mistakes.

Because, despite all the reasons not to, I let him.

Chapter 8

One Year Earlier

Come Sunday morning, I wanted to go home.

And by *home,* I meant Tarble. Wisconsin. The Midwest. I wanted to go where memories of my father had been suppressed, where my guilt had been tamed, where I had felt sane. I hoped what happened in New Orleans—seeing Virginia Woolf in the courtyard and Charlotte Perkins Gilman in the cemetery, not to mention misplacing my thesis notes—was due to a temporary state of stress, provoked by mere proximity to the city. When I left New Orleans, my mental clarity would be reinstated.

And it was, at least at first. In the weeks following our trip, I drowned myself in research, trying to make up for losing my notes—I never did find them—and read much more than necessary or required: two biographies on Woolf and Gilman each, one on Sylvia Plath, articles on Anne Sexton and Sarah Kane, and three psychology texts on female depression and suicide. To those who noticed and subsequently questioned my compulsion—mainly Heidi, and sometimes my mom, when I went home or she came to visit—I explained the importance of these books to the success of my thesis, all the while avoiding their gaze. The only person who could tear me away from my work was Mark. But I spent most of our time together talking about Woolf and Gilman and Plath; too much, it seemed.

"Ruby, I'm starting to feel like a polygamist," Mark said one November night, after we'd finished making love at his cabin.

"Why? Because you haven't divorced Meryl yet?"

He shook his head so solemnly, I wondered if he ever intended on leaving her. Whenever I'd asked about divorce he always said, *these things take time.*

"Because when I'm with you, we're not alone," he said, pulling himself to a seated position, a pillow between his back and the wall. "Virginia Woolf and Sylvia Plath always tag along. It's getting a little crowded for my tastes. I'm a one-woman man."

I questioned his choice of words. He was still married to Meryl, after all.

"You know what I mean," he added.

It was true; I was obsessed. I couldn't keep Virginia Woolf and the others off my mind, even at night. As soon as my head hit the pillow, as soon as I closed my eyes, I saw Woolf draft her suicide letter in drippy ink before loading stones into her pockets; I saw Charlotte Perkins Gilman's fragile white hands administer a lethal dose of chloroform; I saw Sylvia Plath wetting dish towels in the kitchen sink, wringing them out, placing them under the door jambs so the gas from the oven would not seep into the rest of her house, where her two children slept. Just like the nightmares about my father, these visions prompted me to swallow a sleeping pill before bed each night. But I never stopped working on my thesis. Because reading, taking notes, constructing theories, and supporting those theories with concrete information from concrete materials made me feel rational. It made me feel sane. And if I stopped my mind from this cerebral process, I worried I'd see another dead woman writer in time. The irony did not escape me. In order to keep myself from going crazy, I had to study women of questionable sanity.

"I'm sorry," I told Mark. "I'm almost done. You'll have me all to yourself soon."

"Don't get me wrong, I love your dedication. It's every teacher's dream to have a student so fixated on research. And I'm not asking you to slow down your efforts. Actually, I was thinking we should take a break, just until your thesis is complete."

"A break?" My voice cracked.

"Not break. Wrong word. I just meant you should put your thesis first, and let me come second. Just for now, just until you finish."

I sat up then and pulled the sheets up tighter over my bare breasts, suddenly feeling vulnerable and exposed.

"Why do I have to put one before the other?" I asked. "I can do both—work on my thesis and spend time with you."

"I know you can. But you've been . . . I just want you to know I understand if you can't see me much the next couple of weeks. My feelings won't be hurt. In fact, I have a lot of research to do too, before all your papers come in and I'm knee-deep in grading."

"Research? For what?"

"A paper for a literary journal. When the tenure committee reviews me next semester, I have to look prolific. Sadly, it's all about quantity not quality."

"What's your paper about?"

He cringed. "I'd rather not say, until it's completed. It's a creativity thing. Talking about it somehow negates it. You understand. I guess I'm superstitious."

I didn't think Mark believed in superstition.

"Okay," I auto-replied, and then: "Why do I get the feeling that something's changed? Between us? All of a sudden?"

"Nothing has changed." He kissed me then, quick and hard and dry, his lips barely moving. "This is just a stressful time of year, as we near the end of the semester. It always is. But we're grown-ups, right? We understand that sometimes work has to come first. That doesn't change how we feel about each other. Actually, it strengthens our relationship."

I nodded, even though my head and my heart were still trying to make sense of the conversation. "So we're okay?" I asked.

"Absolutely." He patted my shoulder, the way you pat someone's back during a hug, a gesture that always seemed reserved for acquaintances, not friends. "But I should drive you back soon. It's almost midnight."

I swallowed a lump of disappointment. "I thought I was going to stay."

"Did you?" He stood to slide on his jeans. "It's just that I have an early meeting tomorrow morning. And to be honest, I haven't been sleeping well." He pulled his T-shirt on, then ran a hand over his hair to smooth it. "But you can stay. I mean, if you really want to."

"No, I'll go." I stood but covered my body with the sheet until I found my crumpled clothes on the floor. "I need a good night's sleep too."

"See? You get it. Sometimes you need to take care of yourself first, so you can be your best for others, right?"

I nodded hesitantly.

"Right," he repeated, checking the time as he fastened his watch. "Now, let's get you back to campus."

I didn't see Mark much the next few weeks; well, I saw him, but only during senior seminar, to which he always arrived late or let us out early. A few days, he even canceled class, saying we could work on our papers instead. While in class, I tried to get his attention—catch his gaze, share a smile—but he never looked at me. I wanted to believe he was stressed-out from his research and end-of-semester grading. But he showed no signs of anxiety. In fact, he seemed abundantly happy and carefree, with a spring in his step, a glint in his eye.

Since I had no interactions with Mark, my thesis became my one and only concern, and I continued to read, research, write, and revise without abandon, even staying up all night. I submitted my paper early, hoping Mark would see me then, if he knew my work was complete, and I was free and clear of academic obligations. But nothing changed after I turned my thesis in. Actually, it got worse. He flat out ignored me in class, calling on another student when I raised my hand, pretending not to hear me when I called after him in the hallway. When I finally cornered him one afternoon in the faculty parking lot, he apologized, and told me to hold on just a little bit longer. Once the semester was over, things would change, he said.

On the day we were to receive our thesis grades, my mother called in the morning with surprise news: she was flying us to Paris for winter break. We'd leave in two days and be there for two weeks, for Christmas and New Year's. It was not only my Christmas gift, she said, but also a congratulatory vacation for working so diligently on my thesis all semester.

"I don't know how I did yet," I said.

"You always get an A," she teased.

I knew the trip was more than a holiday gift, more than a reward for studying hard. It was an escape—from a Christmas without Dad. We were quickly approaching the one-year anniversary of his death; that was evident everywhere, from the strands of red and green lights lining dorm room windows to the holiday songs blaring inside the local Piggly Wiggly grocery store. If we went to Paris, thousands of miles away, Christmas wouldn't hurt as much. At least, that was the idea.

I'd never been to Paris, and though I'd always wanted to go, I also didn't want to leave Mark. With the papers finally graded, the semester officially over, I hoped time would once again be ours, and I wanted to make up for what we'd lost. But I couldn't say no to my mother, so I reluctantly started packing for two whole weeks without him. If I packed that morning, I rationalized, I'd have more time to spend with Mark that night. Problem was, I didn't have a big enough suitcase. Fortunately, Beth Richards, who lived a few doors down, gladly handed over her paisley print luggage, in which she normally stored extra blankets for chilly Wisconsin nights. I filled it to the brim that morning, even writing my name on the luggage tag, so there would be nothing to do later, so there would be nothing to pry my attention away from Mark, now that the semester was over, now that we could finally be together.

Heidi walked in while I was folding clothes.

"What are you doing?" she asked, hands on her hips. "Are you moving out?"

"Moving out? Why would I be moving out?"

"Then what are you doing?" she asked again.

"Packing. My mom is taking me to Paris."

"You're joking."

"Why would I be joking?"

"I can't believe your mom doesn't—" she started but stopped. "Ruby, what's going on with you?" she asked matter-of-factly.

"What do you mean?"

She drew her head back and flitted her eyelids. "Do you know you left our door wide open yesterday?"

"Did I? Sorry." I walked behind my dresser, where I'd hid from her in the past.

She followed. "I know the anniversary of your father's death is coming up. I think you're depressed."

The thought had crossed my mind too. "You're crazy."

"*I'm* crazy? *I'm* not the one who tore up the room last week looking for my keys, which ended up being in my pocket. *I'm* not the one collecting rocks on the windowsill."

The rocks. Ever since I submitted my thesis, I'd started taking long walks on the beach. And every time, I found a smooth, skipping stone I liked. I kept them on the windowsill next to my bed. I liked rubbing their cool, hard, even exterior.

"Let me help you," Heidi said, sweetly. "Talk to me."

"There's nothing to talk about."

"Really? What about your desk?" She gestured to the books upon books, the Internet articles, the notes covering every available inch of my desktop. "That's hoarding."

"That's research," I argued.

"For a paper you already wrote, already turned in. What is it still doing there?"

I didn't answer.

"Fine, you don't want to talk about the desk. Have you seen yourself lately?"

I stole a look in the mirror. Dark circles rimmed my eyes. My hair shined, but not in that healthy just-out-of-the-salon way. It was oil buildup—I hadn't washed it in five days. My skin seemed a shade lighter than usual. I'd eaten Skittles for lunch three days in a row.

"I haven't slept much lately, that's all," I told Heidi. "Everyone looks like shit lately. It's that time of year. Those of us who have *real* majors had actual papers to turn in."

Heidi, a public relations major, didn't react to my insult. "*Had* papers to turn in. Had. You said it yourself. Past tense, Ruby." She stared at me. "Do you need help? Are you crying out for help?"

"I'm not crying." To prove the point, I dramatically pulled at the skin below my eyes to show they were dry inside.

I looked into Heidi's brown eyes and saw her love for me, the depth of her care, what was missing from Mark's eyes of late, no matter how long I looked, no matter how often. Had he noticed the same changes, the same behaviors in me? Was that why he didn't want to look at me? See me? Did he think I'd let myself go?

"Why are you so angry?" I charged. "What do you care if I wash my hair?"

"Because I'm your best friend." She grabbed my arm. "Or I guess I *was* your best friend. Before you started hanging out instead with Virginia Woolf and Sylvia Plath."

"You're a bitch," I said.

Heidi shook her head, her eyes brimming with tears. She released her grip. "I'm moving into the quad with Rachel and Joy and Amanda," she said. "I'll take my stuff this afternoon when you're at class. I'm sleeping there tonight."

"Fine," I said.

"They'll assign you a new roommate next semester," she added.

I'll pay extra for a single, I thought. Without a roommate, Mark could call me anytime.

"Whatever," I said.

"Whatever," she repeated, before slamming the door.

That afternoon Mark returned our papers, facedown on each of our desks. And then he abruptly ended class, claiming the English department was hiring a new professor for the coming school year and he had to sit in on interviews. I wondered if that was true, or if he was simply afraid of confrontation, afraid I was going to be angry with him.

He'd given me a D, after all.

I should have been angry, hot-cheeked and fuming, but I wasn't. Instead, I walked back to my room in a daze, disoriented by the bold dismissive consonant Mark had written on the front of my thesis. The grade felt less like an appraisal of my work and more like a punishment, a cold slap on the hand. The fury would come later, once the initial sting wore off. But first, I felt something worse than rage. I felt unworthy of his love.

I prepared to call Mark on his cell phone as soon as I got in. But he'd already left a message on my machine, something he never did, for fear Heidi would hear.

"Ruby, it's me," Mark said in his message after an initial pause. "We can't see each other. Not anymore." His voice was higher pitched than usual. "It's the best thing. For you. Right now. You need . . . I'm a distraction, aren't I? You have graduate school ahead of you. And I'm an anchor weighing you down. So it's over. It has to be over. I'm working things out with my wife. She's coming here for Christmas. It's the right thing to do."

I felt as if a string had been looped around my throat, then tied through the very holes of my nostrils. It stung. I stood there unable to move but unable to cry, and I listened to the message again, hoping I'd heard wrong, hoping I'd misunderstood. But the conclusion was the same: he'd broken up with me.

But why did he do it? I thought. Not because he didn't love me. And not because he loved Meryl. But because *it was the right thing to do* and he was *an anchor weighing me down.* He was more concerned about my future—my studies, my getting into graduate school—than he was about his own feelings, what he wanted. He wasn't being selfish; he was being selfless.

Or had he fallen out of love with me? I wondered. I noted the

growing distance in his eyes, his voice devoid of its once earnest tone. And in his message, how he said, "You need . . ." What
did he think I needed? Professional help? Had I somehow driven
him further away these past few weeks? Because I was paranoid and anxious from his lack of attention?

I can't let him put me first, I resolved as I prepared to drive to
his cabin. He would be flattered by the gesture, my determination to talk to him in person. At home, off campus, he would not
be able to deny his love for me.

I would break him.

I parked my car down the gravel road, so he wouldn't hear the
engine when I pulled in, and went by foot to his cabin, stuffing
my hands into the pockets of my coat, bringing them forward
to compensate for it being unzipped. My tears had left my skin
vulnerable to the arctic blast, and the harsh wind whipped
my cheeks like flags. In the dark, cold night, the cabin looked
warm and inviting as an ethereal glow from the fireplace shone
through the sheer curtains of the front window.

"Ruby, please come in from the cold" I imagined Mark
saying, before hugging me until I returned to a normal body
temperature. I would say nothing. One look in my eyes. That's
all it would take.

I knocked on the front door—Mark had never installed a
doorbell—but my cold, gloveless knuckles only skimmed the
surface, and the sound drowned into the heavy wood. I hadn't
heard it myself. Mark wouldn't hear it, either. I moved to the
front window then, and I saw the light grow brighter at the
center of the room. I made out the back of Mark's head a few

inches above the sofa cushions. I saw his elbow rise, then fall. He was drinking something, drowning his sorrows, I presumed.

But just before my fingertip tapped the icy windowpane, I saw a second figure. It neared the couch and straddled Mark, creating a sort of Rorschach inkblot made blurry by the fire. I could no longer discern Mark or the back of his head. The two bodies became one. And then the figure emerged from the blob like a dolphin from water. It grew taller, towered above him. It blocked the firelight in some spots but not in others, smoothly like curves of an ornate wine glass.

Out then in, out then in.

The epitome of woman.

Meryl.

Ducking under the sill, I lost my footing and fell into a snow-drift, singeing my skin on the cold. My heart shattered with the realization: Mark really had gone back to his wife. And there, tucked in the alcove beside the house, was proof. The body of the car blended into the night. But in the moonlight, I could tell it was black, could make out the *license applied for* plate. Be-neath my fingertips, the word Jetta graced the bumper. Obvi-ously Meryl had driven up from Washington, D. C., to spend the holidays with him.

The sight of Meryl through the window, her car in the drive-way, sent a heat through my chest into my throat. My cheeks flared. My hands, however, were frozen by that point, and I reached into my pockets to keep them warm. There I fumbled with my key chain and began to run the tips of my fingers along the jagged edges. And soon, I brought the key with the sharpest ridges to Meryl's driver-side door and dug it deep into the finish until it caught in the groove. I did this more times than I can remember before the key finally slipped in my frozen hand, and I sliced my knuckle.

Sucking on the wound, I drove down the country road, away from Mark's cabin.

It is a devastating taste—the bitterness of blood, the saline of tears.

I drove around for an hour but didn't know where to go, so I returned to Tarble, parked my car in the lot, and walked back to the dorm. The lake appeared wild with rage that night. Thick, gray waves—topped with a white foam that reminded me of a dog with rabies, a sure sign of an impending winter storm—pummeled the rocky shore. Despite this, I decided to take a detour to the frozen sand beside the unruly waters.

Down on the beach, the wind off the lake, coupled by the spray of waves, seemed to drop the temperature another twenty degrees. After a few minutes, the cold actually felt warm against my exposed skin, as it burned my cheeks and mouth, and somehow, lessened the pain throbbing my gut. I was all out of tears by then, my eyes almost swollen shut from crying. I could barely see where I was going, and I didn't care. If I tripped and fell into the water, so be it. The waves would carry me out to sea. I imagined loading the stones from my windowsill into my coat pockets, just as Virginia Woolf had.

I was halfway down the beach when I sensed I was not alone. And from a distance, I made out a figure walking toward me. Man or woman, I could not say at first, thanks to the veil of night, my swollen eyes, and the spray of water. But as it grew nearer, my pulse quickened at the form I eventually discerned.

It was a woman. Dishwater blond hair curled up on the sides, 1950s style. Even at night, her lips appeared dark with what could only be red lipstick. She was wearing a camel-colored peacoat.

I stopped, stared down at the sand, then looked up again. I shook my head, stomped my feet, even grunted, trying to make her disappear. But she came closer, and unlike Woolf and Gilman, she spoke to me.

"Ruby," she said.

And that's when I ran. I'm not sure if she chased me, because I never looked back, not until I arrived at the front steps of North Hall. By that time, no one occupied the sidewalk behind me, as far as I could see.

But the image of a young Sylvia Plath remained.

"Don't try to talk just yet," the nurse whispered, her full lips pursed like a mother ready to kiss the forehead of a baby. "They pumped your stomach. The tube bruised your vocal cords. Your voice is probably hoarse."

I saw the nurse write something on a clipboard, what I assumed was my chart, then made eye contact again. "You have a visitor," she added. "But perhaps you should rest a bit more before seeing anyone."

A visitor. Mark. He had heard what happened, had rushed to the hospital to apologize, to tell me he'd made a mistake. He'd almost lost me forever.

"Who is it?" I tried to sit up but lost energy.

"Trisha, your resident assistant. She was the one who found you and called 911."

"No one else?"

"Your mother will be here shortly, and a few girls, about five of them I think, came right away, but we told them to go back to the college. We didn't know how long it would be. They said they would come back."

"Any . . . men?"

The nurse's eyes filled with pity. "I'm sorry."

A few minutes later, I watched the door inch open. My mother's eyes were a bright green but softened around the edges by sadness or fear or maybe anger. When I saw her, I unraveled. I closed my eyes, but the tears continued to break through the barrier.

"It's okay, sweetheart," she said, getting into bed with me. Soon her arms encircled me fully. She squeezed me, held me in the strength and security of a mother's love. "I'm here."

We sat like that, me tucked into my mother's body, and drew breaths in synchrony, like we must have done when I was an infant still learning how to breathe, still learning the rhythm of life.

"I'm sorry," she said into the silence. "I knew something wasn't right with you, but I just assumed you were stressed about writing your thesis. That's why I wanted to take you to Paris. I thought you needed to relax. I didn't realize . . ."

"I'm sorry about Paris," I said. "Can you get your money back?"

She shook her head, as if to say that money should be the last of my worries. And then she took my hand and held it, securing me to her like the clasp on a mountain climber's rope. "You are alive. By the grace of God, you are still here." She looked into my eyes once more, tucked a hair behind my ear.

"I didn't mean to do it, not really." My voice was hoarse like the nurse had told me it would be. But it was also monotone and robotic, lacking an element that made it sound human. "I just wanted to sleep, so I took my pills. And then I took more. And then I couldn't stop myself. I just kept swallowing pills."

That was true. The sleeping pills were at first a practical idea. I wanted to escape the pain, hoping I'd wake up, and it would all be a nightmare, that Mark would still love me, that he hadn't gotten back together with Meryl. I remembered taking pill after pill from the bottle, placing each on my tongue, counting the pills in my mind. Ten. Eleven. Twelve. Thirteen. Fourteen.

How far had I gotten? I couldn't remember. I only remember seeing Sylvia Plath on the beach. Had she inspired me to do it, to kill myself just as she had?

I knew from my research that the notably bipolar Plath committed suicide at age thirty by sticking her head in an oven full of gas. Many blamed her suicide on the infidelity of her husband, the English poet Ted Hughes. But Plath had tried to kill herself before. While a student at the all-girl Smith College she had swallowed sleeping pills—forty-eight of them—in a failed suicide attempt. She later based her only published novel, *The Bell Jar*, on that experience.

Mom tightened her grip. "Why, Ruby?"

If I revealed who I really was, a woman without morals and values, a woman who sleeps with married men, my professor no less, I feared my mom might never look at me the same way. There would be a small speck of black in her green eyes, a shadow, a deep pocket of disappointment. So I told her everything then, just not about Mark. I told her how Heidi moved out; how I'd been feeling anxious and sad and depressed the past few weeks; how I'd left my dorm room door wide open and collected random objects like the rocks; and how I'd received a D on my thesis, a paper I'd given up a whole semester of my life to write.

"Maybe you can rewrite it," she offered. "Resubmit it next semester?"

I bit my lip. Mark had to have heard the news by then, and he hadn't come. I realized then that things would never be the same. Could I go back to simply being his student? Could I go back to Tarble, now that everyone knew I tried to kill myself?

I looked into my mother's soft, forgiving eyes.

"No," I told her. "I'm dropping out."

December

*I remember a girl in high school did it. A cheer-
leader, the prom queen type. She took some pills—
her mother's Valium—and ended up in the ER. And
the hallways buzzed the following school day with a
burning question: Did she really want to die, or did
she feel like she didn't want to live? There's a difference, apparently. The former is indicative of a much
deeper problem; the latter understandably associated with a response to a traumatic event.*

*If I can't be with Mark, if he doesn't love me any-
more, I don't see the point to living. Over the course
of our romance, perhaps every day we were together,
I imagine I cut a piece of myself off like a strip of
fabric, and worked that section of myself into and
over and under him, so now, there is no way I can
break away.*

We are woven together.

*It hurts. It hurts to get pulled apart by the seams,
every thread exposed, every fiber raw. The only way
I can end the pain, the only way to medicate myself,
is to stop my heart from beating, stop my lungs from
breathing, stop my brain from thinking.*

I want to die. And I feel like I don't want to live.

I don't understand the difference.

Chapter 9

I could not see Lake Michigan from the road, could not distinguish where the murky sky met the steely waters, but as I neared Tarble College on Friday afternoon, I sensed its presence like someone standing behind me; my arm hairs danced, and a cold tingled the canyon between my shoulder blades. Low temperatures and a mistlike rain—as characteristic of a midwestern autumn as amber leaves—had fogged the window of my Corolla by then, and I had to roll it down to view the school from the road.

The Tarble campus was no more than a half mile long, but it stood proud upon its cliff, overlooking the lake to the east and the road to the west. Removed from the main road and a good mile from town, it long reminded me of a miniature village within a snow globe—a utopian world protected by a bubble of glass.

With white knuckles bracing the steering wheel, I approached the school's main entrance. It boasted no fence or gate, just a large stone insignia surrounded by mounds of manicured mums, eye-popping paint splatters of yellow, orange, and red. On instinct, I brought my foot to the brake pedal but didn't press, my boot suspended in air, my leg muscles taut. I watched the windshield wipers whip before me, squeaking each time they doubled back.

You don't have to do this, I thought.

Go home.

Go home.

Go home.

I turned anyway, at the last possible second, a swervy skid onto campus drive. Because it was the onset of Reunion weekend, and classes were still in session, I had to park at the far edge of campus. It was a heart-pumping uphill walk to the academic buildings from there, but I embraced every step, every breath of sand and silt and seagull air before inevitably losing my anonymity. Ahead I saw a herd of students nearing Langley Hall—I recognized their backpack-weighted saunters—and my stomach cartwheeled up my throat. Because some girl will spot me, I thought. Some girl will stop me. Some girl will say "What are you doing here?" And then, before I even answer, her memory will kick in, and her head will flop to the side with pity, and a hush will ensue as she pictures me in a straitjacket. And I will stand there, still and silent in the midst of those buzzing, whirring students, and regret ever coming back.

And therein lies the difference between words and actions. It had all seemed so easy—agreeing to Heidi when she insisted

I stay in her guest bedroom instead of a room at the Lakeview Motel, asking Craig for the weekend off, telling my therapist yesterday and mother how excited I was about reconnecting with old friends at Tarble's Reunion. But it was all talk. Only words. Easy for me to say but not actually do. Now that I stood on campus, in close proximity to Mark's Jeep in the faculty parking lot and the red bridge where we used to meet and the beach where I saw Sylvia Plath and the dorm room where I overdosed on sleeping pills, I wanted to turtle my head inside my body. Thankfully, my oversize umbrella—Mom had checked the weather report and reminded me to take one—veiled me from possible stares and finger-pointing as I reached the main sidewalk and fell into rhythm with the other women's steps.

But the voices came after only a few strides.

"They found her on the floor," one female voice whispered.

"Did she slit her wrists?" another asked.

"Overdose," the first said. "She took the whole bottle."

"Why did she do it?"

"Why does anyone do it?"

The voices, muffled by the white noise of rain, became trapped under the canopy of black umbrella fabric and swirled around my head like twittering birds in a cartoon. I continued walking on autopilot, though, my legs grounded and focused but my mind distant and floating. I tightened my grip on the umbrella handle.

They're talking about me, I thought. *They're already talking about me.*

"Are you talking about Julie?" A third voice asked.

I turned then to see four students walking behind me in an

iceberglike mass, their shoulders slumped and heads drooped in a recognizable act of gossip. Thanks to the spray of rain and lakeside breeze, none of them saw me peeking from beneath my umbrella. Their eyes were glued instead to the sidewalk as they braced the forces of nature with the tops of their sweatshirt-hooded heads.

"You heard?" the first girl replied.

"Everyone's heard," a fourth chimed in.

Tipping my umbrella back, I studied the students lining the sidewalk ahead of me. They were all in clumps too, all consorting, all seemingly whispering on the way to class. The rain was only half of the white noise I'd heard; the other half, their murmurs as they swapped grapevines about Julie.

Julie, Julie, Julie.

Obviously, it was the day after.

As I shook off my umbrella inside the lobby of Langley Hall, the murmurs died to a low humming buzz. The space was alive with people—students, alumnae, and faculty members with red cheeks, taut from over smiling. Scanning the lobby, I saw Heidi standing behind a red table-clothed table, under a WELCOME TARBLE ALUMNAE banner. She looked exactly as I remembered, which was expected after only ten months. Still, the time had passed so slowly for me—it had felt more like ten years—and somehow, I'd expected her to look different, older, changed. But she still styled her chestnut hair into a sleek bob, and her face was still round, her skin naturally pink and dewy, her eyes still a captivating brown.

Only her gregarious smile and blithe spirit were missing. Even from a distance, she looked unusually stern, a wrinkle bridged her eyebrows. And the wrinkle seemed to deepen when she saw me approaching the table.

"Ruby." She handed her clipboard to the bored, name-tagged coworker beside her. "You're here. Already."

"I said one o'clock, didn't I?"

"Of course, you did. Of course." Gripping my shoulders, she moved me several paces from the table. The wet soles of my brown boots screeched on the recently polished floor. "It's just so good to see you."

She hugged me then, holding me longer than necessary, as if saying good-bye rather than hello. She pressed me so hard, my nose smushed into the red fluff of her cashmere sweater, and I smelled grapefruit. She'd eaten one at lunch.

"How was your drive?" she asked after our embrace.

"Fine."

She eyed my umbrella. "It's raining, isn't it? Is it still raining? I was really hoping it wouldn't rain."

I put my hand on her shoulder to quiet her nervous rambling. "Heidi, I know."

She cocked her head at first, as if about to lie, then exhaled a weighty breath, as if resigning to tell the truth. Her voice raised an octave. "You do?"

"Julie," was all I said.

She sighed. "I was going to tell you. Just later, once you were settled."

"What happened?"

Heidi scooted our conversation another foot from the table before saying more.

"Julie Farris," she said under her breath. "She's a freshman.

Smart girl. Sweet girl. Her RA found her unconscious late last night. There was an empty bottle of Tylenol on the floor beside her. She's okay. Alive, at least. She's at Kenosha General. Word is, they're admitting her to the psych ward later today."

I winced. It was the same ward into which I would have been admitted back in December, had my mom not requested I be relocated to the hospital in Oak Park where she worked.

Heidi seized my elbow like a handle then, as if afraid I'd run away. "How did you hear?"

"Word travels fast at Tarble, remember?"

"I'm so sorry, Ruby," Heidi gushed. "If I had known this was going to happen, I never would have . . ."

"Asked me to come?"

She took my hand and squeezed it. "I just wanted things to be perfect."

"It's okay," I lied. "How are you holding up?"

Heidi rubbed the corner of her eye. "I'm exhausted. I've been up since four this morning putting out fires. This couldn't have happened at a worse time. On top of all the Reunion events that have to go on without a hitch in spite of the rain—not to mention the vigil we're planning for Beth—President Monroe has me on damage control. Apparently, someone leaked information to some jerky reporter from the *Kenosha Sentinel,* and he called asking implicating questions, and now it's my job to assure financial backers and alumnae that Tarble isn't some breeding ground for . . ."

"Lunatics?"

She shook her head. "That this isn't an everyday occurrence. It's happened only twice."

Twice, and I was the first.

"Maybe I should go," I said.

"No. Why?"

"It's strange, isn't it? That some student tries to kill herself the night before I come back to campus for the first time? I don't want to make anyone feel weird."

"No one will feel weird. And if they do, then they're weird," Heidi shot back. "Actually, it's a good thing you're here. I mean, look at you. You're proof that life goes on. People heal. People get better. You're not tainted for life. You're totally fine now."

I only look fine.

"Please stay," Heidi begged. "Please? I was so looking forward to this weekend. We were going to order pepperoni and green pepper pizza and watch *Breakfast at Tiffany's* and eat thin mints from the freezer. I had to hunt down a Girl Scout for those, and it wasn't easy. It isn't the cookie-selling season, you know."

I smiled at Heidi's list of our favorite things, her diligent preparation for my arrival. She had tried so hard, put forth a grand effort to welcome me back to campus, back to her life. How could I leave? And why should I? *It's a coincidence,* I thought. What happened to smart, sweet Julie Farris had nothing to do with me.

"Pizza and thin mints, huh?" I pretended to mull things over. "Okay, I'll stay."

Heidi hugged me again. "Let me get your name tag."

She headed to the table, and I followed. I watched her snatch a white peel-back name tag from a sea of identical stickers, and place it on my shirt.

Looking down, I saw my name in italicized Garamond and my class year, even though I hadn't technically graduated. "Why do we have to wear name tags?" I asked.

"President Monroe says it makes you feel important and welcome." She smoothed the curled-up corners of my tag. "And if you feel important and welcome, you'll have a great time. And if you have a great time, then you're more likely to give. It's all about donations."

I pressed the tag again after Heidi did, thinking it was pointless. Everybody already knew who I was: that girl who tried to kill herself. And now, *the one who did it last year.*

I noticed my font color was different than the others. "Why is mine green?"

"They're color coded depending on your major. Just another way to make you feel extra special." She winked. "It's also how we gauge the number of people sitting in on any given class this afternoon. The professors like to know what to expect as far as handouts and such."

"Sit in?"

"Don't you remember? How the alums used to sit in on a class Reunion weekend for old times' sake? It hasn't been so long for you, but the people who graduated twenty years ago get a real kick out of it." She took the clipboard back from her coworker and scanned it. "Looks like your options are English Lit with Suter or American Lit with Barnard."

My stomach flipped. *Mark's here. In the building. Mere feet away.*

I opened my mouth to say I wanted to skip the whole sitting-in-on-a-class experience when someone interrupted us:

"Did I just hear my name? Is that why my ears are ringing?"

I turned to see a woman wearing an A-line royal blue housedress, a belt cinching her thin waist. A messy knot kept her blond hair—an inch of brown at the roots—from her face.

"Professor Barnard," Heidi said. "Ruby, this is Virginia Barnard. She's new this year to Tarble. She teaches American Literature, Feminist Theory, and Women's Gender Studies."

"Good memory." The professor extended her hand but suddenly drew it back, wiping what looked like chalk dust onto her skirt. She held her hand out a second time. "Virginia Barnard," she repeated. "Assistant Professor of English. And you're . . ." She read my name tag. "Ruby Rousseau. Great alliteration."

We locked eyes, and I found the woman sophisticated and charming and warm. And immediately familiar, like a cousin I hadn't seen in a while but could never forget. She seemed to be in her midthirties, younger than most Tarble professors. She had taut cheekbones and a defined chin. Her eyebrows were thicker, a shade darker than the roots of her hair. To me, the overall effect was dramatic. Striking. Her lips were the color of raspberry juice not Max Factor. Her outfit—she'd paired the housedress with boots and clunky earrings carved of mahogany—seemed to suggest she was a bohemian, the kind of woman who dishes out fortunes and guidance from her hut at the edge of the village.

"I see you recently graduated," Professor Barnard said, squinting at my name tag.

I eyed the class year on the tag, a blatant lie. "Oh. Yes. I guess I did."

Heidi saved me from further embarrassment. "I was just telling Ruby about her class options this afternoon."

The professor smiled. "Well, I would be honored to have you in my class today. We were supposed to discuss Thomas Paine's *Common Sense*, but I have something else up my sleeve. Don't let me influence your decision, though," she went on. "I've heard Mark Suter is excellent. Did you have him while you were a student here?"

I nodded, willing my blood not to flush my cheeks at the mention of his name.

"Is he as good as they say?" she asked.

My cheeks grew hot anyway. My throat dry. "He's all right," I managed to say. "But your class sounds fun. American Lit?"

"Yes. I could really use your insights. How are you at poetry?"

"Writing or reading?"

"Analyzing," she said.

"I'm okay."

"Don't listen to her," Heidi interjected. "She's being modest."

"Modesty is a very desirable quality," the professor said. "Walk with me?"

I looked to Heidi.

"Go ahead," she said. "I have to work this table for another hour yet."

Exchanging casual conversation, Professor Barnard and I climbed the spiral staircase of Langley Hall to the second floor, room L219, the same classroom where I'd taken senior seminar with Mark. With a gentle but sturdy hand, she guided me into the classroom and told me to find an open seat while she emptied her messenger bag at the front desk.

I took the seat closest to the door and watched others file into the room, noting which students were old and which were new. The heavyset woman wearing a bright red, never-washed Tarble sweatshirt had, quite obviously, just come from the campus bookstore.

The last to enter were three girls, each carrying a picket sign at her side. They propped the signs—black marker on cardboard, nailed to wooden stakes—upside down against the classroom wall. The one I could read said SILENCE IS CONSENT in bold block letters.

Silence is shame, I thought.

Professor Barnard rushed to speak to the tallest of the three, the one wearing her blond hair in low-lying pigtails, the one still carrying a bullhorn.

"Tia," she said. "You're excused today. Why aren't you still in the grove?"

Tia blew a strand of hair from her eyes, but it fell back to the exact same spot. "President Monroe threatened to call the cops. And my parents said I can't get arrested again."

A ponytailed girl in the second row interrupted their private conversation. "I can't believe you went out there today," she said. "Have you no heart? No compassion? No decency?"

Tia scowled. "Julie wouldn't want us to give up the cause on her account."

Julie. My ears perked.

"It's also futile," the girl shot back. "Nothing's going to change. We all know the board's already made up their minds. Why do you still go out there?"

"Because silence is consent." A spray of angry spit flew from Tia's mouth. "They want to push us out, our customs and our way of life, by admitting men to Tarble. If we are silent, we condone their actions. And like the ancient matriarchies, we will vanish. Our legacy will be lost forever."

"But it isn't *our* legacy," the ponytailed girl countered. "It's the legacy of the women who attended Tarble a century ago, when there were no other educational options for women. Girls today don't need an all-women's college to succeed in the so-called man's world. Women are doctors and lawyers and scientists. They're leaders. I mean, look at Hillary Clinton."

"She went to Wellesley," Tia noted.

The girl belabored a sigh. "Fine, but we *chose* to go here, over coed schools that would have accepted us as equals to male students."

"Equals?" Tia blurted. "You're in *La La Land*, Becca."

"No, *you* are, if you think Tarble can survive in the twenty-first century without admitting men."

"Ladies, enough," Professor Barnard interrupted, moving between the two girls. "Take a breath. Take your seats."

While the girls reluctantly settled, the professor approached the board. I listened fondly to the sound of chalk gliding against its matte black surface. Room L219 was one of the few classrooms at Tarble that still housed an actual chalkboard. The others had been renovated with whiteboards and stripped of all romanticism, in my opinion. Professor Barnard took her time writing the words *I Shall Not Care* in a curvy script. She underlined the title twice before turning to face us.

"Are you familiar with Sara Teasdale?" she asked the class.

Of course I knew Sara Teasdale. The American poet committed suicide in 1933. Like myself and Sylvia Plath, she overdosed on sleeping pills.

After a few head nods and shrugs, the professor went on. "Teasdale was a very popular poet in the early 1900s. Critics loved her; so did the public. But later the critics, especially feminists, discarded her work. They found her too polite and timid." She grabbed a stack of papers from her desk then and began handing them out, licking her finger intermittently to grip the pages, like most teachers do.

Becca's hand shot into the air. "I thought we were discussing *Common Sense* today."

Professor Barnard gave the girl a sly smile. "This is more relevant," was all she said.

It was liberal arts at its best. Students had come to class expecting a lecture on Paine's *Common Sense,* and here that subject had been scrapped on a whim. Looking back on my own college experience at Tarble, I could not count the number of times the class agenda changed on the caprice of one of my professors. If the sun was shining on a surprisingly warm spring day, we had class on the school lawn. If something major happened in the news, we discussed the event at hand and not the pages of Chaucer we'd stayed up until two in the morning to read.

Once the handouts circulated, the professor's eyes bounced around the room. "Now, would one of our brave alums like to take a stab at reading this?"

The heavyset woman cowered in her desk.

The professor's eyes met mine. "Ruby?"

I looked down at the paper, sensing the students' eyes upon me, waiting for me to speak. The black words sprung from the bright white page as I read:

When I am dead and over me bright April
Shakes out her rain-drenched hair,
Tho' you should lean above me broken-hearted,
I shall not care.
I shall have peace as leafy trees are peaceful,
When rain bends down the bough,
And I shall be more silent and cold-hearted
Than you are now.

Tia spoke first. "It's a suicide note," she said.

Professor Barnard leaned against the edge of her desk. "What makes you say that?"

"Her word choice, *When I am dead* and *Over me.* I imagine a cemetery plot on a rainy spring day. I mean, where else would you be dead with a tree hanging over you?"

"What about the rest of you? Is it a suicide note?"

No one responded.

"Well?" the professor prompted.

Becca raised her hand again, and the professor called on her, seemingly annoyed by the formality. The girl twisted in her desk to address the majority of the room.

"I think I speak for the entire class when I say this conversation is uncomfortable," she said. "It's inappropriate, considering . . . what happened."

The room erupted in head turns and sideway glances.

"Considering what happened, it's completely appropriate," Professor Barnard countered. "I know everyone, including the administration, wants to pretend nothing happened last night. In fact, I've been instructed not to talk about it with you, to teach class with a huge elephant in the room. Reunion weekend is supposed to be fun. And we can't have fun if we live in reality, can we? But the fact is, a girl almost died last night. She almost took her own life. And it's all any of us are thinking about today. You want *Common Sense*, Becca? It's only common sense that we process our thoughts and feelings. And what better way to do that than reading poetry?" She cleared her throat. "So, I'll ask the question again. Do you think Teasdale's poem is a suicide note?"

Several students squirmed in their desks, me included.

"No," Becca finally answered.

"Why not?"

"It's a fantasy. She's only imagining what it would be like if she were dead."

"If that's the case, she would have said *if*," Tia argued. "And she said *when*."

Becca pondered this. "But she doesn't sound depressed. She sounds angry. She wants revenge. She doesn't want to die; she just wants to make him feel bad for how he treated her. She wants him to suffer. She wants him to kneel beside her tombstone *broken-hearted*."

"*He*?" The professor crossed her arms. "Why do you assume it's a man? She could be talking about a woman. Her mother, her sister, her friend?"

Becca shook her head. "She's too angry. A woman can't make another woman that angry. Only a man has the power to bring out such feelings of dejection."

"Oh really? What if she's a lesbian?" Tia asked.

Becca rolled her eyes. "Was she?"

"Not that we know of," the professor interjected. "She married a man, but later they divorced."

"Okay, to be politically correct, let me rephrase," Becca went on. "I'm talking about romantic love. That's the kind of love that makes us most vulnerable, the kind that makes us angry and vengeful. And since we know she was heterosexual, I'm going to presume the *you* in the poem is a man."

"Fair enough," the professor noted. "Now let's hear from the rest of you. Is Becca right? Does the author seem angry? And is romantic love the only possible source of such anger?"

"She's definitely angry," one student said. "She wants to be *more* silent and cold-hearted."

"I don't see anger," another student said. "I see . . ."

"Resignation."

I hadn't meant to join the discussion. The word slipped from my mouth.

Professor Barnard walked toward my desk with an outstretched hand. "Can you elaborate, Ruby? Read the poem again. Where do you see resignation?"

My eyes dropped to the page. "In the word *peace*," I said. "She wants peace. Peace of mind. Peace of heart. Like the bough of the tree, weighted down by rain, she wants to succumb. She wants to be numb. She wants to give up. She doesn't want to care anymore. *I shall not care.* I don't think she's angry. Maybe at herself, but not at him. She's defeated. She wants to escape the pain he inflicted on her, and the only way to do that is . . ." I looked up at the rest of the class and swallowed. "To die."

The professor flashed me an earnest smile. "Well put."

While the conversation endured—several other students voiced their opinions on Teasdale's poem—I zoned out, my thoughts drowning out their voices. My hands shook in the aftermath of what I'd said, the snapshot of my soul I'd shared with perfect strangers.

"It isn't a suicide note," the professor divulged once the discussion died down. "Teasdale did commit suicide, but she published the poem long before she took her own life. I think we can all agree, however, that there's a good amount of foreshadowing in her writing."

"How did she do it?" one student asked the professor.

"Sleeping pills."

"Isn't that what Julie took?" another student asked.

"It was Motrin," Becca said.

"Tylenol," Tia corrected.

"I heard she drank a whole bottle of Jim Beam too," one of the other protesters added.

I sat in awe of how quickly the conversation had turned to gossip, how eagerly the students discussed Julie's near suicide once Professor Barnard gave them permission to do so.

"My roommate said a girl tried to kill herself last year too," a student in the back row announced. "Maybe it's a copycat thing."

My chest knotted. They were talking about me, right in front of me, without even knowing it. I looked to Professor Barnard, hoping she would silence them, but she just stood there with her arms crossed, watching the conversation unravel.

"Maybe it's good Tarble is going coed," Becca said. "There's too much estrogen clogging the air. Maybe that's the cause of this whole epidemic, why so many Tarble girls keep trying to off themselves."

"Two girls is not an epidemic," Tia argued.

"Well how many does it take before we admit there's a problem?" Becca asked the entire class. "Three? Four? Ten?"

Another student was about to answer Becca's question when Professor Barnard spoke.

"While I think it's healthy to discuss this issue, I also think candor is paramount," she said, returning to her desk. She pulled out a creaky top drawer, retrieving a stack of blue books from it. "Perhaps a writing exercise is in order."

Professor Barnard's assignment was simple: write your interpretation of Teasdale's poem. If you want to explore tangents, like suicide as a Tarble epidemic, or reflect on a time you felt desperate enough to take your own life, feel free. There are no rules, she said.

Just write.

As soon as she finished her instructions, a hush fell over the class as the girls buckled down to work. Professor Barnard soon approached me with a blue book in one hand and a black pen in the other. She placed the two items on my desk.

"You want *me* to do the assignment?"

"I promise I won't grade you."

I looked to the door. The heavyset woman wearing the Tarble sweatshirt was leaving. "Isn't this my cue to go?"

She sat in the empty desk beside mine, like a waitress sometimes sits with you in the booth while taking your order, and pointed to the blue book. "Would it hurt? To give it a shot?"

I considered the assignment. "Yes."

"That's called risk, Ruby. And writing without risk is not writing at all."

"But I don't know where to start."

"Start *in medias res*," Professor Barnard said. "Start *now*."

And then she walked away.

I stared at the blue book, opened the front cover, and stared some more at the blank page, and then, reluctantly, brought my pen to the paper.

The ink bled onto the page.

I didn't share the details from Professor Barnard's classroom with Heidi until later that night, when we were halfway through watching *Breakfast at Tiffany's*.

"Sounds like she took a real liking to you." Heidi raised her eyebrows up and down several times like Groucho Marx. "Doesn't surprise me. She seems to like the smart ones."

"What does that mean?"

Heidi shrugged playfully, as if she knew exactly what she'd meant. "You're just her type, that's all."

"Her type?" And then I understood what Heidi was insinuating. "You mean . . . she's . . . ?"

"She didn't come out or anything, but she teaches Gender Studies."

"Heidi Callahan," I said teasingly. "You haven't changed a bit. Just because she teaches Gender Studies doesn't mean she's gay."

"The last two teachers before her were. Plus, she isn't married. And she's the adviser for those student protesters, and at least three of them are members of the campus LGBT club. Odds are I'm right. I mean, not that it matters. Not that there's anything wrong with it."

I knew Heidi wasn't homophobic—her favorite aunt, her mother's sister, was openly gay. But she unintentionally fostered the misconception most people have of women's colleges—that they're some sort of lesbian love fest for students and teachers alike. When it came to issues of sexuality, I always employed the attitude Virginia Woolf took in *A Room of One's Own*: "Do not blush. Let us admit in the privacy of our own society that these things sometimes happen. Sometimes women do like women."

I recalled my encounter with Professor Barnard from earlier that day. She had been kind, respectful, encouraging. Was it possible I'd misread her attention? Had she been hitting on me in some strange academic way that I was too oblivious to notice?

I was about to ask Heidi what she knew for certain about Professor Barnard—Where was she from? Where else had she taught?—but was silenced by a solid knock on Heidi's condo door. She opened it apprehensively, thinking one of her neighbors had called the building manager for noise disturbance at our recent rendition of "Moon River." But it was Sarah Iverson, Beth's roommate; her hair was limp and wilted from the rain. I immediately recognized the girl's empty expression, as if her mind were somewhere far off, imprisoned by regret.

Sarah seemed to notice our pajama pants first. "I'm sorry to barge in on you," she said. "But I just found out . . ." She looked to me, and her shoulders crumpled. "Oh, Ruby," she said, before sobbing into my shoulder.

"It's okay," I said, although I knew it wasn't. Her best friend was probably dead. It was only a matter of time before she learned that truth. But I let her cry into my shirt until I could hear breathing in between her sobs. Meanwhile, Heidi turned off the television.

When Sarah's crying turned to sniffles, I gestured to the living room couch behind us. "Would you like to talk?"

She nodded and followed me there. She sat on the couch slowly, as if she wasn't sure it could hold her weight, then accepted a Kleenex from the box of tissues Heidi had nonchalantly placed before her on the coffee table.

"I'll go make some coffee," Heidi announced, giving us privacy.

"I'm trying not to think the worst," Sarah started, her voice shaky. "But I can't help myself. What if . . . God, Ruby, what if Beth's dead?"

I laid my hand on top of hers. "You don't know that."

"Why didn't I see anything on the news?" Sarah's eyebrows arched, her jaw hardened, as if crossing the ever thin line between sorrow and anger. "I feel like I should start a search team or make posters. Offer a reward." She pulled another tissue from the box and blew her nose. "I feel terrible. I didn't know. Not until I saw Jodie Schwerdtman in Newton Center. She said you were the one with all the information."

"Heidi was going to tell you when she saw you," I explained.

"And Beth's mom wanted to call you right away, but she didn't have your phone number."

Sarah wiped her nose. "I didn't know you and Beth were friends."

I detected a hint of jealousy in her tone. "Oh, Sarah. We weren't." And I went on to tell the story about the suitcase.

"It's just strange that you're the one who knows everything. I mean, I'm her best friend. At least, I was. I feel bad. We didn't talk all summer."

I repositioned myself on the couch. "You haven't talked to Beth since graduation?"

She nodded. "To be honest, we weren't talking before that either. It all seems so silly to me now."

"I can't imagine what you two would argue about." It was a question masked as a statement, and I felt a little sick to my stomach after I said it. It was coercive.

"It was silly stuff. Girl stuff." She plucked another Kleenex from the box. "I blamed it all on Beth, but I realized later it was my fault. I was jealous."

"Of Beth?"

"No, of her boyfriend."

I swallowed. "Boyfriend?"

"Some guy. An older guy. I say that because he called our room once, and he sounded really old, like old enough to be my dad. After about the fifth time I asked her about him, Beth finally fessed up and told me he was a grad student at Marquette. She said she met him one of the weekends she went home to do laundry, at an ice cream parlor or pie place, something like that. I was happy for her, at first. I know how hard it is to meet decent guys here. You either end up dating a Kenosha townie or some jerk you already knew from high school. But she was so secretive and always driving up to see him. She stayed the weekends, or sometimes she'd stay on school nights. It was like I didn't have a roommate anymore."

"Did you ever meet him?"

"God, no. She wouldn't even tell me his name. It wasn't any of my business who she dated, she said. He was the reason we were growing apart. I blamed him for that."

"That's understandable," I said, realizing how lonely Heidi must have felt while I was off gallivanting with Mark.

"But it wasn't worth our friendship," Sarah continued. "We got in this huge fight before winter break and we barely spoke to each other after that, other than to say stupid things like 'Hey, are you ever going to do your laundry?' Or, 'Hey, did you use my shampoo?' and it just got ugly and—"

"I'm sorry, but did you just say winter break?"

She nodded.

"Are you sure about that?" I asked.

Sarah narrowed her eyes, as if I had no grounds for questioning her memory. "I'm absolutely sure. She would leave for her English Lit class first thing in the morning and wouldn't come back until dinner, sometimes not until midnight. I started eating dinner with Jodie Schwerdtman."

"English Lit," I said, trying to swallow down a knot. "Was that with Mark Suter?"

She nodded. "And it just got worse after that. I was pissed

because she promised I could use her car to do my education observation hours second semester. But she said I keyed it. Some jerk scratched up the side of her driver-side door, and she blamed it on me. I had to go buy a shitty used Escort."

I grew light-headed then, and held on to the sofa cushion for support. "What kind of car did Beth drive?" I asked.

Sarah crinkled her nose, as if she couldn't fathom why it would matter. "A Jetta."

"What color?"

She paused, still confused by the out-of-context questions. "Black."

That cold, December night came back to me then with twenty-twenty hindsight. It was Beth, her curvy silhouette I'd seen through Mark's front window that night. Beth had straddled Mark on the couch. It was Beth's car parked outside the cabin that night, not Meryl's.

"Look, I knew we wouldn't grow to be old spinsters or anything," Sarah said, refocusing the conversation. "I just never thought we would let a guy come between us."

But I wasn't listening anymore. Because I suddenly knew why I'd been obsessing over Mark and Beth, why I hadn't let go, why I'd agreed to come back to Tarble. I'd known the truth all along, subconsciously, buried under the superficial belief that Beth and Mark's relationship happened months after he broke things off with me, only after his fight to save his marriage had failed. I'd known, deep inside, that Mark hadn't tried to patch things with Meryl.

He'd dumped me for Beth.

And in a split second, Beth Richards was no longer the nice girl down the hall who lent out her luggage. She was no longer Janice's daughter or the brainy photographer. She was not the beautiful, young woman whose life was cut short by a serial killer.

She was the other woman.

Chapter 10

The drive to campus from Heidi's apartment seemed much longer than two minutes on Saturday morning, mainly because I sensed her eyes on me whenever she wasn't looking at the road or the speedometer. Heidi had spent the whole morning watching over me like a mother hen while she cooked us French toast, while we watched the weekend morning news show. She knew my conversation with Sarah had unnerved me. I could see that fact in her flat-lipped smile and pensive eyes.

"So?" she finally said.

"So what?"

"So what do you think of the coffee?"

I looked down at the pink Breast Cancer Awareness travel mug she'd handed me before we left her place. I'd actually forgotten I was holding it. I was still fixated on what Sarah had told me the night before.

I took a sip. "It's good."

"Did you notice the flavor?"

"Vanilla?"

"It's hazelnut," she blurted. "I must not have put enough in. I thought you'd notice right away and say something."

I took an exaggerated sip and nodded profusely. "It's totally hazelnut. I can taste it now."

"I bought flavored creamer when I knew you were coming. The kind we liked."

"I remember," I said. "Thanks."

Heidi kept her eyes on the road this time. "You're welcome."

She was quiet the rest of the ride, so I drank the remainder of my coffee quickly to prove my appreciation, and to get another dose of caffeine to my brain. We were a few feet away from the campus entrance before Heidi spoke again.

"It's still chilly, but at least the rain stopped," she said, resorting to the age-old topic of weather. "Thanks for helping me get things organized for the parade."

The day before, I'd promised to help Heidi with the Reunion parade, when she was stressed-out by everything on her plate—Reunion festivities, Julie Farris damage control, Beth's vigil. But now, the thought of standing in a crowd—gawking at Kenosha's finest middle school and high school marching bands and floats covered in crepe paper stuffed into chicken wire—sounded like a horrendous way to spend the morning. I hadn't slept most of the night, thanks to my discussion with Sarah. Questions had played and replayed in my mind like a song set on repeat. How did it happen? When did it start? Did Beth linger too long after English Literature one day? Had she laughed at all of Mark's jokes over an innocent cup of coffee? Perhaps they drank wine. Maybe Mark gulped too many glasses of Shiraz and couldn't say no when she offered herself to him. Had one thing simply led to another?

And the most pressing question of all: Why did Mark choose Beth over me?

That question festered inside me until I birthed an anger toward Beth Richards I never thought possible. Beth was missing, most likely dead, and yet I hated her. I hated her for taking Mark away from me.

Now in Heidi's car, I started to feel nauseated from drinking the coffee so fast.

"I'm not feeling well," I told her. "Do you mind if I skip the parade?"

"Well, I *can't* skip it. It's kind of my job."

"Can I meet up with you after?"

Heidi turned onto campus drive then, so quickly, I had to grab the *Oh Shit* bar on the inside of the door.

"Where do you want me to drop you off?"

I shrugged. "The library, I guess."

"Your old stomping grounds."

"What does that mean?"

"Isn't that where you went all the time? To work on your thesis? It was always the library or the diner off campus."

"You're still mad at me."

"I'm not . . . Ruby, I don't understand. Everything was fine. Things were going great. You were having fun last night. I saw it all over your face. You'd forgotten all about the Julie Farris thing. And then you had your private chat with Sarah Iverson, and it's like I've lost you all over again. You were acting weird last night and this morning and right now." She sighed, as if exhausted by the recount of the last twelve hours. "What did you two even talk about?"

"Just Beth."

"Beth Richards has you *this* upset?"

"Well, she's probably dead, Heidi."

I immediately regretted saying this, because I was using Beth's likely death as a cover for the awful jealousy I felt toward her. But how could I tell Heidi, an employee of the college, the truth about Beth and Mark, the truth about Mark and me?

"I just wish you'd tell me what's going on instead of shutting me out again," Heidi said. "I thought we were going to make a fresh start."

"I just need a break from all of this Reunion stuff," I explained. "Coming back here was really hard for me."

"Don't you think it's hard for me? Putting our friendship on the line again?"

Her words slapped me with guilt. I hadn't even considered Heidi's feelings.

"I'll help you with the parade," I said.

"I don't want you to." She pulled up to Langley Hall. "If you still want to have lunch with me, I'll meet you back here at eleven thirty."

I nodded and got out of her car, then came around to the driver-side door to say something more.

Instead, I watched Heidi drive away.

The library wasn't open yet. Heidi must have known that, and yet she hadn't told me. So I stood outside the glass doors, waiting for the librarians to unlock them. When I heard someone come through the main entrance of Langley Hall, I expected to see Heidi, thinking she'd come back to apologize for driving off so abruptly. But it was Professor Virginia Barnard. I didn't recognize her at first glance; her hair was down—her weekend look, I supposed. She was wearing a vintage housedress similar to the day before, only red. I watched her blond locks sway across her shoulder blades as she started up the spiral staircase.

She didn't notice me watching her until she was on the third step.

"Ruby," she said, reverting down the stairs toward me. "Ruby Rousseau."

I smiled. "Good morning, Professor Barnard. Good memory."

"Well, don't give me too much credit. It was only yesterday." She pointed at the glass doors behind me. "Are you waiting for the library to open?"

I nodded.

"There must be something more exciting for a girl your age to be doing."

"I like the library. It's quiet."

I noticed the professor carried a large bag filled to the brim with books, papers, and file folders. I gestured at the workload burdening her shoulder. "Isn't there something more exciting for you to do on a Saturday morning than grade papers?"

She looked down at her work as if she'd forgotten it was there. "But I'm a college professor. I've already resigned to a boring life." She smiled at me, her left eye winking. "Walk with me up to my office, will you? We can talk about your essay."

"You promised you wouldn't grade me."

"And my promise is my word. But I wouldn't be able to call myself a teacher if I didn't give you at least *some* feedback."

Hazelnut-flavored stomach acid suddenly rose up my throat.

"Is something wrong, Ruby?" she asked.

"I'm not feeling well," I told her. "Nausea."

"I have just the thing for that. My office is just upstairs."

She started up the steps again, but I paused, remembering Heidi's comment from the night before, about my being Professor Barnard's type. The professor moved so quickly, though, I had no choice but to follow her up the winding staircase to her windowless third-floor office.

"It looks like I live here, because I practically do," she said, removing a dirty coffee mug and half-eaten blueberry muffin from her desk. "I burn the midnight oil, so to speak."

Accepting a seat on a blue-and-white-plaid chair, I perused the room and took in every inch of decor—a collage of photos tacked to a cork board, a poster from a production of Ibsen's *A Doll's House,* the entire three acts of *Macbeth* condensed to one poster, and a 1980s READ poster featuring a young Goldie Hawn curled up with a book. Goldie looked surprised, as if the fake book she was reading had just delivered another plot twist.

The decor seemed mismatched and disparate, and I wondered if the professor had chosen the wall coverings herself or inherited the office that way.

Meanwhile, the professor stood at a makeshift kitchenette, a small pushcart housing a microwave, a hot pot, and a four-cup coffeemaker. She turned the knob on the hot pot, which sent a hissing sound into the small space.

"It's an herbal tea recipe my grandmother passed down to

me: wild yam, alfalfa, ginger, sage, and chamomile," she said. "You'd be surprised how quickly the nausea vanishes. It does wonders for women with morning sickness."

I watched her scoop dried leaves from a bag and place them into a metal infuser ball. I wasn't in the mood for tea, per se. I'd been thinking more about a slice of plain, white bread, something to sop up the bitterness of coffee. But as I relaxed in the high-back chair, within the cozy confines of her office, a cup of tea started to sound like exactly what I needed.

I watched the professor tighten the cap on the ball, then let it swing on its chain below her hand, like a pendulum. "What has brought you back to Tarble?" she asked.

I wanted to play with the syntax of her question, change it to: "What has brought Tarble back to you?" Because it was the suitcase and Beth Richards and *A Room of One's Own* and Mark that tempted me to return to campus, not an innate desire to relive the good ole' days of college.

"Friends," I told her instead. And as if I needed another excuse, I added, "I'm going to the vigil on Sunday, the one for the missing girl."

"Yes, Beth Pritchard?" She gestured to a piece of paper on her desk. It looked like a memorandum from the president about the vigil.

"Richards," I corrected.

"Sorry." She cringed at her faux pas. "Were you friends?"

I shrugged, wondering if Beth had known about me. Had she found pleasure in stealing Mark from under my nose?

The water began to steam above the hot pot then, and Professor Barnard went about pouring my tea into a massive ceramic mug. She dunked the ball into the water several times before handing the cup to me with two hands, gently so as not to spill the hot liquid.

As I sipped the tea I watched her remove a file folder from her bag and from that, a blue book, my blue book from the day before. She didn't hand it to me at first. Rather, she began flipping through the pages.

"How do you like the tea?" she asked.

I nodded my approval.

She concentrated again on my essay. "Your friend Heidi was right; you are modest." She turned the pages slowly, like a mother might stir a pot of chicken soup at the stove while she solved the problems of her children seated at the kitchen table. "Because this is brilliant, Ruby. Yes, you started slow. Reserved. Afraid, even. But by the end, it was the best analysis I've seen from a student in a long time."

I leaned forward to glimpse my handwriting on the page. It looked foreign. Sloppy and dark, as if I had pressed on the tip of the pen with my whole weight.

"Thank you," I said. "But I don't even remember what I wrote."

She handed me the blue book then, as if to jog my memory. I flipped through the pages just as she had.

"It's unfortunate I wasn't teaching here while you were still a student," she said. "I would have been honored to have someone so insightful in my class. I assume you're in graduate school?"

I shook my head no.

"Teaching? Secondary education perhaps?"

"I work for a newspaper in Chicago."

"A journalist?"

I nodded from behind the blue book. "More or less."

"Well, I was particularly impressed by your ability to step inside the author's mind, to feel what she felt, to see things as she saw them," she continued. "I am a big fan of Teasdale and her poetry, and I found your essay eerily intuitive, almost as if you were channeling Teasdale's spirit."

She pointed to her corkboard then, at a photo of a woman wearing a wide brim hat and scarf. Sara Teasdale. I recognized the poet from my research the year before. I set my essay on the desktop then. Uncontrolled, my fingers shook.

She noticed. "Ruby, what's wrong?"

"I'm the girl they were talking about yesterday in class," I said. "The one who tried to kill herself last year."

The professor's lips parted but no words came out.

"So that's why my analysis was so good," I added. "I wasn't writing from Teasdale's point of view, but my own."

She shook her head in self-chastisement. "I apologize, Ruby. I had no idea. Writing this essay must have been very painful for you. I feel terrible."

"How could you have known? Besides, it felt good to read, to think, to write again. Obviously, I needed to get some things off my chest." I gestured at the blue book. "I should consider it free therapy."

"But all of that talk yesterday about the recent suicide attempt . . . you must have . . ." She let out a deep sigh. "The girl, Julie Farris, is one of my protesters. I'm quite fond of her. And I didn't want to just sweep it under the carpet," she tried to explain.

"I understand."

She gave me a small smile. "If you don't mind me asking, did something trigger it? Your suicide attempt? Was it a traumatic event or unexplained depression?"

"My father died the year before," I explained.

"I'm sorry to hear that. The death of a loved one is an unbearable pain." Her eyes fell to my essay, still on the desktop. She stared at it. "Was there something else, though? Besides your father?"

My heart started to beat in my throat. "Why do you ask?"

"Your essay," she said. "Now that I know you were writing from personal experience, I see it differently." She opened my blue book on the desktop and spread it out with her palms as if it were a map. "You're angry."

"I am?"

"And I can't imagine you harbor such rage for your father. So I'm guessing it's like William Congreve said: 'Nor hell a fury like a woman scorn'd'?"

I nodded. I was a woman scorned. "I didn't know I was angry," I said.

The professor laced her fingers. "Ah, that is the miracle of the written word. It beckons our unconscious out of hiding. It tells us things we need to know, sometimes things we don't want to know."

"I don't want to be angry."

"Anger isn't such a bad thing, Ruby. It moves obstacles. Nothing would happen without anger. It's the catalyst for change." She paused. "He hurt you, didn't he?"

"He broke my heart. I dropped out of school. I didn't graduate."

"But you still love him?"

"I think I'll always love him, even though I know he doesn't love me, and that maybe he never did. Why is that?"

She leaned toward me, her voice soft. "Because women love differently than men. We can love without being loved in return. We can love beyond the truth, and even in spite of it."

"When he ended things, I blamed myself," I divulged. "I thought I drove him away. But I know now that's not true. I know better."

"And knowledge is power."

"Is it? Then why do I feel so powerless?"

She shook her head. "I said knowledge is power. I didn't say it makes you powerful. Knowledge is like talent, Ruby. It means nothing unless you *do something* with it. You feel the power later, like an aftershock. You feel it when you figure out what that *thing* is."

We sat silent for a moment, and I stared at my lap. When I looked up again, I caught the professor watching me in awe, as if she saw some aura, some color field of pinks and reds and oranges.

"Do you know much about stars?" she asked.

"You mean, in space?"

She nodded. "Many of us forget they are light-years away. The stars we admire now in the sky are actually light from the past, from thousands of light-years ago. We're just now seeing the image of shimmer. When ships navigated the seas by the stars, they literally sought the future by their understanding of the past."

"That's interesting."

She shook her head, as if to say she wasn't even close to

making her point. "The past is a funny thing, Ruby. It is nature's most underestimated ghost. It is still very much alive. Its heart still beats. It haunts. And it is always impacting, always dictating the future, which eventually becomes the past. You see, it multiplies, this enigma. It grows larger and larger until at the end, it swallows your entire life. Every day, every moment becomes the past."

I said nothing this time, waiting for her to finish.

"I think the real travesty happens much earlier, when we are young, when we become so aware of this future, this daunting day when our past consumes our life, that we stop living altogether. When we simply give up."

She lifted my essay from her desk and handed it back to me like a torch.

"It is the fight against the past that keeps the spirit alive and well," she said.

I regretted leaving Professor Barnard's office as soon as I shut the door. The four walls of her simple space, her home away from home, had embraced me long enough that I'd grown accustomed to their warmth, and the hallway now felt cold and barren. Gwen's office had never had that effect on me. In fact, I always left our Thursday night sessions fluttering for freedom, like a butterfly let go from the trap of a Mason jar. In a mere twenty minutes, Professor Barnard had done something Gwen had never been able to do during ten months of therapy.

She'd empowered me.

I walked back down the spiral staircase into the lobby of Langley Hall—the blue book still rolled up in my hand like a torch—and found myself right where I'd started that morning, just outside the library doors. I stood there a second, unsure of where to go or what to do. The pseudotorch, now growing wet with perspiration from my palm, shed no light on the subject.

And then I saw her—myself. The me before Mark, before my father died. Two years younger, she is fresh-faced and confident, an auburn-haired senior with a backpack slung on her right shoulder. There's a bounce in her step, a calm but almost mischievous smile at her lips. She knows where she's going and where she's been. Her future is unwritten, but that doesn't seem to faze her. In fact, she's empowered by the thought of everything that can be. Her whole life is in front of her, a blank page full of promising stories. And so I followed her—this memory of myself—out the front doors of Langley Hall into the clean, crisp air of late morning.

From a distance, I saw campus drive was blocked from the parade; onlookers, some standing and some couched out on collapsible chairs with cup holders, flanked both sides of the street. Avoiding the crowd, I headed toward North Hall, the northernmost dormitory on campus, hence the name. As I neared the thin, angled building, my eyes traveled up its ivy-covered facade to the third floor, finding the fourth window in from the right. The curtains were open in room 318, but I could picture only darkness in my old dorm room.

Fortunately, the side door had been propped open with a brick, something students did from time to time to skip the hassle of swiping an ID card, and I entered with ease, walking through the first-floor hallway with stealth, as if coming in past curfew. When I reached the front lobby, though, I was stopped by the smell—the unmistakable scent of women's perfume laced with bleach. The lobby sat empty and quiet that morning, and yet I saw it bustling with students, saw my resident assistant at the front desk, and saw that younger version of myself round the corner and disappear into the stairwell. Standing there in the lobby of North Hall, surrounded by the familiar smell of my youth, I wondered if somehow, I could bring that girl back from the dead.

Could I save Ruby Rousseau? Even if I could no longer save Beth Richards?

I climbed the stairwell to the third floor, where I passed room after room in decreasing sequence, 330, 328, 326, and 324. The students' names were written on red and orange construction paper leaves sprinkled with gold glitter, something the RA must have crafted in her spare time.

I stopped first in front of room 324. It had been Beth Richards's room, the one she'd shared with Sarah Iverson. The last time I'd seen Beth she was outside that very door, the day I borrowed the luggage. I paused there a moment longer, as if the door were her tombstone.

Just a few doors down, I came to room 318. It was now Sheila and Lisa's room, according to the names on the door. I brushed a fingertip across the brown wood, then laid my hand flat on the door. I expected to feel heat, some sort of high-voltage energy, but instead it felt cool under my skin. Inhaling and exhaling, I tried to blow a sudden sick feeling out of my body, but after several heaves, the feeling formed a knot in my stomach and grew sour. And I couldn't move. So I simply stood there, arm extended, palm on wood, breathing in and out.

"They're not here," someone said.

I sprung my arm from the door, as if it were actually hot to the touch, and saw a girl standing a few feet away. I didn't recognize her. She was probably a freshman. I wondered how long she'd been watching me.

"Who?" I asked.

"Sheila and Lisa." The girl gestured to the door. "Isn't that who you're looking for?"

"No. I used to live on this floor," I tried to explain.

The girl eyed me closely then, neared me slowly, as if preparing to tell a fantastic ghost story. "You went to school here?"

I nodded. She came closer.

"Is it true?" she asked, once she stood before me. "What they say about that room?"

"I guess that all depends. What do they say?"

"I heard a girl died in there. She killed herself. Is that true?"

Thanks to Julie Farris's suicide attempt, rumors had already grown like vines from mouths to ears, twisting truth. *But she's right,* I thought. A girl did die in that room. The girl I used to be.

"She overdosed on sleeping pills," I said.

"And?" the girl prompted.

"Not *and*," I corrected. "But."

"But what?"

"But she didn't die," I told the girl. "She lived to tell about it."

Chapter 11

Heidi was still waiting for me outside Langley Hall when I walked up five minutes late.

"I wasn't sure you were coming," she said, her round, cherubic face lit with a smile.

"About earlier—" I started.

"Are you feeling better?"

"Much." Thanks to Professor Barnard's magic tea, the nausea was gone. What had she said was in it again?

"Then let me treat you to lunch," Heidi said, linking her arm through mine, as if she'd already forgiven me.

The Lakeside Diner was a likely choice—it was where Heidi and I had always gone to study, talk, or cry over carrot cake. It had been our retreat, when things had gotten rough, as they so often did in college. It wasn't gourmet or classy, but I found its location near the Kenosha harbor and subsequent nautical theme charming. A chalky, ocean blue ceiling contrasted the sky blue pleather booths. Watercolor seascapes of boats and seagulls flanked the walls. And it always smelled of deep-fried perch and lemon.

We filled our first minutes in a corner booth overlooking the water with simple things, like ordering coffee, reading the menu, and asking the server to explain the specials. We didn't say more to each other than "The Thai chicken salad sounds good" or "Remember, for a dollar more, you can add a slice of pie." We knew our conversation would have to go down that road: a twisted, bumpy one mired with feelings of abandonment and guilt. But for the moment, we set our emotions aside and indulged in mindless activities and friendly banter.

"I'm going with a cheeseburger." Heidi flopped her menu down, then stretched her arms above her head and yawned, as if it were the end of a very long day. "You?"

I decided on the roast turkey, complete with mashed potatoes and gravy. I'd pay the extra buck for a slice of cherry pie too.

After we ordered our meals, we gorged on the bread basket, spreading butter on pumpernickel like it was jelly. I downed a whole slice before saying what needed to be said:

"I had an affair with Mark Suter."

Heidi's forehead initially creased in confusion, but soon her eyes grew wide with understanding. *"Professor* Mark Suter?"

I told Heidi the whole story then, about that afternoon in Mark's office, our discussion about my thesis, the coffee shop in Racine, and the kiss in his Jeep. And New Orleans. But for all those moments of euphoria, there were those moments of shame, insecurity, and despair, and I shared those too. The disapproving look from the woman at Café Du Monde. The D on my thesis. The sleeping pills.

The visions of dead women writers—those, I kept to myself.

After I finished, I looked out onto the harbor and watched a boat sail on the horizon, and cross over the line between lake and sky. Heidi said nothing, and I held my breath.

"I'm not being quiet because I'm judging you," she finally said. "I'm just trying to piece things together. I guess the first thing I should say is thank you for trusting me." She spoke slowly, as if still trying to solve a riddle. "He's the reason you were so distant? Why you pulled away from me that semester?"

"You understand why I couldn't tell you? I didn't want us to get caught. I was ashamed."

"Of course you were. I mean, not that you did anything *wrong*."

"It was wrong," I said. "He was married. *Is* married."

"But he was your teacher. He took advantage of that."

"I was a consenting adult, Heidi."

"But he was in the power position. He's twice your age. He should have known better."

Heidi seemed to stare off at the same boat on which I'd been transfixed earlier.

"This makes a lot more sense now," she said.

"You mean, my behavior?"

"Yes, that does make more sense to me in hindsight, but actually, I was talking about . . ." She checked the dining room for familiar faces or perked ears. "Look, you have to *promise* not to tell a soul. I could seriously lose my job over it."

I traced an x on my chest.

"You know Julie Farris? The girl? The one who took the Tylenol? Well, just a few days ago, she made some allegations against Professor Suter. A sexual harassment kind of thing. She told President Monroe that he made sexual advances, and when she said no, he punished her with a bad grade."

A chill tickled the back of my neck. "Did he deny it?"

"I'm not sure it went that far. It was still being investigated when she . . . you know." She sighed. "Do you think that's why she did it? Maybe she was embarrassed? She regretted coming forward?"

"Or maybe they were involved," I offered. "And he broke her heart like he did mine."

A wave of sadness crossed Heidi's face then, and I realized she carried the burden of my near suicide with her as much as I did.

Just then the waitress arrived with our food, and we accepted refills on coffee and extra napkins and a bottle of Heinz for Heidi's fries.

"Something has to be done," Heidi finally said, whacking the side of the ketchup bottle to get it to flow. "He can't be allowed to teach."

I ran my fork tines through the mashed potatoes and let the gravy ooze into the tracks. I remembered what Professor Barnard had said about anger moving obstacles, about knowledge being power. "Are you asking me to come forward?"

Heidi bit into her burger without abandon. She licked an errant drop of ketchup from her lips. "Would you?"

"It was hard enough for me to tell you just now. And my

mom." I set my fork down on my plate. "I don't want my mom to find out."

Heidi stopped chewing when she realized I'd lost my appetite. "Oh my gosh, Ruby, I'm sorry. Please eat. This is just me rambling. Thinking out loud. I don't expect you to say or do anything."

Only when I took a solid bite of turkey, did she continue.

"I just hate him now. I can't explain it to you. I used to feel indifferent about him. Never thought he was cute like most girls do—no offense. But I didn't think he was a dick or anything. But now, I absolutely hate him. For breaking your heart. For ruining our friendship. For being a sleazy, fat pig."

I smiled. She was a dedicated friend.

"Okay, okay. So he's not fat," she corrected. "I meant fat-headed."

"But what good would it do?" I said, once the pressure was off. "If I did speak up? It's been almost a year. Would anyone believe me? It would only embarrass me, and let's face it, I've already embarrassed myself enough. Showing my face around here this weekend was a big enough test of my courage."

"It *was* courageous." She patted my hand. "But somebody needs to stop him from preying on his students. It's totally unprofessional and gross. He should be fired."

Heidi let out an excused belch, then covered the remains of her burger and fries with her napkin and pushed it aside, as if she never wanted to see food again.

"I'm leaving room for the alumnae dinner tonight," she explained. "It's fifty bucks a plate. The good stuff."

I didn't respond. My thoughts had traveled back to the evening I visited Janice Richards. Beth hadn't been back to the Tarble campus since the beginning of the school year, Janice had said. Is that when things went sour between Beth and Mark? Did Mark dump Beth for Julie?

"Yoo-hoo." Heidi waved a hand before my eyes. "You have that 'off in your own world thing' going on."

"Sorry. I was thinking about Beth Richards."

Heidi narrowed her eyes and looked past me then, as if attempting to bring Beth clearly to mind. Then, her eyes shot to mine with intention.

"You want to know something weird? Something I just realized?" She shook her head then, as if she couldn't believe what she was about to say.

"What?"

"Julie," she said. "She looks an awful lot like Beth."

Clearly we were being wooed: the endless supply of beer and wine, the butlered hors d'oeuvres, the Chilean sea bass with honey lime sauce and pimiento risotto. When I bit into the flourless chocolate torte smeared with a dark ganache, I understood why Tarble College had gone to such lengths to welcome the alumnae back to campus with a formal dinner Saturday night. The torte was so rich, so decadent, I considered an equivalent monetary gift to my alma mater.

Swallowing the last bite of torte with a sip of cabernet, from my third glass, I felt warm and full inside and relished having been the center of attention that night. My former classmates—Amanda, Brandy, Joy, and Rachel—had swarmed around me like bees when I'd come into the banquet room. I'd felt like the bold, yellow center of a flower. Hug after hug, their perfumes swirled into a heavy, obnoxious cloud of scent that had made me dizzy.

Now, feeling confident from the alcohol, I scanned the banquet room for Mark, and although I saw many professors, including Virginia Barnard, I didn't see him. Licking the last drop of ganache from my fork tines, I dared him to walk through the door.

My euphoric, almost arrogant state lasted until President Eileen Monroe approached our table. Like most Tarble students, I both admired and feared the Tarble alum who had run the school for the past fifteen years. It was her hair: black with a regal, signature stripe of gray, smoothly swept to one side, lying in place like a helmet. Always. That evening, her hair looked unbelievably perfect, as if it had been styled and set on a mannequin the night before and affixed to the president's head only moments before her appearance. It complimented her impeccable first lady red suit.

"Good evening, ladies." The president positioned herself behind the vacant chair of Heidi, who had left us to tend her alumnae coordinator duties. "I trust you enjoyed the meal?"

After hearing many "yeses" and one "delicious," she cleared her throat with something more sophisticated than a cough. "I personally want to thank you for attending Reunion. I know Tarble can rely on your support as we embark on this new chapter of excellence in education. It will not be an easy road, but change never is. One thing that will never change, though, is this school's ability to persevere."

We nodded, eager to please her.

"Will we see you at the vigil for Beth Richards tomorrow morning?" she asked.

Again we nodded, this time solemnly.

President Monroe grimaced. "It was a truly difficult decision to go on with Reunion festivities in light of the news about Beth. But canceling events would signify a loss of hope, and we mustn't lose hope. Beth is a Tarble girl, after all. Resilient. Courageous. We must believe the best possible outcome. We must keep Beth and her family in our thoughts and prayers. That's just what we have to do. "

"And what about the other girl?" asked Joy, the only one of us bold enough to raise the topic of Julie Farris. "How is she doing?"

I noticed a vein throbbed in the president's forehead.

"Yes, Julie. A sad situation as well. But she's fine, dear. Still recovering in the hospital but hopefully getting the help she needs." She sighed. "Now, my intention was not to talk your ears off all evening. So please, enjoy another glass of wine. Sit back, relax, visit. And again, thank you for your support."

We followed her orders. While some of us stood to grab another drink from the bar, and others resumed side conversations, President Monroe sat beside me in Heidi's chair.

"Ruby, it is a pleasure to see you back on the Tarble campus." She gave my shoulder a motherly pat. "I want you to know—and I mean this sincerely—if you would like to return and finish your degree at Tarble, we welcome you with open arms."

I blushed, not expecting her to single me out. I thanked her before my eyes betrayed me with tears, which I wiped embarrassingly on my white cloth napkin, staining it with mascara.

"My dear, I didn't mean to make you cry."

"It's just very kind of you."

"Well, Tarble is a family," she said. "And we take care of one another. I understand how stressful college can be for a young woman, the immense pressure to succeed. It can get the best of us, sometimes."

She spoke loudly, too loudly I thought for what should have been a private conversation, and I wondered if she was truly sincere or whether it was, as Heidi had called it earlier, *damage control.*

Before I could say more, the president excused herself to tend to a matter that was, judging from the direction of her gaze, on the other side of the banquet hall. I watched her glide across the room, as if by chariot, and land near the door.

And that's when I saw Mark. But it wasn't the Mark I remembered. In fact, he'd aged in the past year. Where I remembered only fine lines, his skin was creased. I used to think his nose was distinguishably pointed, but it now appeared beaklike. His blue eyes looked more slate than sky, and they'd succumbed to a redness only alcohol could induce. He was either very drunk or very sad, or both. If he was distressed over Beth's disappearance, he was doing a poor job of masking it. And he wasn't alone. Soon a woman sidled up next to him, snaked her arm through his, and playfully laid her head on his shoulder. Her blond hair and red fingernails contrasted with her black cocktail party dress, making a bold and flashy statement. When the woman caught me watching, and lifted her eyebrows, as if to ask, "May I help you?" I realized who she was. I'd seen a picture of her in Mark's office once.

I bolted from my chair to find Heidi, who was on the opposite side of the room schmoozing financial backers of the college, as she'd been directed to do.

"He's here," I whispered. "And so is Meryl, his wife."

"Bastard," Heidi whispered back.

I spent the following hour in a tense, deliberated state, acting like an undercover cop. I watched Mark's and Meryl's every move but pretended not to, engaging in polite conversation with my friends, exchanging *hellos* with a few of my former professors.

As the night proceeded, Meryl, who at the onset of the evening had rolled beside him like some sort of ball and chain shackled to a prisoner's foot, stood several feet away from her husband. She dug her long red fingernails into Mark's chest, a litany of words falling from her equally red-tinted mouth. Presumably reaching a breaking point in the argument, Mark pushed her away, but she pushed back, knocking him hard enough to stumble and spill the remains of his gin and tonic. After that, she beelined to the door.

Once Meryl left, I saw Mark scan the room for judging eyes, and soon, his gaze landed on me. I swallowed hard but matched his stare. I thought my knees might buckle under me. I thought I might smile or cry or even laugh inappropriately. But oddly, I didn't feel anything. Maybe it was the three glasses of wine at work, but I stood my ground.

And then he looked away, without a note of recognition; no smile, no head nod, not even a sour purse of the lips.

It was as if he hadn't seen me.

Just before ten o'clock, I saw Mark give a half bow to a group of colleagues before heading for the door. Following, I was almost to the doorway when I felt a tug on my sweater.

"You're not going after him, are you?" Heidi asked, still holding a patch of gray wool. She seemed out of breath, as if she'd chased me two blocks, not through a half-crowded room.

I nodded and tried to keep walking. Heidi held me back.

"What about his wife?" she asked.

"Meryl left an hour ago."

"Do you think you're up for this?"

I nodded again, even though a voice in my head begged to differ.

Heidi finally let go. "If you're not back in twenty minutes, I'm coming to look for you."

I pushed the swinging door with force, as if to prove my strength. And just before it closed behind me, I heard Heidi whisper something like "be careful."

Of course, there was no sign of Mark in the lobby of Newton Center. Heidi had held me back long enough to lose his trail. Which way had he gone? I wondered. He was drunk, and he knew it. He wouldn't get behind the wheel of a car, at least I hoped not. He would need to sober up first by taking a walk or a nap.

Where could he sleep on campus undisturbed?

I headed toward the north doors then, cutting through Newton Center by squeezing past a few L-shaped couches. I banged my knee on the wooden edge of one and whimpered into the empty lobby, but kept going. And once outside, I saw someone walking in the distance on the sidewalk, heading toward Langley Hall. I followed.

Once I stood outside Mark's office door, I noticed it boasted a new nameplate: Mark Suter, *Associate Professor* of English. Below that, he had posted a copy of his course schedule. He was still teaching some of the same classes, like Classics. He had added a special course on Arthurian Legend, though, and his office hours had changed.

I heard a bump then. Pressing my ear to the door, I listened for evidence of life, a snore. But what I heard was the sliding of a drawer, then the slamming of a drawer, and finally the sound of breaking glass. He hadn't gone to sleep, I thought. He'd gone into a rage.

I turned the knob.

Meryl was crouched on the floor near the filing cabinet, picking up shards of glass from a broken photo frame. She muttered profanities under her breath. I stole a peek at the rest of the room, which looked like it had been jostled by a tornado. The papers on Mark's desk—his disorganized piles—had avalanched to the floor. The cushions of the couch had been upturned. Several books had been knocked from the shelf.

I pulled the door back slowly, but it creaked, and Meryl spun around to face me. Holding a gleaming, cleaverlike piece of glass, she approached me. I diverted my eyes to the floor but found no solace there. The sharp toes of Meryl's black heels pointed at me like accusations.

"Sorry." I feigned confusion. "I think I'm in the wrong place."

With her pointed shoe, Meryl stopped the door from closing and let out a cross between a laugh and an exasperated breath. "You're one of them, aren't you?"

She was so close, I could smell her breath. It was sweet, as if she'd just drunk a glass of iced tea. But her lipstick looked untouched: a smooth, satin red.

"I'm not," I snapped, realizing a second too late that the correct response was *One of whom?* I looked again at the floor but could still feel Meryl deconstructing me with her eyes.

"Honey, you're a horrible liar." She stepped back, relaxed her shoulders. "Now, my husband? He's got his Ph.D. in bullshit. Knows just what to say and how to say it. Knows the precise amount of detail to add to any story to make it believable but not far-fetched. Knows the right questions to ask, to make you think he gives a shit."

I said nothing but listened for the sound of footsteps down the hall, for a door opening, something to distract the woman's attention. Then I eyed the shard of glass still in Meryl's grasp. It looked sharp enough to kill someone.

Meryl looked down at the glass too and shook her head in disbelief. "For heaven's sakes, I'm not going to hurt you." She tossed the shard carelessly into the wastebasket. "My guess is you've already been hurt enough."

"I'm so sorry," I blurted.

She didn't respond. Instead she returned to the pile of broken glass on the floor. I stood there, frozen, wondering if I should leave while her back was to me. But I moved only a step before she said, "I didn't mean to break it. Honestly. It fell from my hand." She blew a dusting of glass from the photo and held it out to me. "I barely recognize myself."

Perhaps it was the slight shaking of her hand as she reached out to me, or the resignation of sadness lacing her voice, but I decided to accept the photo. It was the picture I remembered seeing in Mark's office, of Meryl in a teal shirt standing by a redwood tree. I'd studied the picture countless times when Mark wasn't looking. I'd gravitated toward it, hoping to see something ugly, something marred and tainted. But each time, I always saw something I was not, something just beyond my reach. I stared now at the photo, then back at Meryl's blond hair and red fingernails.

"You look different." I regretted the comment immediately. It was girl-talk, evidence that I wanted to continue the conversation.

She shrugged and swept her bangs out of her eyes, streaking blood across her forehead. She must have cut her hand on the glass. "I'm trying to save my marriage."

The guilt festered in my stomach. It had been so easy to be with Mark without Meryl around. It was as if she'd existed only by name, like some fictitious character who lives inside the story after you shut the book. But here she was, standing before me, flesh and blood.

Bleeding.

"Do you know where I found this?" she asked, taking the

photo back, running her finger along the frame. "In the file cabinet. Under *M* too. For *Meryl*. He literally filed me away."

"I'm so sorry," I said again, seeing Meryl for what she really was, the victim. I wanted to tell her how much I'd been hurt too but knew it would solicit no pity.

She shrugged again, as if she no longer cared, as if she had no fight left in her, or rather, it had been beat out. "I bet you thought you were pretty special," she said. "That you were the first. But the fact is my husband's been fooling around with his students for years. I'm not sure what number you are." She laughed again, as if crying had done her no good in the past. "And you're just one of the girls who said *yes*. How many said *no*?"

She was right. I had thought I was the first. I knew Beth and possibly Julie Farris had come *after* me, but I had yet to think that anyone had come *before* me. From my perspective, Mark and I happened unexpectedly. A meeting in his office had simply spilled into a cup of coffee. It had all been so new, so surprising, so forbidden. For me, at least.

"I guess I was naïve," I said.

"He's manipulative," she went on, setting the frame on the desk before grabbing tissues from a box and winding them around her hand. She'd finally noticed the blood. "He told me working at different colleges so far apart would allow us to focus on our careers. If our marriage took a backseat, so what? When you're educated, when you're mature and secure, you don't need someone to hold your hand, caress your cheek, and whisper *I adore you*. If your husband doesn't dote on your every word, it doesn't mean he's having an *affair*." She applied pressure to her wound. "Now that's naïve."

She looked resilient to me, despite what she said. And I wanted to know how she did it; how she stayed with him, knowing he'd been unfaithful. I'm not sure I could have stayed, and yet I wondered if I'd have been strong enough to leave.

She stared at me, long and hard. "You're wondering why I didn't leave him."

I nodded.

"I knew in my heart it was just sex, not love. Until . . ."

"Beth." Her name dribbled from my mouth.

"So you know about her? Mark's *one true love*?" She snickered, the resignation suddenly absent from her voice. "No one compared to *her*. He even told me so. Right to my face when he asked for a divorce."

My mouth dropped open—Mark had never spoken of divorcing Meryl when he was with me—but I camouflaged my surprise.

Meryl wasn't looking anyway. She was pulling the tissue, soiled with blood, off her hand. "He was ready to throw it all away for her. But karma's a bitch. Turns out, she didn't want to marry him. When she threw his ass to the curb, he came groveling back to me. And like a fool, I took him back."

Her words struck me, because I hadn't considered the scenario, that Beth had broken things off with Mark and not the other way around.

"But he still loved her," Meryl continued. "He was obsessed." A sudden flash of horror crossed her face. "And I keep thinking about that saying, something about a fine line between love and hate?" She looked me squarely in the eyes then. "Did you hear? That Beth Richards is missing?"

I nodded.

"Missing girls don't usually turn up, do they? And who's the first person they suspect?"

"The husband," I answered. "Or the boyfriend."

She nodded solemnly. "I thought I knew my husband. I thought I knew what he was capable of. But now . . . I don't know." She tossed the broken photo frame into the wastebasket. "I don't know anything."

December

How is it possible? That I could feel so connected, that I could tie my life and my body up with someone so cold?

How could he make love to me one day, and the next, tell me it's over?

How does he sleep at night? Does he ever think of me? Does he ever feel guilty?

If I knew that, if I knew he boasted one shred of humanity, just enough to make me a thought—even a fleeting one—then maybe I could forgive him. Maybe, one day, I could love again.

But I fear he has already forgotten me, forgotten what I look like, forgotten the curve of my face, the shape of my eyes. He has erased me from his memory to the point that he could pass me on the street or see me across a crowded room, and not even recognize me. He could look right at me, then look away without any note of recollection.

Then again, I don't recognize myself.

Chapter 12

The next morning, I decided to call Detective Pickens.

Maybe I had watched too many episodes of *CSI,* but it was possible, I reasoned after my discussion with Meryl, that Mark was responsible for Beth's disappearance. Could Beth have gone missing—or worse, died—in the most cliché, soap opera kind of way? In a crime of passion? If Mark couldn't have Beth, then no one could?

As much as Mark hurt me, I didn't want to consider him a suspect. I didn't want to think I'd ever been in love with a man who was capable of murder. And yet I felt a responsibility to speak up, to tell the detective what I knew. I couldn't handle the guilt of wondering anymore.

I was fishing in my purse for his business card when Heidi came through the bedroom door, her expression grave.

"I think you better come out here," she said, her voice flat and lifeless.

Running a hand over my bed head, I followed her into the living room, where the television flickered.

"It's all over the news," she said.

Still groggy, I didn't understand what she meant at first. Then it dawned on me. "Beth?"

Heidi nodded, then flipped from channel to channel until a picture of Beth Richards filled the screen. It was the same photo Janice had shown me. Beth was smiling; a small dimple marked her right check. She looked wholesome, the girl next door.

" . . . has been missing since last week," I heard the reporter say in a voice-over. "The Milwaukee native flew to Pittsburgh for a photography workshop but never arrived."

I stared back at the screen and realized one of two things had to have happened overnight: they either found Beth Richards's body or the suspect confessed.

"Police have had this man, John C. Grenshaw of Pittsburgh, under surveillance for an undetermined amount of time. They arrested him yesterday after finding a gun and other suspicious items in the trunk of his blue Chevy Camaro."

I turned my head when they showed the man. He was Caucasian, average-looking, but with bright orange hair and a mustache. His green eyes pierced mine, even through the television screen.

"Last night, Grenshaw confessed to raping and killing Beth Richards," the reporter continued, "telling authorities he dumped her body in the Monongahela River. Divers are currently searching for the body. Police believe Grenshaw is linked to two other homicide cases in the Pittsburgh area. Chief of Police Jack Blumberg will provide a statement today at noon. We will continue to update you on this breaking story."

Heidi raced through more channels. "All of the major stations are running it, if you want to see more."

I placed my hand over her trigger finger. "I've seen enough."

Heidi turned the television off and shivered. "Did you see his hair? Like a leprechaun."

I shivered too.

"You okay?"

I nodded. Unlike Heidi, I'd been prepared for this impending news, but somehow it stung harder than I had expected. My emotions about Beth Richards had run the gamut—from indifference to sorrow, from jealousy to anger. And now, I felt a deep pit of regret and loss in my stomach. But I also knew one thing for certain: Mark was innocent. I breathed a sigh of relief that I hadn't called the detective only moments before to point an accusatory finger at him.

"I guess this changes the nature of the prayer vigil today," Heidi said.

"We were supposed to pray for Beth's safety."

Heidi nodded. "Now, we have to pray for her salvation."

Heavy and still, the air inside Frieburg Chapel was pregnant with the news of Beth Richards's murder. Everyone had either watched the news or heard about it over coffee and powdered sugar doughnuts in the lobby. I noticed people bowed their heads lower, their gestures contained and voices solemn. It was as if a storm cloud had fallen from the sky and seeped indoors, muting everything, even the vibrant hues of the chapel's stained glass.

A few hours earlier, when the newscasts began, Tarble administrators had considered canceling the vigil, because by definition, a vigil is a state of wakefulness, a watch. It implies hope. But President Monroe, who had personally telephoned Heidi to confer about the issue, insisted the ceremony still take place. Beth's murder, she said, was all the more reason for the Tarble community to come together and pray.

The vigil-turned-memorial had not escaped the attention of local newspaper reporters, who had jumped on the story of a young, beautiful woman murdered. Journalists from the Kenosha- and Milwaukee-area newspapers were on hand that morning with notepads and digital recorders, interviewing Beth's former classmates and professors. Technically, I should have been doing the same. Come Monday morning, I was supposed to submit an article to Craig about Beth's disappearance. No doubt he would expect one on her murder instead. But I knew there would never be an article. It was the epitome of conflict of interest.

As Heidi and I sat in the first pew, I watched the people—I estimated there were almost 150—enter the chapel. No one talked, and the silence magnified their heavy footsteps on the wood floor. I saw Sarah Iverson, holding a tissue up to her red, swollen eyes, take a seat a few rows behind us. The other girls from my class were there too, as well as Professor Barnard.

"It is customary to address you with Good Morning," President Monroe finally said from the pulpit as the crowd settled.

She wore a black pantsuit instead of her telltale red or blue. "But it is a morning of great sorrow. Today, we were to pray for Beth Richards, to send her the strength and the courage she needed to find her way back home. But we have learned unfathomable news. A sick, misguided man has confessed to taking her life."

The president lowered her eyes to the podium and sighed. A wave of response trickled through the rows of people as they sighed too.

The president seemed to struggle for words, her face contorted in what seemed to be utter shock. "How can we make sense of this tragedy?" she asked, regaining composure. "I assume it will require reflection and prayer and perhaps, forgiveness. And that requires time. For now, we must remember Beth for her life, not her death."

The president went on to describe Beth Richards as an "intelligent, graceful student who was passionate about science and life." Then she invited Beth's former classmates and professors to come forward and speak. Many people did. One professor shared an anecdote; another a warm memory. Even Sarah Iverson spoke, telling the crowd in a shaky voice about the time she and Beth pulled an all-nighter before finals junior year, only to find out later Beth had already aced her exams.

While Sarah spoke, I saw Mark stand up across the aisle. No sign of Meryl. I hadn't known he was there. Was he daring to offer a speech about Beth? No. I watched him wrestle with knees and feet as he scooted out of the pew with his head hung low. And then, he disappeared into the lobby through the glass doors.

When the room grew suddenly silent and microphone vacant, President Monroe said a simple prayer, then encouraged us to begin a dialogue about ways to find peace among men.

Heidi and I met up with the other girls in the lobby, where we hugged and cried and stood in silent circles, still trying to wrap our minds around the news. We'd all taken a cup of coffee and a doughnut hole and a paper napkin on which to hold it, but no one seemed to eat or drink. Instead, we babbled small fragments of thought.

"Hope he gets the death penalty," Joy said.

"Her poor mother," Amanda added.

Janice, I thought. *Poor Janice*. How had she taken the news? Did she pass out, or collapse or scream at Detective Pickens and beat his chest with her fists? I could imagine her repeating the word "no" a thousand times, as if saying that simple word would negate the truth about her daughter's fate. At some point, she'd have to accept the loss, and do things she never thought she would have to do, like picking out a casket and burial plot, setting a date for a wake and funeral, running obituaries in the local newspapers. I had stood beside my mother through that entire process for my father, and remembered it only as a lucid dream, a wakeful nightmare.

I was about to take a bite of my doughnut hole, or at least lick off some powdered sugar, when I felt a tap on my shoulder. It was Tia Clark, the leader of the student protesters. I recognized her from Professor Barnard's classroom on Friday.

"Sorry to hear about your friend," she said, tugging self-consciously at her too tight T-shirt, which read WELL-BEHAVED WOMEN SELDOM MAKE HISTORY. She guided me by the elbow away from my circle of friends. She held my arm so tightly, I winced, but I thanked her for the kind words.

Tia's mouth appeared clenched though, as if holding back what she wanted to say. "Look, it may not be the most *appropriate* time, but I'd like to talk to you about this Beth Richards girl."

"I can't think of a more appropriate time," I told her. It was, after all, Beth's vigil turned memorial.

Tia's expression turned sour. "It doesn't have anything to do with her murder, per se. It's just kind of weird. I thought you should know, that's all." She pulled a paper from her back pocket, the creased program from that morning's service. "I talked to Beth Richards about two weeks ago," she said. "I didn't know it was Beth at the time. But when I saw her picture today . . ." She pointed to the program with Beth's senior picture gracing the front. It was the same photo they'd plastered all over the news. "I'm positive it was her. She came to talk to Julie last week."

A thud sounded in my chest. "Julie Farris?"

"We were protesting in the grove, and she walked up asking which one of us was Julie."

"Did Julie talk to her?"

"She was at class."

"Did Beth say what she wanted?"

"Nope. Don't think I didn't ask. She said it was private."

I stared back at Tia's blond pigtails and hard expression and wondered about the direction of our conversation. "I'm not sure I understand," I said.

"Seems sort of strange, doesn't it? That Beth would go looking for Julie and then, well, end up dead? Right around the time Julie tried to kill herself?"

It's stranger than that, I thought, considering Mark's connection to both of them.

"I don't understand why you're telling *me* this," I clarified.

"You're Ruby Rousseau, right?"

I nodded.

"Well, when I talked to Beth, she had something in her hand, something I assumed she'd brought to show Julie. And, you know, I tried to see what it was, because I'm nosy."

"What was it?"

"A magazine of some sort. Not a glossy one, something more professional-looking. I only made out the words *Midwest* and *Council*. The rest was covered up by a yellow sticky note."

"Okay?"

Tia tugged at her shirt once more. "She'd written some girls' names on the sticky note. Four names. Julie's name was at the very top."

I shrugged, as if to say I still didn't understand.

She hesitated. "And your name was written directly below it."

Chapter 13

Beth Richards knew about me. At least, she knew *something* about me. She'd written my name on some sort of list, a list that also included Julie Farris. I had two things in common with Julie: Mark Suter and my suicide attempt. What other names had Beth jotted down? Was it a list of Mark's conquests?

I could think of only one person to ask.

I had to wait twenty minutes before visiting hours began at the psychiatric ward of Kenosha General Hospital, and then, it was another ten minutes of protocol—metal detector and pat down, labeled bright orange name tag, car keys inventoried inside a clear plastic bag, and the escorted walk through two keypad-accessed doors—before I actually saw Julie Farris.

I was surprised by the level of security. I'd only been a patient in a psych ward, not a visitor. And as I endured each step of the process, I imagined my mother having to do the same, all the times she came to see me before I was discharged. What does it feel like, I wondered, to be patted down to see your own child? I'd hurt my mother more than I'd known.

I met Julie in a communal visiting room full of hard couches and sterile table and chairs. Because she was on suicide watch, a nurse stayed in the room while we spoke, ready to act at the first possible sign of self-harm.

My mouth hung open when I saw Julie's long blond hair and tall, slender frame. Heidi was right, she looked like Beth Richards, not only in hair color and body type, but also the unique details of her face. Close-set blue eyes. Narrow bridged nose. Pouty lips. *They could easily be sisters,* I thought. Maybe even twins.

"I wasn't sure you'd agree to see someone you didn't know," I said.

Julie didn't respond but twisted in her chair. "Could you give us some privacy?" she asked the nurse.

"You know the rules," the woman said.

Reluctantly, Julie faced me again. "I know who you are," she finally said. "Actually, I was going to call you once they let me out of here."

"You were?"

She tugged at the neckline of her hospital-issued gown because it slanted to one side, exposing her left collarbone more than her right. "We have a lot in common, don't we?"

"How much do you know?" I asked.

"You first."

I paused, caught off guard by her straightforward approach, her cool, calculating voice.

"You filed sexual harassment charges against Mark Suter," I finally said. "But my guess is that it was more than that. You had a relationship, didn't you? You love him."

She snickered. "Not anymore."

Two nights in the psych ward had obviously worked wonders on Julie. A year had passed, and I still loved Mark. I worried I always would.

"You also said he gave you an unfair grade," I added. "When you refused to sleep with him."

"Okay, so I didn't refuse him. But he did give me an unfair grade. I know a lot of people can't be objective about their writing. But I can. And I wrote a kick-ass paper."

I admired her confidence but was also confused by it. Was this girl—a girl who had tried to kill herself just two days prior—really so certain of herself, or was it an act? Was she trying to appear self-assured, so the doctors would release her sooner?

"Why did you do it?" I asked.

"Because I deserved an A."

"No, I meant, why did you take the Tylenol?"

"Oh." Her cheeks suddenly sunk. "Because I was devastated. Naturally. He messed with my head. He did this to me, just like he did it to you."

"You know about me?"

"Everyone knows about you."

Obviously the Tarble gossip mill had ensured my notoriety for decades to come.

"But how did you know about my relationship with Mark?"

She tugged at her gown once more. "He told me."

I couldn't fathom why Mark would tell Julie Farris about me. To what gain? I was a skeleton from his past, an embarrassment. But I didn't press the issue. I saw the nurse check her watch. We had a limited amount of time, and I had more important questions to ask.

"Did a girl named Beth Richards come to talk to you recently?"

Julie didn't blink. "Yeah, my friend Tia said some girl with that name came looking for me one day in the grove, but I never talked to her. I don't know what she wanted." She furrowed her brow, as if suddenly intrigued. "Why do you ask?"

I paused, unsure of what piece of information to share first.

"It was all over the news this morning," I decided to say. "She was murdered."

Her eyelids flitted in surprise. "Wait. Who is she?"

"She went to Tarble. Graduated last year." I glanced again at the nurse overseeing our conversation. "She was involved with him too. I think that's what she came to see you about."

I told Julie then about Beth's list, though I didn't know what other names graced that sticky note. "My best guess is she was trying to rally us," I added. "Get us to all come forward and file claims against him."

"And now she's dead?"

I nodded. "Tia said she had some sort of publication with her too, with the words *Midwest* and *Council* on it. I Googled it. I'm guessing it was a professional journal published by the Midwest Collegiate English Teachers Council. Does that mean anything to you?"

She shook her head no. "Do they know who killed her?"

"Some guy in Pittsburgh. Actually, they think it's a serial killing."

This tidbit should have unnerved Julie, noticeably creeped her out, but it seemed to put her at ease. Maybe for a moment, she'd also considered Mark a suspect.

"Why were you going to contact me?" I asked.

"To do the same thing. To ask you to file a claim against him. Will you?"

"You still want to go through with it?"

"Why wouldn't I?"

I assumed, because of her suicide attempt, that Julie would drop the charges against Mark. I thought it was a sign she'd lost her will. I wanted to see Julie as I saw myself—innocent and wounded. But something about her sharp eyes and quick tongue made that impossible.

"How come you never said anything?" she snapped. "Last year? When it happened?"

Because coming forward would have been like saying the relationship was wrong, I thought. That it wasn't love, but something inappropriate. Something disgusting. It would have made me feel the way I did that first night in New Orleans, the night the woman in the café said *tsk, tsk* under her breath, the night I couldn't get the powdered sugar stain out of my dress.

"I didn't want anyone to know," I said instead.

"And what about now?"

I shrugged.

"It's his fault you tried to kill yourself, you know. And why I did too. He needs to pay for what he did to us."

"He didn't put the pills in our mouths, Julie."

"But we almost died. I would be dead right now, had my RA not come to check on me."

I didn't want to play the blame game. I'd played it a number of times with Gwen. We agreed that I couldn't blame myself entirely, but I had to take responsibility for what I'd done. It was my choice to swallow the pills.

"Okay. Let me ask you this," Julie charged when I didn't respond. "Did Mark ever give you a bad grade, one you didn't deserve?"

"My thesis. He gave me a D."

"First D you ever got in your life, right?"

"The only D."

Julie crossed her arms smugly. "Then maybe it's time for a second look."

I found Professor Barnard grading essays in her office that Sunday afternoon—another half-eaten muffin, this time lemon poppyseed, beside her. But she graciously agreed to procure a copy of my thesis from the English Department office without much explanation. After my chat with Julie, I remembered I'd turned in two copies of my paper last year per Tarble College policy—one to be graded by Mark and the other to be filed in a portfolio for the department.

Now, she was at her desk, reading about *A Room of One's Own* and the trials and tribulations of women writers trying to create in a field dominated so long by men. Waiting for her to determine a reasonable grade, my heart beat hard and fast, and I could no longer sit and watch her. I paced her office, reading every inch of her bulletin board.

Soon Professor Barnard raised her eyes and smiled, broad and all-knowing. Her expression told me the verdict was good. But what was *good* news? Did I want to know Mark had been honest, that he had graded me fairly? Or would I rather learn I had written a quality paper?

The professor set the document down and removed her reading glasses, but she didn't speak. Her mouth tugged to one side, as if chewing on words. "I would have given you an A minus," she finally said.

"That's good to hear," I said. "Because Professor Suter gave me a D."

"Grading essays is always subjective, but there's absolutely no justification for a D." She paused. "Unless, of course, it's plagiarized."

"I wouldn't do that."

"Maybe not intentionally, but . . . I have to be honest with you, Ruby, I feel like I've read this before."

"How is that possible?"

She shrugged. "You tell me."

I let out an astounded huff. "Every word in that paper is mine, Professor Barnard, except the quotations." I looked her directly in the eye, to prove I wasn't lying. "I didn't steal anything."

She held my gaze. "It's just so familiar . . . I . . . ." She let it go with a wave of her hand. "I suppose it doesn't matter now, does it?"

"It matters," I said. "It matters to me whether you believe me."

Her eyes softened. "I believe you. But I'm not sure where we're going with this. Why did you have me read this? You want to refute the grade? Why now? Why didn't you say something last year?"

I swallowed. "I guess I cared more about him than the D."

Her lips parted in surprise. "You mean, it was Suter? He is the *he* you wrote about in my class the other day?"

"We had an affair," I said, even though I hated everything the *A*-word connoted. It was the best word, however. The most accurate descriptor. It wasn't love. At least, it wasn't to him.

The professor sighed. "I guess I'm not surprised. I know his type. Arrogant but charming. Intelligent but emotionally immature. I've dealt with countless men like him at every level of my career. I knew he was slime—even back when I interviewed for this position." She shook her head in true disgust. "I'm assuming it didn't end well?"

"The day he handed out grades was the same day he told me it was over," I explained. "And that's the same day I tried to kill myself."

"Did you report him?"

"I just wanted to forget it ever happened."

"And did you? Forget?"

I hung my head in silence.

"Look, Ruby, I'll be happy to support you if you decide to refute this grade. But you need to answer a very important question first: What do you care more about now?" She gestured at my thesis. "Suter or the paper?"

I grimaced. "It isn't so black and white. Odds are, I'll have to come clean about the affair. And I can't do that. I don't want anyone to know. I don't want my mom to know."

"I understand how you feel. But men like Suter can't control their need for power, their need to dominate. If he did this to you, I'll bet he's done it to others. If you come forward, others might too."

"Another girl already did," I said. "Julie Farris filed sexual misconduct charges last week."

"Julie? Don't tell me she was involved with Suter too."

"She was devastated when he ended it," I said. "Just like me. That's why she did it, she said."

"You spoke to her?"

I told the professor then about my visit to the psych ward.

The professor clucked her tongue. "I wish Julie had come to me. I could have helped her." She paused. "How is she? You know, emotionally?"

I recalled Julie then, her cool confidence, uncharacteristic for someone who'd recently attempted suicide. "Surprisingly well. She still wants to get Suter fired. And she asked me to help."

"Is that what you want to do? Get Mark Suter fired?"

I shrugged.

"Why do you want to protect him, Ruby?"

"I don't. I want to protect myself."

"But silence is consent. That's why my protesters go out to the grove every day."

"Silence is also dignity," I countered.

"But if no one stops him, he'll just keep doing this. To more girls. Over and over. And look at the ramifications. You and Julie both tried to kill yourself. Fortunately, you both failed. But one day, a girl could . . ." She paused and swallowed. "A girl might succeed."

My stomach churned with guilt.

"Maybe you don't have to say anything about the affair," she offered. "Just focus on the grade. That alone could get Suter fired."

"He'd get fired for grading one paper unfairly?"

"Two papers," she corrected. "I'll review Julie's essay as well. I'm certain I won't agree with his assessment. Trouble is, how do I get my hands on her paper? If Julie complained about the grade, there's probably a copy of it in her student file. But I don't have access to those. Only administrators do."

Heidi, I thought. Heidi has access to student files. But did I want to drag her into this? Despite all the bad things Heidi used to say about Tarble, I could tell she really liked her job, and she was good at it. I didn't want to put her career in jeopardy. But I also knew she wanted Mark to be fired—she had said so at lunch the day before—and she hated him.

"What if I could get a copy?" I asked.

Peering outside her office door, Heidi looked both ways down the hallway. All areas were clear, as Langley Hall sat as still and silent as Sunday. She motioned me inside.

"Did you get it?" I asked, following.

"Oh, I got it." She closed the door behind us. "And then some."

She handed me a small sheet of dusty blue paper then, the Tarble emblem visible at the top. The paper's edge still showed a sliver of glue from being ripped from a desk tablet. I stared at what Heidi had written there in black ink, and then asked the question to which I already knew the answer.

"What's this?"

"The other girls Suter screwed over," she said.

Chapter 14

Tina Beyers and Madeline Kohl.

I stared at the two names Heidi had written on the paper, and wondered if they were the same names on Beth Richards's list.

"You got these from Julie's file?" I asked.

"From Suter's." She jingled a gold key on her chain. "My master key works on every door in the building, including Human Resources."

According to Mark's private employee file, he had been the subject of not one, but three claims of sexual misconduct over the past two years. The other two claims—submitted by Tina Beyers and Madeline Kohl—had later been withdrawn. Why they withdrew their complaints, I couldn't say. But at least they'd tried. Like Julie Farris, they had done something noble, something brave, something I never did. Whether they had a full-fledged relationship with Mark, or were simply the object of his affections, they broke their silence about him.

Could I follow their lead?

"Both of them dropped out of Tarble," Heidi went on. "You all have that in common. But none of you look alike. If Suter has a type, I'm not seeing it. Here, I'll show you." She moved to her computer screen at her desk.

I pulled a chair beside her. "You have student photos on your computer?"

"Tarble switched out hard copy files for electronic ones a few years ago," Heidi explained. "Cool, huh?"

I nodded.

"Okay. Here's Tina Beyers," she said, clicking the mouse.

I studied the girl's small, childlike features—thick brown bangs swept to the side revealing a short forehead—and found it hard to believe Mark had ever had a sexual relationship with Tina, or even hit on her. I wasn't sure what his type was, considering I had auburn hair and Beth and Julie had blond, but regardless, Tina Beyers just didn't seem to fit.

"Now check out this Madeline chick," Heidi said, sensing I was ready to move on.

Once the photo loaded, my mouth hung open. Madeline. The girl's black cropped hair was unforgettable. There was no doubt in my mind, she was the girl who'd sat crying in Mark's office that afternoon, the day he and I had gone out for coffee, the day everything began between us. I recalled what transpired in his office, how Mark had told the girl to come back in an hour, and how later he'd blown her off to stay and chitchat with me.

She'd probably waited outside his office door all afternoon.

"I know her," I said.

"Really? Who is she?"

I stared at the photo a moment longer. "The girl Mark dumped to be with me."

Heidi let me use her office phone to make the call, and I pressed each number carefully, double checking each digit with what Heidi had written. I let the phone ring eight times before hanging up and dialing again, thinking that despite my focused precision, my nerves had caused me to press a wrong number. The phone rang ten more times, and I prepared to hang up. But just as I pulled the phone away from my ear, a woman answered.

"Is Madeline there?" I asked.

"Speaking," she said, soft and hesitant.

"This is Ruby Rousseau," I started. "You probably don't remember me but—"

"I remember you."

Her tone was so cold, I actually shivered. Madeline Kohl remembered me, but she didn't do it fondly.

"We went to Tarble together," I rambled. "I was a senior when you were a fresh—"

"I know who you are. What do you want?"

There was no roundabout way to get to the point, so I just got to it. Madeline's reaction would speak volumes, I thought. "I want to talk to you about Mark," I said.

Silence. And then, "What about him?"

"He was seeing you when he got involved with me." It wasn't

so much a question as a statement she could either confirm or deny.

Madeline remained quiet on the other end.

"Hello?" I said, thinking she'd hung up.

"I'm here." Her voice was airy and apprehensive. She sighed. "He told me he was getting back together with his wife. But I knew it was a lie. I knew about you. How could I not? How could I pretend I didn't see how he looked at you when you came into his office that day, or how many times I saw you going into his office after? I was watching. I watched it all unfold. I watched it all crash down around me. Until I couldn't take it anymore."

I heard a vacancy in her voice, a hollow murmur that reminded me of my own. It was unfathomable that I'd played a part in hurting this girl without even knowing it. I wondered if I'd ever seen Madeline hanging outside Mark's office door, or hiding behind a pillar in Langley Hall, watching us.

"Is that why you dropped out?" I asked.

"My doctor thought it was best."

"Doctor?" My heart sank. "You mean, like a shrink?"

"I didn't want to live anymore."

"Did you . . . ?"

"No. I ran a knife against my wrist once," she divulged. "But I didn't have the guts to apply any pressure. I got help before I did anything stupid."

Stupid, like what Julie and I did by overdosing. I shivered at how much the three of us had in common.

"I didn't know about you, Madeline. Honest," I said. "At least not then. But I want you to know, he gave me the same line he gave you, about working things out with Meryl. It was a lie. He just moved on to yet another girl."

"Do you want my sympathy or something?" she snapped.

I couldn't blame Madeline for her anger; it was the same fury I'd felt toward Beth when I'd found out she was the shapely figure I'd seen straddling Mark through the cabin window.

"Mark didn't just do this to you and me," I told her. "There are two others. Maybe even more. And if I could be as brave as all of you, if I could come forward to say what happened, well, there's strength in numbers, isn't there?"

"As brave as me?" Madeline balked. "What are you talking about? I didn't do anything brave. I did the most cowardly thing of all. I ran away."

"I'd hardly call filing a complaint an act of cowardice."

"I didn't file anything. What makes you think I did?"

I couldn't mention Heidi or what she'd risked to help me, nosing in those private files. But I didn't understand why I had to. The report was in Mark's file. Why would Madeline lie about it now?

"So you didn't say anything to the Tarble administration about what happened between you and Mark?" I clarified. "You didn't charge him with sexual misconduct?"

"No. And I never told anyone either. Mark made me promise not to. He was worried he'd lose his job."

"How did you do in his class?" I asked. "I mean, did he grade you fairly?"

"My essay on *The Scarlet Letter*," she said. "That's the paper we were talking about when you came into his office. I worked so hard on it too, to impress him, to show him I was smart and creative." She paused. "He gave me a D."

And Madeline made three.

I returned to Professor Barnard's office armed with a copy of Julie Farris's essay, and handed it to her proudly, like an eight-year-old showing off her first batch of brownies from an Easy-Bake oven. "I already read it," I said. "And it's good."

She smiled but held the paper by her fingertips at first, as if it were tainted. "Ah, yes. Anne Bradstreet. The first American poet," she said, scanning Julie's essay with a keen eye. "I won't ask how you got this."

"Good, because I can't tell you." I paused. "But there's more."

When she raised her eyebrows in intrigue, I told her everything I'd learned while we were apart, about the other sexual misconduct claims in Mark's Human Resources file and my subsequent conversation with Madeline Kohl about her essay on *The Scarlet Letter.*

"Even though these girls withdrew their claims, I can't believe Suter still has his job." Professor Barnard shook her head. "Three accusations are enough to raise eyebrows. The administration obviously dropped the ball here."

"But that's the strange part," I added. "Madeline said she never filed a claim."

"But she had to have, if it was in his file." The professor crinkled her nose in confusion. "What did the other girl, this Tina Beyers, say when you talked to her?"

"I couldn't get ahold of her, but I'll keep trying."

"Do you think there are more of you out there?"

I shrugged. "There were only four names on the list."

"List?" She narrowed her eyes. "What list?"

I cringed when I realized my slip. I never intended to mention Beth's relationship with Mark—not to Professor Barnard, not to Heidi, not to anyone. But it was too late. I considered lying, telling her I misspoke, but the professor seemed too smart for that. So I had no choice but to tell her the truth, how Beth was the reason Mark broke up with me, how she came to campus looking for Julie Farris with the list of names and the journal published by the Midwest Collegiate English Teachers Council.

"I have no idea what a professional teachers' journal has to do with Mark," I added.

The professor's mouth popped open. "The new teacher orientation," she blurted.

"The what?"

She stood then and began sifting through the contents of her magazine files on her bookshelf. "Back in August, at my orientation, I remember they gave accolades to certain professors for various achievements, and Mark Suter was one of them. He published a paper in a recent issue of the MCETC journal. I'm almost positive. It's here. I know it's here."

After knocking a few books from the shelf, she pulled out several quarterly issues of the journal in question, and we began rummaging through them, flipping pages violently. We didn't even bother to sit down. Instead we stood side by side, the journals open before us on top of the shelving unit. The professor spoke first.

"Here it is," she said, before reading the title. "'Feminine

Depression and Literary Creativity: Revisiting the Works of Woolf, Plath, and Gilman,' by Mark Suter, Associate Professor of English, Tarble College."

My jaw dropped.

"He stole your work," she said.

I fixed my eyes on the article again and started reading it, my finger gliding over the words, hoping to find word choices and syntax and phrasing different from my own. A word or two had been changed, a paragraph had been omitted, but the majority of it was mine. Word for word.

I hope you don't mind, I remembered Mark saying in New Orleans, after the symposium, *but I shared some of your ideas . . . I gave you credit, of course. Not by name. I just called you my star pupil.*

What a liar, I thought. I didn't lose my notes in New Orleans. He stole them.

The professor stabbed at the article with her index finger. "That's why I couldn't shake the feeling that I'd seen your thesis before or heard something to the same effect," she noted. "No wonder he gave you a D. He couldn't have you thinking your paper had value."

I swallowed a pool of saliva that had formed in my mouth from not breathing and looked again at the article, at Mark's name in the byline. Heat flushed my cheeks.

"He was always talking about how many papers he had to publish to please the tenure committee, how he needed to look prolific," I said. "So instead of doing the work himself, he took it from me."

"Not only you. I'm willing to bet he stole work from Julie and

Madeline too." The professor returned to her desk to pick up Julie's paper. "I bet Suter has this exact essay about Anne Bradstreet saved on his hard drive right now, only with his name at the top, ready to submit, another paper to add to his obnoxiously long CV."

Mark's computer, I thought. *What would I find there, if I had a look? More papers he stole from his students? Evidence of his countless affairs? Love letters to Beth?*

Certainly, Heidi's master key would open his office door.

Heidi wanted to do more than give me her master key; she wanted to snoop in Mark's office alongside me. But she'd already risked losing her job by prying into private files. I couldn't let her become a full-fledged accomplice. Begrudgingly, she let me go alone. She wanted to wait for me in her office, but I told her to go run errands instead, and come back to campus in an hour. That way, if I got caught, she wouldn't be on campus, and I could lie and say I stole her key.

The air inside Mark's office was stale and musty, and I wondered if he'd been there since Meryl had trashed it the night before. Items—like the sofa cushions and paper piles—had been replaced but sloppily. Tissues, stained with Meryl's blood, still sat in the wastebasket. Odds were, Mark wouldn't return to his office until the next morning, but I moved swiftly and stealthily toward his desk, just in case.

I booted up Mark's computer but paused when the security log-in page loaded. I forgot that it would be password protected, since he used it to access the college's main computer system and enter grades. I nosed around his desk for the password, even looking under the keyboard, thinking maybe he'd written it down in case he forgot. He didn't. So my only option was to guess his password accurately before too many invalid tries locked me out.

I looked around the room for clues. Was it something simple and straightforward, like his name? Or perhaps the name of an author? Was it an acronym of some sort? Or his birthday? My eyes soon went to the wastebasket, where Meryl had tossed the bloody tissues the day before. What had she called Beth? Mark's *one true love*?

I typed the word *Beth* into the blank space and held my breath as I clicked enter. No luck. *Invalid password* popped up on the screen. Staring at those two red words, I realized the odds were against me. I knew I'd just end up trying two more times, unsuccessfully, and the system would lock me out. Ditching the mission, I turned the computer off and got halfway to the door when I stopped abruptly at a thought. I raced back to Mark's computer for another try. This time, a successful one.

Beth was too short to be a password, I realized. But *Elizabeth* wasn't.

Once I had access to Mark's computer, I saw he kept his hard drive as messy as his desk. Files and icons covered the entire desktop. I read the titles of the file folders quickly, hoping he'd named them simply, hoping he'd unknowingly made this task easy for me. Skipping folders generically titled *Assessments* and *Book List,* I clicked on one marked *curriculum vitae.*

Mark's professional résumé was, as Professor Barnard presumed, obnoxiously long. He'd included the standard credentials—his B.A. from Tulane and his M.F.A. from

Northwestern—but also an exhaustive list of conferences he'd attended, as well as every paper he'd published professionally. His paper on Woolf, Plath, and Gilman—the one he stole from me—was his most recent publication credit, dated from that summer. But the entry listed just before it, titled *Deconstructing Hester*, also caught my eye. According to his CV, he'd published an essay on *The Scarlet Letter* just four months after his affair with Madeline Kohl ended, just four months after he'd slapped her essay on Hawthorne's Puritan novel with a D. It couldn't be a coincidence.

There were a number of blank files on the desktop with no actual content. A couple of files were story starts, snippets of novels or short stories he never finished. Despite a concerted effort, a thorough check of his documents, I found nothing on Anne Bradstreet, nothing to suggest he'd also stolen ideas from Julie Farris.

I found something more disturbing than that.

The document was titled *Her Fractured Mind: Where Creativity and Insanity Collide* and that alone piqued my interest because it related to my thesis topic. I assumed it was another reworked version of my ideas. But once I opened the document and saw the words SUBMISSION—*PSYCHOLOGY NOW,* DRAFT at the top of the page, I questioned that assumption.

What would Mark write for a psychology publication? I wondered.

The answer was there in the text:

Looking back, I'd liken her mind to my hometown public library, jam-packed with facts and stories and ideas. And like a precocious schoolboy, I wanted to read every book on her shelves. But I can't sugarcoat the truth: she was delusional. She saw things that weren't there.

How could a mind so beautiful, so imaginative, malfunction? Why did it drive her to the brink of suicide? Was her mind predisposed to breakdown, to self-destruct?

i.e. Was she destined to be crazy?

The words—*delusional, malfunction, suicide, crazy*—bombarded my eyes like flashes of light as I tried to make sense of Mark's essay. Checking the document's properties, I saw Mark had created the file in December of the year prior, right after my near suicide. And my cheeks grew hot, my throat tight. My fists clenched.

It's me, I thought as I printed a copy of the document. *I'm the delusional she.*

Chapter 15

Professor Barnard had finished reading Julie's essay by the time I returned to her office. It was close to three o'clock by then, and I saw the day wearing on her; her makeup had worn off, particularly under her eyes, and she was yawning when I came in the door. I knew she would have gone home by then, if I hadn't asked for her help, and I felt bad I'd ever questioned her intentions, especially based on Heidi's comments about her sexuality. She may be quirky, and she may be radical, I thought. But she's loyal. And in the end, that's all that really matters.

"Did you find anything?" she asked. "Anything on Bradstreet?"

"No, but he published a paper earlier this year on *The Scarlet Letter*," I said, pointing out the notation on Mark's curriculum vitae. "He probably lifted it from Madeline Kohl. And I also found this." I handed her Mark's unfinished submission for *Psychology Now*. "It's about me. I know it is. He created the document around the time I tried to kill myself."

"A psychology publication? But why would he . . . ?" She trailed off once she started reading. "Oh my," she said. "I don't understand. If this is about you, what does he mean by *fractured mind* and *delusional*?"

I paused. Up to that point, I'd told only two people about my visions, Mark and Gwen. "Before I did it, before I overdosed on sleeping pills, I saw . . . You're going to think I'm crazy."

She shook her head no. "What did you see?"

And so I told her about Virginia Woolf, Charlotte Perkins Gilman, and Sylvia Plath.

"Woolf, Gilman, *and* Plath? Is that why you did it, why you tried to kill yourself?"

"I thought I was going mad," I explained. "I didn't know if I was seeing ghosts or hallucinating. My therapist later said it was *reality manifested into surreality,* something to that effect."

She frowned, and I could tell she questioned my sanity, even though she said she wouldn't.

"Can you believe his audacity?" I went on. "To write about me, like some sort of clinical subject?"

She exhaled, deeply, through her nose. "What are you going to do?"

I finally understood what Professor Barnard meant the day before when she talked about stars. I was never going to move forward, never going to be healed, until I faced my past head on, until I looked it in the eye and said, *You don't own me anymore.*

"I'm going to tell President Monroe everything," I said.

She smiled, her lips closed but her eyes wide and beaming, the way my mother had smiled when I made my First Communion, when I got my driver's license, when I graduated from high school. And though she didn't say it, I knew the professor was proud of me for making the right decision, a decision only I could make.

"Can you prep me?" I asked. "Help me organize what to say and how to say it?"

"I'd be honored," she said. "Monroe is tough. I suppose that's how she got where she is today. Sweet and nice doesn't exactly move you up the administrative ladder. But she's also a facts-and-figures person. She likes data. So you'll need to go to her with as much concrete proof as you can. Keep trying to contact Tina Beyers. Secure a copy of Madeline's essay if you can, and a copy of Suter's paper."

I nodded earnestly, as if taking notes during a lecture.

"With the coeducation vote only days away, it's going to be hard to get an appointment with her on such short notice," she added. "So you'll either have to go first thing tomorrow morning or better yet, tonight."

"Tonight? But it's Sunday. Her office is closed."

"I meant go to her house," the professor explained. "She lives on campus for a reason. She's supposed to be accessible to students at all times."

I recalled the president's home at the south end of campus. It was not a mansion but close to it. Orange brick with wide, white columns and a manicured landscape, it had always reminded me of the Louisiana plantations I'd toured as a child.

Just then, my cell phone rang. The *Chronicle* number appeared on the screen, and I answered, thinking it was exceptional timing for Craig to call. To buy time, I would have to tell him I was still working on the article about Beth, only now with a different slant. I would need to stay at Tarble another night to complete it.

"Did you hear what happened?" Craig asked after I answered. "About that girl, your friend?"

"The serial killer? Yeah, I saw it on the news this morning."

"I'm not talking about this morning." He paused. "The Pittsburgh PD just released a new statement. Sounds like that Grenshaw guy lied. They haven't found Beth's body in the river yet, even though they've had divers in there all day."

"But why would he lie?"

"I'm guessing to finagle a sentencing plea for the girls he *did* kill. Or maybe he was just dicking the police around for spite. Doesn't matter why, really. They're on major image protection mode now. They're scrambling to find another suspect. And you know how these things usually go. It's usually the boyfriend or husband. But she wasn't married, was she?"

Mark.

"Beth was seeing someone," I blurted. "They broke up before she went missing."

"What?" Craig's voice was loud, as if he was trying to communicate to me over a bad connection. I didn't hear any interference on my end.

"I said, Beth was—"

"No, wait, Ruby. Not you. Georgene is waving her arms at me. Something else just came in. Can you hold on?"

While I waited I listened to murmurs and phones ringing in the background. I could almost see the gray peacoat wool partitions of my cubicle, and I realized I hadn't missed work in the least.

"What's going on?" the professor asked, a wrinkle of concern separating her eyebrows.

I was about to answer but Craig came back on the line. I held up a finger to say I would explain it all in a minute.

"You're not going to believe this." He panted, as if he'd just run up a flight of stairs. "But a woman has come forward. The woman who sat next to Beth on the plane to Pittsburgh." He caught his breath. "She's saying that after seeing all the photos of Beth on the news this morning, she's certain the woman who sat next to her was *not* Beth Richards."

"But didn't the flight attendant verify Beth was on the plane?"

"I suppose the person sitting next to Beth would remember her better than the flight attendant." He paused. "Do you know what this means, Ruby? I mean, if this woman is right, if she's telling the truth? Think about it. They've been looking for Beth in Pittsburgh."

I realized where he was going. "You mean, Beth could be anywhere?"

"Maybe she never left Wisconsin. Maybe someone just posed as Beth on the plane, someone who looked enough like Beth to pass through security. It's ingenious, don't you think? It certainly set the police on the wrong track."

Someone who looked enough like Beth, I thought. *Thin and tall. Blond hair. Light skin.*

"Craig, I have to go," I said. "I have to call the detective right away."

His tone turned serious. "What's wrong?"

"I think I know who was on that plane," I said.

I didn't have to explain much of the conversation to Professor Barnard. She got the gist of it from hearing only my end and reading my body language. But I relayed the most relevant information Craig told me.

"So who was it?" she asked. "Who was on the plane?"

"Julie Farris. She's the spitting image of Beth Richards," I said, looking in my purse for the detective's business card. "I've got to tell the police about this. Mark's a suspect too. Maybe he put Julie up to it."

"You mean he found out what Beth was up to and tried to silence her? And used Julie to cover his tracks?"

"Maybe that's why she tried to kill herself. She felt guilty. Unless she was the one who did it." A shiver shimmied up and down my arm, remembering how calm and confident Julie had been when I visited her in the psych ward. "Either way, I have to call the detective and tell him what I know."

"What should we do about all of this?" she asked, gesturing to the mess on her desk, the paper trail we'd collected on Mark. "What about talking to President Monroe?"

I shrugged. "I guess it'll have to wait."

My call to Detective Pickens went to voice mail after three rings, but I left a message, saying it was urgent, that I had crucial information about Beth Richards's case.

Once I hung up, Professor Barnard grabbed her messenger bag. "Would you mind if we stepped out for some fresh air?" she asked. "I've been cooped up in this office all day."

"Of course," I said, standing too. "I get better reception outside anyway."

"I should probably run home too," she added. "I just got a puppy a few weeks ago, and if I don't let her out soon, it's borderline mistreatment." She placed a hand on my shoulder. "Will you be okay? By yourself?"

I nodded. "Why wouldn't I be?"

She gave me a perplexed look, then lowered her voice. "What if Mark Suter really did do something to Beth? To keep her from exposing him? He might know you're on to him too. He might try to . . . I'm just worried," she said. "For your safety."

I remembered what Meryl had insinuated about Mark the night before. I too had no idea what he was really capable of. "I'll be okay," I said, checking my watch. "And Heidi will be back soon."

The professor nodded her approval. "It should take me twenty minutes. Tops," she said. "Where should we meet up again?"

"You don't have to come back, if you don't want to."

"I have to," she said. "It's too late. I'm way too invested now."

We decided to meet behind Langley Hall, on the boulders lining the beach. It was not only the best-known spot for cell reception—I didn't want to miss the detective's call—but also the best hiding place on campus. Tucked between the water and the academic buildings, it was where Tarble girls often took boys to do more than make out. If Mark was on campus, if he was looking for me, he wouldn't see me there.

Sitting on the second set of boulders, my cell phone in my hand ready to answer, I looked out onto the vast blue lake and marveled at the range of emotions I'd experienced over the weekend. The apprehension of being back on campus again, the anger toward Beth for stealing Mark's affections, the guilt of meeting Meryl face-to-face, the sadness at the news of Beth's murder, the rage toward Mark for plagiarizing my work, and the gut-wrenching dread that he—a man I'd truly loved—was responsible for Beth's disappearance. My watch's second hand moved slowly, and I stared at my silent cell phone, willing it to ring. I couldn't stand waiting, so I called the detective again, this time dialing the station number. I left a message with the cop on desk duty, who said she'd get the information to him ASAP. Doubt laced the woman's voice, though, as if she'd fielded many calls over the years from crackpots with *important information.*

I called Heidi too but got no answer, so I just sat there, gazing at the water, waiting.

I was in such a deep trance that I startled when my phone finally rang; the cell slipped in my moist hand like a wet bar of soap. I answered it without even glancing at the caller ID.

"Ms. Rousseau?" a man said.

"Detective Pickens." I recognized his voice. "Thanks for calling me back. I need to—"

"Actually, I was about to call you," he interrupted. "I need you to answer a few more questions about Beth Richards."

The change in subject stunned me. I had planned to tell him about Julie Farris and Mark.

"Did Ms. Richards ever seem depressed during the time you knew her?" he asked. "Withdrawn?"

"No."

"Did she ever mention hurting herself? Or reach out to you for help in any way?"

Hurting herself? "No. Why?"

He ignored my question. "Mrs. Richards said Beth had a roommate at Tarble," he went on. "A girl by the name of Sarah Iverson. Do you know how I might reach her?"

"Yes, I saw her this weekend but . . . Detective, I called to tell you something. Something I think is really important to Beth's case."

He paused. "Okay," he finally said. "But make it brief."

I told the detective everything I knew then, about Julie Farris's resemblance to Beth, her connection to Mark Suter, how Beth had tried to contact Julie before she died. He was silent on his end while I spoke, and I assumed he was taking notes.

"All right," he said when I finished.

"All right?" I repeated. "Does that mean you believe me? You're going to question Mark Suter and Julie Farris? Because Julie's in the psych ward at the hospital here in Kenosha," I added. "But I don't know for how long. She may have already been released."

He cleared his throat. "Psych ward?"

"She tried to kill herself a few days ago."

A long pause. "I see."

I heard nothing on the other end and wondered if he hung up. "Hello? Detective Pickens?"

"Yes?"

"Why did you ask me if Beth was depressed? Or tried to hurt herself?"

He let out a cross between a sigh and a groan. "Look, I didn't want to get into this with you right now. Not yet. But . . . there's a possibility Beth Richards killed herself."

Saliva stuck to the back of my throat. I pushed it down with a painful swallow.

"I just talked with Janice Richards," he explained. "Apparently, Beth e-mailed her the day she left for Pittsburgh. A suicide note. For some reason, she just got the e-mail today. We're not sure why there was a delay, but we're looking into possible scenarios. Our tech experts are looking over the e-mail, verifying its origin."

"But . . ." I was at a loss for words. Something Janice said came back to me then. Beth hadn't been feeling well before she went to Pittsburgh, she'd said. She'd been fatigued and lethargic. She'd also withdrawn from her friends, like Sarah Iverson. The symptoms of depression were there all along.

After the detective and I hung up, I couldn't help but wonder: Was Mark attracted to emotionally unstable girls? Or did he make us that way?

I was considering the answer to that question when a pair of hands flashed in front of my eyes before I was blinded by a white rag. I suffocated in its thick terry cloth texture.

I squirmed and kicked and thrashed until I grew dizzy.

Then everything faded to black.

December

    I can't stop thinking about the baby. Our baby. My baby. I wonder if he—or maybe it was she, I'll never know—has forgiven me.

    Then again, I haven't forgiven myself.

    When my stomach rumbles from hunger or gas shoots inside me like a pinball machine, I imagine it is him, or her. Kicking me. Flipping over. Doing somersaults. Waving its tiny fingers through amniotic fluid. When this happens, I rub my belly and say, in a singsong voice, "I love you, baby." And every time, my voice echoes off the hollow chamber, and the emptiness consumes me. There is no baby, I realize for the hundredth time.

    There is no baby.

    There is no baby.

    There is no baby.

Chapter 16

Her voice—high-pitched and sweet—woke me like a robin chirping outside your bedroom window on an early spring day.

"Ruby," she whispered. "Ruby, wake up."

I couldn't lift my eyelids; they were swollen with lethargy. Obviously, I was still under the effects of whatever chemical had saturated that white rag. It all seemed so distant: the boulders, the lake, the hands, the struggle. Had that been a few hours ago? A day? A week? In the wake of temporary blindness, my other senses heightened, and I took in the damp, almost sweet smell of mildew, of water aging in floorboards like cabernet in oak barrels. I lay on a soft surface, what seemed to be a bed, and I felt a hand on my shoulder, shaking it to dislodge me from sleep.

"Ruby," she whispered again. "Please. You need to wake up."

Wherever I'd been taken, I was not alone. And this girl with the soft, syrupy voice was not my captor. Trying to open my eyes once more, I saw her like a silhouette, hazy and dim.

"Who are you?" I whispered back.

"It's me." She paused. "Beth."

A spark of mental clarity zipped through me then. My eyes shot open and I blinked repeatedly to keep them that way. I saw her then, slightly gaunt, her lily white skin a shade lighter, her blond hair darker and oily. It was tucked behind her ears on each side.

"You're alive," I said.

"I'm alive," she repeated.

"Where are we?" I asked as she pulled me to a seated position.

But I knew the answer to my question as soon as my eyes adjusted to our surroundings. The room was dark—the boarded windows let in only a stream of light through the slats—but I saw white paint chipping off the floorboards, a stone fireplace, wall-to-wall wood.

We were inside Mark's cabin.

He had changed a few things since I'd been there last, though. The twin bed with a frilly comforter on which I sat, set flush against the wall like a daybed, was new. So was the rustic table and three chairs in the corner. There were valances above the windows; a shag carpet to warm the floor; pictures on the wall.

"Beth . . ." I started, my voice gaining strength in tone and volume.

But she placed a finger to her lips and shook her head as she eyed the door to the front of the cabin, where the kitchen was.

"We need to be quiet," she whispered. "She'll hear us."

"S*he?*"

Beth paused before whispering the name. "Meryl."

As Beth and I whispered back and forth, I sensed night falling outside the cabin. The beams of daylight peeking through the slats of the boarded windows diminished. Beth sat mere inches away, but the details of her face grew fuzzy.

"Can we escape?" I asked, maintaining a whisper.

She shook her head. "Don't think I haven't tried. She dead bolts the door."

I eyed the windows. "Can't we kick those boards through?"

"I've tried that too. I think she double boarded them, thick wood and fat nails. They don't budge. When she's not here, I scream and scream, hoping someone, someday will hear me. I screamed so hard my throat was sore for days. We're in the middle of nowhere, Ruby."

We'll call for help on my cell phone, I thought. But where is it? And where's my purse? I had both with me on the boulders. I patted my pants pocket and the bedspread beside me in vain. Meryl must have taken them.

"Can't we wait for her by the door," I suggested instead. "And attack her when she comes in? Is there anything we can use to hit her with? One of these floorboards?"

"She has a gun, Ruby." Beth hugged her stomach protectively. "I can't risk it."

I recognized her gesture. "You're not . . . Beth, are you pregnant?"

She nodded.

"Is it Mark's?"

She nodded again. "And I think Meryl wants it." Her voice cracked then. She was on the brink of sobbing. "I think she's keeping me alive until I give birth. And then . . ."

"We'll escape by then," I whispered. "Or someone will find us."

I thought back to reading the words *Like Cassie's Cabin* in the margin of *A Room of One's Own.* A sudden chill quivered my body at the thought: Beth had left a clue to her whereabouts without even knowing it. I wondered who else knew about the cabin. Heidi came first to mind. Had I told her about it? I couldn't remember. Were Heidi and Professor Barnard looking for me? Would they have called the police?

"The police are probably looking for me right now," I assured her.

"And what about me? Are they still looking for me?"

"There was this serial killer," I tried to explain. "And you fit the description of his other victims, and at first, they thought you were . . ."

"Dead?"

I nodded. "But your mom—"

"My mom?"

"Your mom swore you were alive, Beth."

I told Beth about the suitcase then. "You probably didn't think I put my name on the tag, since I never went on my trip."

She gasped. "I left your tag on my bag?"

"You didn't know?"

"I packed quickly. Wait. My bag was on the plane?"

"Of course it was. Didn't you check it?"

She shook her head. "Meryl took me from the airport. She

must have . . . Oh my God, she checked my bag to make it look like I was on the plane."

"I think she did more than that," I said. "She pretended to *be you*, Beth. The police thought you were on that plane, that you went missing in Pittsburgh. Well, until today."

I told Beth then about the woman who'd sat next to her, or rather, next to Meryl on the plane. The woman had been keen enough to realize the Beth Richards she'd sat beside was not the same girl she'd seen on the news.

"So it's only a matter of time before they figure out what happened," I reassured her. I was trying to convince even myself of that fact. I retraced everything I had said and done over the weekend, every clue I might have left for the police to find me. Find us. And that's when I remembered my phone conversation with Detective Pickens and realized Meryl must have faked the suicide note to Beth's mom. I didn't want to mention the note to Beth, though. It would only upset her. She could find out later, after we escaped.

"You knew about me," I said instead. "And the other girls? You wrote our names down."

"Meryl told me about you. All of you."

"Did you know Mark stole my work and passed it off as his own?"

She nodded, then placed her hand on top of mine. "But, Ruby, for the record, I didn't know Mark was seeing you when we got involved. I never meant to hurt you."

"I know." I thought of Madeline Kohl. "You fell in love with the wrong guy. We all did."

"But I didn't. I never loved Mark."

"You didn't?"

She scrunched up her nose, her lips turned downward. "I was just trying to pass English."

"You used him?"

"I'm a biology major. I should have known better than to take English Lit to fill my stupid humanities prerequisite. Shakespeare and Wordsworth?" She rolled her eyes. "I was close to flunking. And I couldn't have that on my transcript. So when I caught Mark looking down my shirt one day, I thought, hey, maybe it would work. It wasn't hard. A few giggles and winks, and he took me out to dinner."

"And you passed his class."

"I got an A."

I couldn't help but feel slightly resentful, since Mark had given me a D on my thesis. "But you still dated him, even after the semester was over," I noted, remembering Beth's many trips to Tarble over the summer. "Why didn't you break up with him?"

"The sex was good," she said frankly. "And he was so over the moon for me, he did anything I wanted. I'm not gonna lie, I took advantage of that. Plus, I was afraid he'd just end up hounding me if I broke up with him during the school year. He seemed so obsessed with me, I wasn't sure how he would react if I called it quits. So I decided to wait until summer to do it. And then the summer came, and, I don't know, I guess I was a little bored, so I kept it up."

"You told your mom you were staying with Heidi Callahan," I added.

"Yeah, Heidi was my cover, because she worked at the college.

But once school started up, I knew it was time to end the whole charade. So the last time I went to Tarble, I broke up with him."

I couldn't imagine anyone cutting Mark loose; he seemed to be the one who broke hearts.

"He didn't take it well," she went on. "Crying. Pleading. On his knees, even. Begging me to give him another chance. He said he'd just asked Meryl for a divorce. He was leaving her for me. He even rented a house in town, thinking I was going to move in with him. He was delusional." She made that disgusted look again. "It was pretty pathetic. At one point, he wouldn't let me out of his office, said he wouldn't let me go until I agreed to stay with him. I got so pissed off, I threatened that if he didn't let me go, I would tell President Monroe about our affair. I'd get him fired."

"Did it work?"

She nodded. "But on my way home, I stopped for gas, and that's when Meryl confronted me. I left one psycho only to deal with the other one."

"She followed you?"

"She was on campus. Apparently she heard everything that went down between us in his office."

"What did she want?"

"That's the weird thing. I assumed she was going to tell me off or slap me or call me a whore, but she didn't. She was actually really pleasant and understanding. That's when she told me Mark had slept with a lot of his students. And she asked if I was serious about reporting him to the Tarble administration."

"Were you?"

"Not then. I just said that so she'd let me go. But the following week, Mark starting stalking me. Waiting for me outside my anatomy class, sitting out in front of my house at night, calling me and e-mailing me nonstop. It was so bad, I had to change my number and my e-mail address."

"You should have gotten a restraining order."

"But how embarrassing is that? Going to the police? Having to tell them about me and Mark? And I didn't want my mom to find out. It was hard enough to hide the fact he was stalking me. So I tried to take things into my own hands. I figured the only way to get him to leave me alone was to threaten him. So when Meryl called to see if I'd reconsidered, I agreed to meet up with her to discuss how to get him fired. She gave me the list of names. You. Tina. Madeline. Some girl named Julie Farris. She said if we all came forward, we could ruin him and his career. She showed me the paper he'd written for that journal and swore it wasn't his writing. She was sure he'd stolen it from one of you."

"It was me."

She nodded. "You know, I really didn't want to get him fired. I didn't want anyone at Tarble to know about our relationship. I just wanted him to leave me alone. But I figured the more information I had, the more ammunition, the better chance of him backing down."

I remembered what Julie had said at the hospital: she'd never spoken to Beth. "Did you ever talk to any of the girls on the list?"

"I went looking for that Julie girl but couldn't find her, and then shortly after that, I found out I was pregnant. I couldn't believe I had been so careless. I didn't even love Mark, would never, ever have considered having his baby in a million years. So I stopped my pseudo investigation, because I had bigger things to worry about. I wanted him out of my life." She paused. "Out of my body."

"You wanted to have an abortion?"

She paused again, and I heard in her delay the weighty sigh of remorse.

"It's not that I didn't want *a* child; I just didn't want *his* child," she finally said. "I tried doing it at a clinic in Milwaukee, but I chickened out when I saw this girl I knew from Sunday school working in the building next store. I couldn't do it, not so close to home. I didn't want a physical memory—a place I'd have to drive by all the time and remember what I did. So I picked Pittsburgh. How random is that? I'd never been there before, didn't know anybody from there. I never planned to go there in the future. It just sounded like a dreary, horrible place where you could go to have an abortion."

"Your mom said you were going to take a photography workshop," I noted.

"It was my alibi."

I formulated a timeline in my mind. "So Meryl kidnapped you *before* you could do it? How did she know you were pregnant?"

"I told her. That was my stupid mistake. She kept hounding me, asking how things were progressing and when I planned to present my case to the bigwigs at Tarble. When I told her I had changed my mind, she flat out asked if I was pregnant. It's like she knew. And I don't know why—maybe I felt guilty for having the affair with her husband—but I told her the truth. How could I have known she'd want to take my baby?"

"Did she take you from the airport?" I asked.

Beth didn't hesitate to reveal the details of her disappearance. She said Meryl had approached her in the e-ticket line, saying she needed to talk to her, even offered to buy her a cup of coffee. Beth agreed because she had gotten to the airport early and didn't consider Meryl a threat. They did go for coffee, during which Meryl pleaded with Beth not to have the abortion, not to let Mark dictate her future. But Beth would not change her mind.

"I can only guess she slipped something into my cup at some point," Beth explained. "Because I started to feel really lightheaded. She offered to let me sleep in her car for a while, and I did, because I was too dizzy to think clearly. I remember lying on my side in the passenger seat. 'I'll take care of you,' Meryl said. 'I'll take it from here.' And that's all I remember. Until I woke up in this cabin."

"How scary," I said, imagining her distress the past nine days.

"You know, it's not all bad here," Beth said. "I've slept most of the time because I'm so exhausted. I guess that's normal at this point of pregnancy. I wake up mostly to eat. And she feeds me. Wonderfully delicious things. Omelets and fresh fruit and orange juice. Spinach salad. Chicken breast, even."

"You eat the food she prepares you? Aren't you afraid she's poisoning you?"

"No. When I figured out she wanted my baby, I realized she

wouldn't give me anything harmful. This baby is my lifeline, Ruby. It's saved my life."

"When did you figure out she wanted the baby?"

"It came to me in bits and pieces. She talked a lot about the baby, whether it was a girl or a boy, and how she hoped it didn't look like Mark. How I was so lucky to have conceived, to have this special gift growing inside me." Beth paused, as if Meryl's words had convinced her of that fact. "She takes good care of me. She gives me prenatal vitamins. And in the morning, for my nausea, she serves me this wonderful tea. It's herbal. It has chamomile and rosehips and yam, all sorts of wonderful things."

My entire body froze, every limb, every finger and toe, every organ. I didn't breathe or blink or quiver. Everything ceased moving, except my brain, which exploded with the horrific discovery.

"Tea?" I managed to say.

"It's a recipe passed down from her grandmother."

I didn't respond. And Beth sensed I was quiet for too long.

"Ruby?" she said, reaching for my hand.

"It's not Meryl," I got out.

"*Who's* not Meryl?"

But just then, I heard the unlatching of a dead bolt and saw the door open, a beam of light from the cabin's front room shot across the floor and forged an arrow at us.

Watching the dark figure in the doorway, I prepared to see a very familiar face.

Chapter 17

She flipped the light switch, and once our eyes met, a wave of anger coursed through me. If it had been someone like John C. Grenshaw keeping me captive, I would have been scared. But anger won out against Virginia Barnard. Frankly, I was pissed.

"What are you doing?" I blurted.

Professor Barnard held up a hand, as if I might charge her any minute. "Ruby, please. I'm not the enemy here. Just let me explain."

"Explain why you pretended to be Meryl?" I shot back.

"You're not Meryl?" Beth cried, as if lying about her identity was the worst of our captor's actions, not the actual abduction. "Then who are you?"

"A pathological liar," I said. "Her name is Virginia Barnard. She's a professor at Tarble."

Beth blinked several times and shook her head, her eyes fixed on nothing as her mind processed the information. "I don't understand," she said. "If you're not Meryl, why did you take me? Why did you keep me here?"

"To protect you," she said. "*Both* of you."

Earlier that day, I had marveled at the closeness Professor Barnard and I shared, but now it made me wiggle with repulsion. It was flat out creepy. "Protect us? From what?"

"From Mark."

It was the first time Professor Barnard had ever referred to him as Mark, not Suter or Professor Suter. And the way she said his name—the breath in her voice, the high pitch of the vowel sound—revealed she was not as impartial to him as I'd once believed.

"I never wanted to lie to you." She came toward us then, cocking her head in surrender, like a dog showing its tummy. "But it was for your own good. And I know you'll understand my actions once you let me explain. Trust me, the end really does justify the means."

Beth and I exchanged glances, but neither of us protested an explanation.

The professor, now standing a few feet before us, paused to inhale and exhale several times. I saw her eyes turn glossy and reflective as she fought back tears.

"You have to understand how much I loved my sister," she finally said. "And how much she loved me. We were soul mates. We should have been twins. But Jenny was six years old when I was born, and because of that, her feelings for me bordered on the maternal. She used to say I was better than any baby doll she'd ever had. Because I was real. And because I loved her back. She called me *butterfly sister* because I was born on the same spring day the monarch butterflies hatched from their cocoons in her first grade classroom. And she never ceased looking at me with curiosity and wonder, never stopped reminding me of my beauty and goodness and grace. And I, in turn, adored her. Everything she did, the way she walked and talked, the way she braided her hair, the way she danced and roller-skated and sang without effort, was pure magic to me. Watching her was like watching my favorite television show. My eyes never wavered. I was fascinated by her. I'm telling you this, because you need to understand what we meant to each other, how we needed each other to brave this world. We slept in the same room because we wanted to, not because we had to. And on the nights my father came home drunk, we lay beside each other in my twin bed, our fingers laced in the ravine of space between us, fearing he'd grow tired of beating on our mother and drag us out of bed. He never did. But I knew if he had, Jenny would go. Jenny would always go before me."

Beth and I made eye contact again, and on her face, I read the same confusion I felt. But neither of us interrupted, and the professor continued her story.

"We were inseparable, even when our age difference started to matter, even when Jenny became a woman, and I was still a girl. If she could, she always took me with her when she left the house, without thinking, like grabbing your purse on the way out the door. And when it came time for her to go to college, she didn't want to leave me behind. But she was very talented, a gifted actress, and she got a theater scholarship—an offer she couldn't refuse from a school out of her reach—and she took the opportunity. It was three hours away, and she promised to come home whenever she could, and in the meantime, she would write to me. And she kept her word. I received a letter from her every two to three days. I relished every detail she shared, about her roommate and dorm life, about her classes and auditions. I lived through her, vicariously, and at twelve years old, without my own set of life experiences, I had the capacity to feel whatever she felt, just by reading her letters. When she got the lead in the play, I felt like I did too. And when she fell in love, I fell also.

"He was a senior. Three years older. And oh, was he handsome. That smile, those eyes. She sent me his picture, and I tacked it above my bed and stared at it, even at night in the split second when a car passed our house and headlights lit the room. I fell asleep thinking about him, dreaming about him. She said he could have had any girl on campus, but he chose *her*. And in my mind, he chose me. Maybe if our father had been more attentive, if he hadn't been a drunk, if he hadn't cheated time and time again on our mother, we wouldn't have fallen so hard. But we did. And I cherished the story of how they met. That he'd seen her from afar, fallen in love at first sight, and I imagined him sitting on that bench outside her class, waiting for her to walk by so he could ask her out, ask me out. She fell in love with him the way you do the first time, when youth is still on your side, in a very physical way, with her whole heart and mind and soul. He became part of her identity. My identity. Like life support, we could not breathe without him."

A warmth filled my chest then and bubbled up into my

throat, before falling over my shoulders and down my arms like a sprinkling of rain. I'd heard this story before. From Mark.

Jenny, that was the name of the emotionally unstable girl Mark dated at Tulane, the girl who'd gotten the lead in *The Mikado.*

"And he gave her a most precious gift." The professor's voice cracked on the word *gift,* but she recovered by clearing her throat. "She became pregnant with his child. To many girls, this would have been a horrific discovery, but not to Jenny. Sure, it would compromise her education and her career, but she didn't care. She had *his* baby growing inside of her, and in this way, they could never be separated. He would have to love her forever. But he pleaded with her not to keep the baby." She lowered her voice an octave. "'What kind of future will we have together if we don't finish school?' he said. 'I want to marry you, Jenny, but I want to do it the *right* way. If you love me, a baby can wait.'"

The professor bowed her head. "Jenny believed him," she said, her eyes still on the cabin floor. "She took to heart his promise of their future together. And she ended the life of the child."

I looked to Beth. Her hand immediately went to her stomach and stayed there like a barrier, a road block.

"I'm not going to let you take my baby," she cried.

Professor Barnard smiled. "I'm so happy to hear you say that. Because I don't want your baby, Beth. I just want you to want it."

Beth narrowed her eyes; she looked hurt, bewildered, frightened.

"Why did you take her then?" I interjected.

"May I finish the story?" she asked.

We nodded, and she went on.

"A few weeks after the abortion, he stopped returning Jenny's calls. Just like that. He'd made love to her one day and the next, forgotten her very existence. He avoided her. She'd come by his apartment, but his roommate would say he was out. She'd look for him in all their usual meeting places, but never found him. It was pure torture, and one day, she decided enough was enough. She had given up *a child* for him, ripped a life out from inside of her. She would *make him* talk to her." On each syllable, she pounded her fist on the palm of the other hand, violently, as if pretending it was his skull. "So she waited for him outside one of his classes, just as he had for her in the beginning.

"But when she finally confronted him, he made a fool of her, in front of everyone," she cried. "He called her a freak. He said he didn't love her. He had never loved her."

I imagined it all vividly. The girl crying, tears streaking her face, a crowd of students gawking at the scene.

"It was the same day *The Mikado* was set to open. She was so distraught, she couldn't perform," the professor went on. "The understudy had to do it. She couldn't eat, couldn't sleep. She was comatose. It was the guilt. She had *murdered* her child, her own flesh and blood for a man who did not love her. And the guilt ate away at her heart, gnawed it until one day, in a moment of deep despair, she swallowed all of her roommate's painkillers. They didn't find her until it was too late. They couldn't revive her. She was gone, and I lost the only person in this world who loved me, the only person I had ever felt close to. I know in my heart, my sister didn't want to die. Like most young girls who overdose on pills, it was a cry for help. She never would have left me alone in this world, not on purpose. She thought someone would find her. Or maybe she didn't think. She was acting on feelings, not thoughts."

Professor Barnard dropped to her knees before Beth. The sudden movement caused her hair to fall from its knot at the nape of her neck. "Don't you see why I *had* to take you, Beth?" she pleaded. "I was protecting you from the pain of the decision you were about to make. A decision that could have destroyed the rest of your life. You didn't understand the gift you had growing inside you. You didn't know the pain and guilt ahead of you. I had to stop you. I had no choice."

I stared at the professor then, at her wild wisps of hair and agonized expression, and I understood her pain. She'd lost her sister; I'd lost my father. But I also saw the worst-case scenario of my future. That twenty years from now, I'd still be telling stories about how Mark hurt me. I'd still use him as an excuse for not dating, for not writing, for not living. I'd be forever crippled by my past.

"I'm truly sorry for your loss," I said. "But I don't think this is about Beth. It's about you and your sister. You want revenge. You want to punish Mark for something that happened decades ago."

Beth's eyes grew wide. "Mark?" she repeated. "You mean, *he's* the guy?"

"She tracked him down," I said. "All these years later, she went looking for him."

"But I didn't. He came to me," the professor said. "You did too."

"Me?"

"It was destiny, I think. After my sister died, I inherited all of her belongings—her books, her diary, her pictures, letters she never sent, and I pieced together what had happened. I blamed Mark for her death. And as easily as I fell in love with him, I began hating him. Loathing him. The anger I harbored for him suppressed my sadness about my sister. Years later, when I was old enough to leave home, I moved to New Orleans because that is where Jenny died, where I felt her spirit, her soul. I went to school there too, majored in theater just like her, and English. And I lived there many years, never thinking of Mark Suter. But then one night, I couldn't sleep, and something prompted me to go out for a coffee, and not ten minutes later, there he was. I recognized him immediately, the moment the two of you walked into the café. That arrogant saunter and condescending smirk. And you, another victim of his good looks and lies."

A memory flickered inside me then, but before my mind could even conjure it, my body sensed it. Every hair lifted off my skin, every pore opened and gasped for air.

"You," was all I got out.

"Yes, Ruby. It was me," she said. "Do you know it was a year ago? Almost to the day?"

My mind fumbled through the memory of my first night in New Orleans with Mark. The woman at Café Du Monde writing in her notebook had hardly looked like Virginia Barnard. That woman's hair had been brown and wiry. She'd worn glasses.

"You said mistress," I said, recalling her disapproving look. "You called me his mistress."

"Oh, honey, did you think that?" She reached for my arm, but I pulled away. "I said, 'Don't trust him.' I was trying to warn you. The very sight of him sickened me. Because I saw he'd gotten older, but he hadn't changed. He was still preying on young girls with fresh, vulnerable hearts. And I knew one day he would cast you aside like a bone stripped of its meat, just like he did Jenny. He would ruin you, suck the future right out of you. And that's when everything clicked, that's when I vowed to keep him from doing this to another girl."

"So that's why you got the job at Tarble?" I asked. "To stalk him?"

"To *watch* him," she corrected. "I knew you couldn't be the first student to swoon at his charm, nor the last. And he had to be stopped. He had to be punished. I wanted to bury Mark in his own lies. He had to be publicly humiliated, his moral indecency splattered in the news. He had to be ruined. But even more than that, I wanted to liberate you. All of you. He had to pay for what he did, and you had to be the ones to deliver that punishment. I could guide you, assist you, nudge you, but ultimately, I wanted you to do it. I knew you had to, if you ever wanted to move forward with your life."

"So that's why you pretended to be Meryl?" Beth clarified. "To persuade me to come forward?"

"I couldn't tell you who I really was, could I? You wouldn't have believed me. I had to be Meryl. She had an obvious incentive and unquestionable knowledge. And I knew you were the one who could rally the others. Because you had a power they didn't. You didn't love him, Beth. You never loved him. I knew that the day you broke it off. I heard it in the distant, steady tone of your voice. He had no hold on you, and that's why you were the one, the one who could bring him down, the one to lead the others. But then you found out you were pregnant. And you not only wanted to quit the fight, but you also wanted to do something I knew would hurt you more than Mark ever could."

Beth stared at her. "Did you know I was pregnant, even before I told you?"

The professor nodded. "I followed you that day to the clinic. And I was hopeful when you didn't go through with it, thinking you'd changed your mind. But you hadn't, and I took you, thinking if I couldn't change your mind, I would keep you until it was too late, past the point of no return. And I decided to get the rest of you to come forward, one at a time if I had to. I started with Julie Farris. It was pathetic, how Mark tried to replace Beth with a look-alike. As if she were a *dog* and he could just go to a pound and pick out another one just like her. When he dumped her too, I called Julie, pretending to be Meryl, and she agreed to file charges. But her conversation with President Monroe didn't go as expected. Monroe wanted to sweep it under the carpet. She was too worried about disgrace and losing financial support for the school's coeducation plans. So we decided Julie should fake her suicide on the eve of Reunion weekend. Talk about disgrace. It not only put Monroe in her place, but also added to the mounting evidence against Mark. Because now two girls had tried to take their life over him."

It made sense then, I thought, why Julie was so put together during my visit to the psych ward. Because she hadn't tried to kill herself over Mark. She wasn't depressed. She was vengeful.

"What about Tina and Madeline? Did you approach them too?" I asked.

"I wanted you to do that."

"But you gave me a list with their names on it," Beth argued. "How did you know they'd had relationships with Mark?"

"I didn't, not for certain. I only knew Ruby dropped out of school because of Mark. But I cross-referenced the list of students who had dropped out of Tarble with his class rosters, looking for overlap. Tina and Madeline fit the bill, and I figured there was a good chance one of them had been involved with him."

"What about those sexual misconduct charges Heidi found in his HR file?" I asked.

"They were fake. I put them there."

"You thought they would convince me to come forward?"

Her eyes shot to mine. "Didn't they? We were so close, Ruby. We had him right where we wanted him. But then that woman on the plane . . . I had to act fast. I couldn't expect another lucky break, not like that whole serial killer thing. So I had to take you too."

"And now, you can let us go," Beth begged. "If what you said is true, that you took me to keep me from having an abortion, you can let me go now. Mission accomplished. Because I love my baby. I'm going to keep it." She looked to me. "And you can let Ruby go too. We won't press charges. We won't tell the police anything. We just want to go home."

Professor Barnard seemed to consider her plea. "I understand you want to go home. And I will let you go. I want nothing more than for you both to live happy, productive lives. But I can't let you leave until I know for certain Mark can never hurt you or anyone else again. And there is only one way we can guarantee that."

I read the gravity of her expression. "Guarantee?"

"Oh my god," Beth cried. "You want to kill him?"

The professor shook her head. "The only way to stop him is to take away the thing that gives him power, the thing that makes him Mark Suter."

Beth and I exchanged glances. We didn't know what she was talking about.

"If he had raped my sister, no one would question his punishment," she went on. "But in a way, he did rape her. Just not physically. He used her and abused her, stole her goodness and love, and in the end, took her life." She smirked. "And you know what the punishment for rape used to be, don't you?"

She didn't have to say it.

Chapter 18

Beth started to dry heave then. Over and over again, her stomach wrenched, as if she had a virus or food poisoning. As she vomited nothing but saliva, I watched her face contort at the sour taste of stomach acid.

"You're upsetting her," I said.

"Her stomach's just empty," the professor countered. "She needs to eat. Beth, dear, you need to eat. You always get nauseated if you go more than two hours without putting something in your stomach."

Professor Barnard guided Beth by the hand to the table then, and Beth, worn out from the ordeal, let her.

"Come on, Ruby. You too." She pulled out a chair. "We can discuss this over dinner."

I crossed my arms and said nothing. I didn't want to partici-
pate in the professor's fantasy, the three of us sharing meals at
the cabin table like the sisters in *Little Women*.

Besides, my curiosity had been sated, now that the professor
had explained who she really was and why she took us. There
was nothing keeping me there, nothing forcing me to listen to
her crazy notions any longer. Earlier, Beth had mentioned Professor Barnard's gun, but I had yet to see one. So when the professor rushed to the kitchen, presumably to get Beth something
to eat, I followed, hoping to take her off guard somehow. But she
was one step ahead of me. Turning the kitchen corner, I walked
right into the end of the revolver she aimed at my chest. Looped
around her other hand was a piece of rope.

"I didn't want to do it this way, Ruby," she said, pushing me
back into the main room. "But now you've given me no choice."

"You wouldn't shoot me," I said, as she lowered me to the
chair across from Beth.

She didn't respond and instead, using the rope, she tied my
left wrist to the base of the wooden dining table, all the while
watching Beth for any sudden movement. I thought about
reaching for the gun, which she'd set down at the far end of the
table so she could tie my hand, but before I could put thought
into action, she was done.

"Do I need to tie you up too?" she asked Beth.

Beth shook her head no.

The professor left the room only briefly—not long enough
for Beth and I to whisper or gesture anything coherent to each
other—and she returned with a steaming platter, what looked

to be a whole roasted chicken, mashed potatoes, and peas, and my stomach ached with hunger. I had eaten nothing but a doughnut hole that morning.

I watched Beth push chunks of chicken and forkfuls of mashed potatoes into her mouth with vigor. I couldn't blame her for indulging. She was, after all, eating for two. The professor also made me a plate, which she set before me. She then sat down and began eating. I eyed the food. The chicken was not the least pink, the peas a vibrant green, the potatoes a creamy white. Could poison look so nutritious?

Professor Barnard seemed to read my mind. "Why would I poison you?"

It was a rhetorical question, and I didn't answer. Instead, I stuffed a tablespoon of peas into my mouth. They were delicious—fresh and definitely not canned.

We ate in silence, less the ting of cutlery and chewing, until I looked around the room and asked, "How did you get access to this cabin?"

"I'm renting it, from the woman Mark sold it to," the professor explained as she started to clear our dishes. "In fact, she's the person I pretended to be when I called. I told Mark I wanted to sell the cabin back to him. And I knew he'd be interested. He only sold it to make himself more alluring to you, Beth, so you would marry him. And now, distraught over losing you, he needs the comfort of something familiar."

"You called Mark?" I asked.

"I had to, if I wanted him to come here."

"He's coming *here*?" Beth said. "When?"

The professor checked her watch, and her eyes widened. "In

less than an hour, so we better discuss the plan." She spoke coolly, as if planning an annual fund-raiser.

"Why do you want to do this?" Beth pleaded. "Why can't we just get him fired, like you wanted to do in the first place?"

"Because I realize now, that's not enough. He'll just keep hurting girls. Over and over and over again."

The professor's voice was tight, stretched like a rubber band ready to break, and her eyes were desperate, dark, and vulnerable. And I knew we'd never leave that cabin, never escape, unless we indulged her. Unless we pretended to go along with her plan.

"If we do this," I said. "If we . . . you know . . . then you'll let us go?"

"You have my word," she said.

Beth and I locked eyes then, and an unspoken understanding passed between us.

"Okay," Beth said. "We'll do it."

The cabin grew chilly once the sun went down, and Professor Barnard started a fire. The flames, primitive and ritualistic, cast an eerie orange glow on everything—the floor, our faces—and set the tone for what Professor Barnard wanted us to do that night. The plan was simple. Get Mark to admit what he'd done and apologize for his cavalier behavior and dishonesty, then punish him in the worst way imaginable to a man.

Beth and I were in position beside the fire when we heard a car on the gravel road. The hum of the engine struck me. There was a whirring, a slight whistle, and I knew it was Mark's Jeep. Beth seemed to know it too. Soon, we heard a knock—one long and two short, like a code—and waited until the professor answered the door before speaking.

"How are we going to do this?" Beth whispered. "Without really doing it? She cares more about hurting him than she does us. I'm afraid she'll shoot us if we diverge from her plan."

I heard the front door squeak open and gulped down the knot forming in my throat. "When we see a chance to disarm her, we'll take it," I said.

We heard Mark's immediate surprise when he saw his colleague, Virginia Barnard, answer the cabin door. "What are you doing here?" he asked.

"I live here," she said.

"Really?" He let out a huff. "Small world."

"Good thing," we heard her say. "Or our paths would not have crossed again."

"I'm afraid you've lost me," he said.

"A long time ago, Mark. But I found you."

"I'm sorry?"

"You will be," she said.

We heard the cock of a gun then. I held my breath, and I heard Beth do the same.

"What the fuck?" Mark blurted.

Professor Barnard pushed him through the doorway then, digging the gun into his back. "Didn't your mother ever tell you?" she said. "Not to use that kind of language in front of a lady?"

Mark's face seemed to crumble at the sight of us. It lost all structure of cheekbone and turned to a wobble of surprise.

"Beth!" he called before darting for her. But Professor Barnard held him back by the arm and dug the gun farther into his back. His body was contained, but his voice carried the distance. "Beth, you're alive!"

Mark's eyes watered. I could see the dampness shimmer in the firelight.

"I'll kill you," he spat at Professor Barnard's face. She kicked him in the leg then, hard enough to make him wince, and pushed him into the chair we'd set up for him. And that's when he finally noticed me.

"Is that Ruby?" He stood from his chair in another wave of anger.

There was no time for truth. It wasn't in the script, and it would have to come out later. Once Professor Barnard held the gun to his temple, we worked quickly, tying his hands behind his back and his feet together, and both to the chair. I tried making the knots loose, but the professor noticed.

"Tighter, ladies," she scolded. "Tighter."

Once Mark was secured to the chair, she let him have it.

"You're a disgusting excuse for a man," she said, before elbowing him in the face.

Despite the force, he took the blow well, as if trying to prove he was a man who could take a hit from a woman. His face contorted as the beginning of a bruise crossed his cheek.

"Apologize to these girls," she said.

"Me? Apologize? You're the crazy bitch who took them."

This outburst earned Mark another elbow to the jaw. When he grunted through the pain, I felt Beth flinch beside me. I watched Professor Barnard for any sign of weakness, but her hold on the gun was still tight. We'd have to forge ahead.

"Then apologize to me," Professor Barnard said.

"You?" He threw her an incredulous look. "What for? I hardly know you."

"You have no idea who I am?"

"A deranged lunatic?"

The professor butted the gun against his cheek like a slap to the face. "Does the name Jenny Barnard ring a bell? Have you forgotten what you did to her? What you did to my sister?"

He stared at her, at first hard and cold and unsympathetically. It had been more than twenty years since Mark had dated that girl at Tulane. But suddenly, his expression turned somber. It was the same sadness I'd seen cross his face on the Tulane campus, before he lied and said Jenny had gone into the Peace Corps.

"She trusted you, Mark," the professor hissed. "With her heart. With her body. And you stole from her, stole her love, stole her virginity, stole her innocence. You threw her away like a piece of trash, like a worthless banana peel."

Mark closed his eyes and shook his head. "I was young," he said. "And stupid. I . . . I never thought she would . . . hurt herself."

"She didn't hurt herself. *You* hurt her. *You* killed her baby. *You* killed her."

"I'm sorry," he said. "I'm so sorry. Just let Beth go. Please, let Beth go."

For a moment, I saw a look of satisfaction cross Professor Barnard's face, but it was soon replaced with malice. "Sorry isn't good enough," she spat.

"Then why the fuck did you make me say it?"

She whipped Mark with the butt of the gun again, causing his nose to spurt blood. It dripped down his chin onto his chest.

"You used my sister, and you used Ruby. And Tina. And Madeline. And Julie."

He whimpered. "Tina? Who's Tina?"

"Say it," she screamed. "Say you used those innocent girls."

"Okay, I used them. There, I said it. You have me. Now let Beth go."

Beth, I thought. It was Beth he saw the moment he came into the cabin, not me. It was Beth's freedom he was willing to trade his life for, not mine. *He never loved me,* I thought. Not like he loved her, not like he still loves her now. And for a moment, I pitied him. Because I knew Beth didn't love him in return, and she never would. She hurt him just like he hurt me. And still he loved her. He'd do anything—even give his life—for her. At that point, my anger toward Mark eclipsed everything else.

"You stole my work," I blurted.

Professor Barnard looked at me then like she had earlier that day, when I decided to come forward about my relationship with Mark. She was surprised I spoke, but proud.

"My thesis," I went on. "You gave me a D, then published it under your name, didn't you?"

He didn't answer at first, and the professor pressed the gun to his temple. "Answer her," she charged.

"Yes," he said.

"You stole Madeline's work too. And Julie's."

"Yes," he repeated.

"And you wrote about me. You used what happened to me as material for publication."

He shook his head. Another drop of blood fell from his chin. "I never wrote about you."

"But I saw it on your computer, Mark," I argued. "What you wrote after I tried to kill myself. *Her fractured mind.* You called me *delusional,* and said I *saw things that weren't there.* You wrote that about me."

He paused. "I wrote that about my mother."

"Your mother?"

"She was . . . schizophrenic."

"You never told me that," Beth said.

"It's not something I wanted to tell. She was everything that word connotes. She heard voices. Saw people lurking in shadows. She was paranoid. And she tried to kill herself a couple of times when I was kid." His eyes circled the room. "In this cabin."

Looking at Mark, with blood staining his face and shirt, I saw him not as a manipulative womanizer but as a young, innocent, and vulnerable boy wrestling with his mother's insanity, struggling for her affection, wondering why he wasn't enough reason for his mother to want to live. Professor Barnard must have sensed my sudden sympathy for Mark, because she pulled a utility knife from her pocket then and handed it to me.

"That's enough talking," she ordered. "Let's get this over with."

I looked down at the knife; its blade gleamed in the flicker of firelight. My heartbeat thumped in my head. "But I thought we were going to tie—"

"That's for his pants," the professor spat. "You'll have to cut them off."

"My pants?" Mark huffed. "Ruby, what is she talking about? Beth? Beth? What is she talking about?"

"He said he was sorry," Beth pleaded.

Professor Barnard tightened her grip on the gun and kept her eyes on me. "Ruby, do it."

I knelt before him, and a loose nail head in the floorboard dug into my kneecap.

"What are you doing?" Mark yelled. "You're not . . . oh, God, you're not going to . . ."

"Don't fight it, Mark. Or it will hurt even more," the professor said.

I looked into Beth's panic-filled eyes and saw she was on the verge of tears. Will she be able to overtake Professor Barnard? I wondered. How far will I have to go? How far will I have to take it?

Though he wriggled in the chair, I held Mark's leg firmly and cut into his khakis, just above the knee. Then I pulled the small tear I created, splitting his pants all the way up until I saw his underwear under the shredded ends of fabric. When the outside air hit the tender skin of his inner thigh, Mark sucked in a breath.

"Ruby," he screamed. "Don't!"

"Keep going," the professor commanded. "Cut his underwear."

Looking at Mark's crotch, at the fine hair lining the inside of his thighs, I felt like I was going to vomit. At one time, the sight of Mark undressed was alluring and intimate. Now, it was repulsive.

"Faster," the professor charged.

Mark flinched when I brought the knife back to his crotch, and he writhed in the chair again, enough to jostle my arm and prick the inside of his thigh with the knife. I held my breath as I pulled the front of his underwear away from him with my thumb and index finger and worked the knife through it enough to make a hole. I ripped the rest like I did his pants. The flap of underwear lay over him like a loincloth. My hands began to sweat.

The professor took the knife from me then and replaced it with a long strand of kitchen twine, the kind I imagined she used to truss the legs of the chicken. My hands felt suddenly empty, and I regretted not acting when I had the knife. It was a weapon, the only weapon she would willingly give me, and I hadn't used it against her. I knew I had to do something before it was too late, but I couldn't seem to cross the line between thought and action. I assumed Beth felt the same.

"Now tie it," the professor said.

My hands shook. "I can't."

She pointed the gun at Beth. "Do it, or I'll shoot her."

"You wouldn't do that."

Professor Barnard fired the gun into the rafters. The sudden bang of the gun jolted me into tears. I covered my head as sawdust sprinkled us like snowfall.

"Tie it," the professor ordered. "And it has to be tight to cut off the blood flow."

"Oh, fuck," Mark cried. "Fuck. Ruby, don't do it."

The professor stuffed a cloth napkin into Mark's mouth to quiet him. "Do it," she said.

I heard Mark's muffled cries as I lifted the twine and dragged it under the flap of underwear, but my hands shook uncontrollably, and I didn't have the dexterity to make a knot. I tried three times before I got the twine looped, but I didn't pull the ends.

"Pull it," the professor ordered. "Tight! Tight!"

"I can't," I cried again.

"Let me do it," she hissed. She shoved me away to take my position, and I slammed into the wood floor, my cheek burned by the jagged wood. I heard Mark's stifled wail as the professor pulled the knot tight. But a second later, I heard a body thump to the floor, and the gun skid across the cabin. I turned to see Beth holding a fire poker. She'd obviously hit the professor with it.

"Ruby, grab the gun," Beth yelled as the professor bolted from the floor.

As I ran to retrieve it, the professor lunged at Mark, and Beth tried to stop her again with the poker. The two wrestled, their movements jerky and erratic, and I saw Mark's chair tip over and land beside the fire. He was still bound to the chair, and his screams—sharp, screeching wails—told me the fire had begun singeing his skin.

I grabbed the gun and prepared to shoot but Professor Barnard was already on the floor—Beth had whacked her again with the poker—and I stood above her, ready to pull the trigger. Meanwhile, Beth pulled Mark's chair from the fire and began slapping at the flames on his face and hair and chest with the napkin that had been in his mouth.

"Mark," Beth yelled, once she'd patted away all the flames. "Where are your keys?"

Professor Barnard let out a cackle then, even though she lay perfectly still on the floor. "Go ahead and look," she said. "You won't find them."

"Then we'll call 911," I said. "Mark, do you have your cell phone?"

Mark motioned to his pants pocket, the lining still visible via the exposed crotch of his pants. Beth pulled the phone out and read the words on the screen. NO SERVICE.

"Don't you remember?" the professor said. "No cell towers for miles. You've all spent enough time at this cabin to know that."

"Then let's start walking," Beth said. "We'll tie her up until the police get here."

"We can't expect Mark to walk to the main road in his condition," I argued.

"But he can't stay here," Beth countered. "He'll kill her."

"Ruby can stay," Mark muttered through his burnt lips.

"I'm not leaving Ruby here alone," she barked. "The three of us go. That's final."

"I'll tie her up," I offered, giving Beth the gun. I wanted it out of my hands.

After I tied Professor Barnard's hands to the daybed, Beth and I untied Mark and pulled him up from the floor. It was hard to tell how much tissue damage had occurred, but he moved past us with a sudden burst of energy, as if to deny he'd even been hurt. Beth and I followed him a few steps before turning to look back at Professor Barnard. She should have looked vulnerable there in the dark, on the cold cabin floor. But she didn't.

She looked peaceful, as if everything were right with the world.

I checked Mark's phone every couple of yards, so I could call the police as soon as I got service. It was a slow, dark walk to the main road. Fortunately, the display screen from Mark's phone allowed us a small amount of light, which I cast on the gravel road from time to time to ascertain whether we had drifted off course into the woods.

We walked in silence for what seemed like a long time until the road glowed in the dark, as if the moon had moved directly above us, lighting our path. We heard the stir of gravel next, and saw headlights appear in the distance. A moment later, we saw the flash of red and blue lights flicker above the car.

The police car stopped before us, and at first, I saw only black figures emerge, my eyes blinded by the lights. One of the cops— the thinner of the two—barked orders into the radio, and the other, a large ball of a man, approached us. Soon I made out his trench coat and mustache. It was Detective Pickens.

"Where's Barnard?" he asked.

I pointed behind me. "Back at the cabin. Tied to the bed."

The other police officer talked into the radio again while Detective Pickens moved closer. "Is anyone injured?" he asked.

I gestured to Mark.

The detective's eyes shot in his direction and opened wide with alarm.

"Send *two* ambulances," he shouted to his partner, before rushing to Beth's side. "Have you been shot?" he asked her.

Beth shook her head no, but soon, her eyes followed to where the detective's had been. And my gaze, in turn, followed to see the crotch and thighs of her pajama pants stained in a bright red blood.

Beth touched the red, as if she didn't believe it was there, then brought her shaky hands up to inspect the evidence on her fingers. She collapsed then, falling into the detective's arms.

"She's pregnant," I blurted.

And that's when Mark dropped to his knees.

Chapter 19

Upon arriving by ambulance at Kenosha General, Beth and Mark were whisked away to more intensive areas of the hospital, while I ended up in an ER room with only partitioned curtains. Under my mother's watchful eye—she'd announced she was a certified RN the moment she arrived—the nurses checked my blood pressure, heart rate, breathing, and reflexes. In the end, I was treated for a mild case of dehydration and given an antibacterial cream for my scraped cheek.

Throughout the examination, Mom ran her palm over the top of my head, smoothing the curls on my forehead like she did when I was a kid. She asked, over and over again, if I was okay, never broaching the subject of Mark or my relationship with him, or how little I'd told her about what had happened at Tarble, the events that led me to be abducted by Professor Barnard. It was simply understood we would tackle these subjects when the time was right.

It was a quarter to midnight by the time Detective Pickens pushed open the curtain. His expression was stiff, but his eyes were soft. He brought my purse. They'd found it hidden in the cabin.

"How's Beth?" I asked.

"Stable."

"And the baby?"

"There's a heartbeat, though considering the bleeding, it's a threatened miscarriage." He paused. "Suter will undergo skin grafting soon. Most of his burns are second-degree, but some areas are third."

"What about Barnard?" I asked. "Is she in custody?"

He grimaced. "Not yet. We found on the cabin floor the rope you used to tie her up. She must have taken off in Mark's car. We searched the cabin, though, and took evidence. A team is out looking for her. She'll turn up. The most important thing is that you and Beth are safe."

"How did you find us?"

The detective took a seat then in the small chair by the bed, the one my mother had refused to sit in, preferring to stand by my side. "First of all," he said, "I want to apologize for not responding to your concerns immediately." His fat fingers danced in front of him, acting out his feelings, what was missing in the emotionless void of his brusque voice. "We wasted our time on Grenshaw when we should have been focusing on Barnard."

"But how could you have known it was her? I certainly didn't, not until it was too late."

"We could have, had I followed through."

"What do you mean?"

He repositioned his large body in the small chair and threw a glance at my mom. "The book belonged to Barnard, not Beth."

I stared back at him in confusion. "*A Room of One's Own?*"

"It wasn't Beth's handwriting," he explained. "The name and phone number inside the front cover and those notes in the margin? About Cassie's Cabin? Beth didn't write any of that. I didn't find that out until I showed it to Janice earlier today."

I tried to make sense of the detective's news. "So Barnard put the book inside Beth's suitcase? Before she checked it?"

"Before, or it could have been after, when she brought it to you."

"Brought it?" I choked on the words. "To me?"

"Barnard was the delivery woman, the one who dropped the suitcase off at your house. It wasn't a legitimate service, Ruby. And I would have found that out sooner had I followed through with a phone call to the airline. Beth's luggage was never lost. Barnard simply retrieved it after her travels, then brought it to you."

My mind traveled back to that evening over a week ago, to the woman in the brown shirt and culottes, her ponytail pulled through the back of her hat, the East Coast accent. A chill cascaded over me then like a cold rain.

"She planted the book inside the suitcase," I said. "And the postcard about Reunion. She wanted me to come back to Tarble."

I wondered what else Virginia Barnard had orchestrated over the weekend. Had she designed the lesson and essay about

Sara Teasdale's poem specifically for me? Had it all been part of her plan? She wanted me to bring Mark to justice, to take over where Beth had left off. And I'd fallen into her trap.

"But how did you figure out *she* was the delivery woman?" I asked.

"Let me backtrack a bit. When we realized Beth might not have flown to Pittsburgh, I ordered a team to start looking through the Genereal Mitchell Airport security tapes from the day Beth disappeared. The Pittsburgh PD had already looked at the PIT tapes, but we had no reason to watch the ones from the Milwaukee airport, not until the Grenshaw case fell apart."

"Did they see Barnard on the tapes?"

"Yes, though initially, we didn't know who she was. She was wearing another disguise."

"She was pretending to be Meryl," I explained. "That's who Beth thought she was."

He nodded. "And then she doctored up her appearance to look younger, more like Beth so she could fly to Pittsburgh in her place. We're not entirely sure where she kept Beth during that time."

"Her car," I offered. "Beth told me she felt really drowsy all of a sudden and fell asleep in Meryl's—Virginia's—car. When Beth woke up again, she was in the cabin."

The detective pulled a pen from his breast pocket and made a note. "Barnard must have drugged Beth pretty heavily then, considering she flew to Pennsylvania and back again. At any rate, watching the tapes verified Beth willingly walked away with this unidentified woman. Meanwhile, I was with the tech team, trying to pinpoint an origin for the suicide note Janice received in her e-mail. It was a new account, created just that day. It took some time, but we tracked it to a computer on the Tarble campus."

"But you said the e-mail, the suicide note, was dated the day Beth disappeared," I said. "How did Barnard manipulate the time?"

"Simple. She reset the time and date on the computer she was using. The e-mail she sent entered Janice's in-box under the time and date of the source computer, and not the receiving one. Janice just assumed it had been stuck in cyber space. Truth is, Barnard sent it just minutes before Janice received it."

"She knew about the woman on the plane," I explained. "She was trying to throw your investigation off track."

"And soon after that, your mother called, saying she hadn't heard from you. She'd tried calling but couldn't get ahold of you."

"I just knew something was wrong," Mom added, breaking her silence.

"Then I went over everything you'd told me about Mark Suter and that book," the detective continued. "And once Janice insisted it wasn't Beth's handwriting in the book, I checked the number on the business card from the delivery service, which I eventually traced to Barnard. By the time I got to Tarble, it was too late. She was nowhere to be found, and neither were you. Neither was Mark Suter. But I did speak to your friend Heidi. She filled me in about a few things."

"I didn't tell her everything," I said with remorse. "There was a lot she didn't know."

"She knew enough. We found you, didn't we?"

"But how did you know to come to the cabin?"

"The notation in the book, *Cassie's Cabin*. Meryl Suter told me where it was," he said. "Look, for the record, I rarely admit I'm wrong. And I was wrong. If I had listened to you, I could have saved you, your mother, Beth, and her family a lot of pain and suffering. If I could go back and do things differently, I would. But I can't." He stood then and took my hand in his, covering it with his other. "I'm sorry, Ruby."

It was the first time he'd ever called me by my first name.

"What if you don't find Barnard?" I asked.

"We will."

"I don't know. She's . . ." I paused. After learning she'd not only tricked Beth into thinking she was Meryl, but also me into thinking she was a delivery woman, I couldn't find the right word to describe her. No wonder she'd looked familiar. After all, I'd unknowingly seen her twice before that, the first time at Café Du Monde.

"Cunning?" the detective offered.

"Resourceful," I said.

The detective nodded. "Do me a favor," he said. "Check your purse. Make sure everything's there. Barnard may have stolen a credit card."

"It doesn't look like anyone's been in here," I said, after unzipping it. My wallet was there. Driver's license, credit card, library card, cell phone. Twenty bucks cash.

"Anything missing?" he asked.

I shook my head as I checked the side pockets. One was empty but the other still held the photo of Beth and Mark. "I have a confession to make," I told the detective. "I took this from Beth's bedroom."

"You can return it to her," he said.

I studied the picture like I had the day I found it; but this time, my eyes zeroed in on the woman in the background, the one wearing the wide-brimmed hat and draped scarf, the one I'd initially taken to be a stage performer.

"It's her." I tapped the picture. "Barnard. In the background."

The detective snatched the photo to inspect it. "*That's* her?"

I remembered the photo of Sara Teasdale tacked to the corkboard in Professor's Barnard's office, the wide brim hat and scarf.

"I better take this with me," the detective said.

Too dumbfounded to speak, I closed my eyes as an epiphany bubbled up inside me and prepared to explode. And I willed the police to find Professor Barnard, wherever she was hiding.

She had some explaining to do.

An hour later, Mom stepped out to see if I could be released, and I fell asleep. I had the miniature television on, but the volume was so low, it might as well have been off. And I shut my eyes for a moment, lulled by the inaudible television noise, the sound of a cart rolling, the beeping of a machine.

When I heard the curtain slide, I opened my eyes to a new shift nurse in off-pink scrubs—more salmon colored than those of the other staff—and large tortoiseshell glasses. Her blond hair, flat and dull, was pulled back into a tight bun, which minimized her forehead wrinkles and made her look ten years younger. Despite her disguise—apparently one clever enough to fool the police officers in the waiting room—I recognized Virginia Barnard by the browns of her eyes. And I immediately pawed at my white blanket, searching for the power cord with the important buttons, especially the one that alerts the nurses' station in an emergency. But it was buried in the folds.

"Please. Don't. I'm not going to hurt you," she said.

I finally found the button under another blanket crease and rested my finger on the switch like the trigger of a gun. "Then why are you here?"

"To check on you. Both of you." She sighed. "I hope Beth doesn't lose the baby."

I was surprised she knew about Beth's threatened miscarriage. "Did you go see her?"

"No, but the nurses talk. They also said Mark lost a lot of skin. He may be permanently disfigured. That's so unfortunate." She smirked. "He was so handsome."

"There's no way you're getting out of here a free woman," I said.

"I'll take my chances."

"All I have to do is press this button."

"But you won't," she said, removing the phony glasses as she neared me.

I held the power cord tighter, took a deep breath, and said, "It was you."

"Yes," she said. "I brought you the suitcase. Just like seeing Mark at the café, it was all a matter of fate. I looked down at Beth's suitcase and there you were—your name and address on the tag—begging me to find you, to inspire you to come back. And so I put the postcard and book in there for you. It was my sister's copy."

It made sense to me then. Jenny Barnard had written *Like*

Cassie's Cabin in the margin. It was her affection for Mark I had sensed from the notation, not Beth's. I remembered my discussion with Mark that afternoon in the coffee shop. He'd drawn a comparison between his mother's cabin and Woolf's book. Had he stolen the idea from Jenny, or had she gotten it from him?

"I'm not talking about the suitcase," I said. "I'm talking about Virginia Woolf and Charlotte Perkins Gilman in New Orleans, and Sylvia Plath here on the beach."

She shook her head. "I never pretended to be Plath."

"Don't lie to me. You were on campus for the English Department interviews then. You said my name. It was you."

"Yes, it was me on the beach. But I wasn't pretending to be Plath, Ruby. I was just dressed as myself that night. I said your name because I wanted to talk to you."

"But I thought . . ." I recalled the 1950s-style clothing the professor had worn all weekend and considered the woman on the beach, her camel-colored peacoat and blond hair. Could it have been Professor Barnard I saw? Had I morphed her into being Plath because I'd been predisposed to do so?

"But Woolf and Gilman?" I argued. "That was you, right?"

She nodded. "You have to understand, when I saw you in the café, so young and innocent, I saw my sister twenty-some years ago. And I vowed to remove Mark from your life as soon as possible. I knew his mother had been schizophrenic. He'd told my sister. It was in her diary. And when I read your thesis notes, it all became clear to me how to save you."

My mouth hung open. "*You* stole my notes?"

"Yes. I knew you would end up telling Mark about your visions—you'd been so open and honest with him in the café when you talked about your father—and I knew he would be reminded of his mother. He would either lose interest in you or love you more, but I gambled on it being the former. He was going to break your heart eventually, I just expedited the process."

"But you made me think I was going crazy," I said. "You were more concerned with removing Mark from my life than you were about my sanity. You thought you were saving me from your sister's fate, but you helped drive me to it."

"I'm sorry, Ruby. I never meant to hurt you. In my mind, I was also haunting Mark, trying to remind him of what he'd done to my sister."

I stared back at the professor. Anger throbbed through my veins. But another feeling soon overtook it. Relief. Everything that had happened —Woolf, Gilman, and Plath, those haunting visions of dead women writers—were nothing but this insane woman's plot to toy with my life.

I wasn't crazy after all.

The professor's hand went to her heart. "I made up for it, didn't I? I brought you back to Tarble. I forced you to face your past, to confront Mark. I resurrected you from the dead." She reached behind her back. "Look, I don't have much time. Either you're going to press that button or a real nurse is going to push back this curtain."

I stiffened, wondering if she was armed. But she didn't pull out a weapon.

"This is for you," she said, handing me a leather-bound notebook, similar to the one Mark had given me in New Orleans.

I held the book in my hands but didn't open it. Instead I ran a finger along the paper edge. "What is it?"

"Jenny's diary. I want you and Beth to read it, so you under-stand."

I glared at her.

"You can pretend to be angry, Ruby," she said. "But I know how you really feel about me. When it comes to showing our feelings, it is what we do, not what we say, that matters. And you proved everything to me tonight when you tied me to the bed. You left the knot loose."

"I didn't," I argued. "It was tight."

"Was it?"

I thought back to earlier that night, when I bound Profes-sor Barnard's wrists to the bed. By the time the police arrived at the cabin, she had gotten herself free. It was impossible, I thought, that I had wanted Virginia Barnard to get away, that I had helped her escape. But then again, maybe I had.

Because after she left, I waited a good long minute before pushing the call button.

Epilogue

One Year Later

The only thing I miss about the Midwest are the autumnal colors. Come fall, the trees do not change color in New Orleans, but it's also eighty degrees, and I spend most of my afternoons outside—perusing the French Market, reading in Jackson Square, writing at the café in Pirates Alley. The splendor of the Quarter is literally at my doorstep, since Mom and I started renting an apartment above an antiques shop, just two blocks from St. Louis Cathedral. Mom has her eye on a ranch in the suburbs, though, and when she buys it, the apartment will be all mine.

It didn't take us long to adjust to living here again. In fact, it's as if we never left. The unexpected news from the New Orleans Police Department played a hand in that. Almost three years after my father's hit-and-run, they finally pinned down who was driving the car that night. It turned out to be a sixteen-year-old girl, driving her parents' car just one week after she'd gotten her driver's license. Wracked with the guilt for so long, she turned herself in, and with her to blame, I could no longer fault myself for my father's death. But the funny thing is, I can't hate her. I want to, but I can't. Because if I learned anything from the ordeal a year ago, it's this: anger cannot bring my father back.

Now that we are back home, Mom and I have started some new rituals; like every Sunday morning, we walk to Café Du Monde for breakfast. But this morning in mid-October, I am alone. Mom flew back to Chicago for the closing of our house in Oak Park, and though I offered to accompany her, she refused, saying I shouldn't miss school. And she's right. I'm taking an overload this semester at the University of New Orleans to complete my degree. I can't afford to miss a day if I want to start an M.F.A. in creative writing next year.

The café is bustling as usual this morning, but I snatch a recently emptied table in the back. The waiter has yet to bus it, but I know he'll be by shortly. In the meantime, I decide to look through the stack of mail I've collected since Mom left. I was never good about opening mail in a timely fashion. And that's too bad, I realize, because it's brimming with good stuff.

After weeding out the flyers and advertisements, I see my very first paycheck from the *Times-Picayune*, seventy-five bucks for a freelance article on last month's Seafood Festival. It's a start, I think, and I remind myself to send Craig Hewitt an e-mail to let him know the good news. Although my former boss and I flirted a bit after I returned from my weekend at Tarble, it never amounted to anything serious. Fresh from the whole ordeal, I wasn't ready to date anyone then. And although I'm still not dating anyone now, I feel ready to meet the right person. I'll know when it's the right person this time around. Gwen and I agreed on that at our last session.

Behind the paycheck, I find a postcard from Tarble College, announcing the school's first annual Homecoming later this month. Despite protests, the Tarble board of trustees voted unanimously for coeducation, and Homecoming would replace the annual Reunion festivities this year. I smiled when I saw what Heidi wrote on the back of the card: "I know you can't make it, but see you in NOLA for Thanksgiving!"

Coeducation was not the only change to occur at Tarble College. Mark was no longer on the faculty. I'd followed through with charges against him, not for sexual misconduct but for plagiarism. Julie and Madeline had done the same. I eventually spoke to Tina Beyers, but Professor Barnard's assumptions about her had been off base. Yes, she had been in Mark's class, and yes, she had dropped out of Tarble, but the two factors were unrelated. Regardless, in response to our claims, and the unveiling of his many relationships with his students, President Monroe was prepared to fire him, but he resigned.

I'm not angry with Mark anymore. I've let go, because after some reflection, I realized he was equally haunted by the past. Growing up without a father but with a schizophrenic mother had shaped Mark—his beliefs, his values, his attitudes toward women. Obviously, he loved his mother. He spoke so affectionately about her that day in the café. And he was attracted to women like her—creative, emotional, passionate women. But he also resented her for having those very qualities. He was conflicted, and that juxtaposition of feelings played out in his relationships. That is why he could be so understanding yet so condescending. For as much as he loved his mother, he wanted to punish her. I understand this now. It doesn't help to be angry anyway. After all, he's already been punished for his wrong-doings. Thanks to the flames that marred his face and neck, Professor Barnard got her wish. That night in the cabin, she'd wanted to take away Mark's power. And though he still had his manhood, his disarming good looks were forever gone.

Of course, Virginia Barnard was no longer teaching at Tarble either. She was charged with abduction and falsifying informa-tion, although she didn't go to jail. Instead she was sent to live in a Louisiana state mental health facility just north of Baton Rouge, only an hour's drive from me now, which sometimes gives me pause. Fifteen minutes after I pushed that call button to the nurses' station, the Kenosha police captured Barnard in Mark's car in front of a Burger King six miles west of the hospital. Found to be unfit for trial, Wisconsin officials even-tually relocated her to the facility in Louisiana, where nearby relatives could oversee her care. Despite everything that hap-pened, Beth and I agreed the facility was the best place for her, not prison, and the judge took our perspectives into account when making the decision. In the end, neither of us could hold her in contempt. Although we could never condone her actions, we understood them.

We read her sister Jenny's diary, after all, the one she'd kept over twenty years ago, when she was a freshman at Tulane. It detailed every emotion of her breakup with Mark, from why she fell in love with him in the first place—it was his blue eyes, she said—to her guilt about aborting the baby. Eerily, it had all happened in December, the same month I'd overdosed on the sleeping pills many years later. And in every entry, in every word, I saw a piece of myself.

I could have written that diary.

Jenny's diary was cathartic in another way too. It served as the springboard for the discussion I'd been meaning to have with my mom since I dropped out of school. I ended up telling her everything—about Mark and New Orleans and visiting Dad at the cemetery—all the things I swore I'd never tell her. And even after she heard it all, even after she found out I'd had an affair with my married professor, there was not a speck of brown in the green of her eyes.

The waiter interrupts my thoughts to clear the table and take my order, and I ask him for a café au lait and an order of beignets before I go on to the next piece of mail in my stack, a thank-you note from Beth Richards for the baby gift I recently sent. She didn't miscarry after all, and in May, she gave birth to a darling girl—Renee, which means "reborn" —with fine blond hair, a button nose, and petal-like lips the color of a rose. I know Janice Richards was beside Beth as she gave birth, holding her hand with every push, unspeakably gracious for the miracle of outcomes: her daughter alive and a granddaughter too. So far, and much to Beth's satisfaction, the baby looks nothing like Mark. He will, however, be a part of his daughter's life. Beth is allowing him visitation rights because she realized that having a father—even an imperfect one—was better than not having one at all. And Mark will have plenty of time to see his daughter on weekends, since he and Meryl divorced in the spring.

I look at the photo of baby Renee that Beth included in her card—the baby is now five months old and cutting a tooth—and marvel at the fragility of human life. Had Virginia Barnard not kidnapped Beth, she would have boarded that plane to Pittsburgh, and under the cover of attending the photography workshop, aborted the baby now smiling back at me.

Little girl, you owe your life to a crazy woman, I think.

Then again, so do I.

True, what Professor Barnard did—pretending to be the ghosts of dead women writers—played a key role in my suicide attempt. But she wasn't entirely to blame. Mark played his part too, and ultimately, so did I. In the end, I chose to swallow the pills. It was my insecurity, my desperate need to be loved, to fill the void my father left when he died, that brought me to that point, not the visions of Woolf and Gilman and Plath.

But when it came to picking up the pieces of my life, I have to credit Professor Barnard. Had she not brought the luggage to my house, had she not put the book and Reunion postcard inside, I never would have returned to Tarble. Because of her, I confronted Mark, confronted the pain, confronted my past, and in doing so, finally embraced my future. I often reflect on the story the professor told us in the cabin about her sister. Not of Jenny's suicide, but of their deep bond of sisterhood. I never had a sister, but I imagine if I had, she would have gone to the ends of the earth to protect me. There would be no bounds to her love. And so I've come to see Professor Barnard in another light. Because truth is, she came into my life softly and unexpectedly and briefly, but inspired a metamorphosis. She changed me, altered the course of my life.

She was, as her sister Jenny so whimsically put it, my *butterfly sister.*

The waiter brings me my coffee and beignets then, and I set the mail down to savor them.

I finish my café au lait but take the other two beignets with me in a paper sack. *For Dad,* I think, deciding it's the perfect day to ride out to the cemetery. I leave the café and cut through Jackson Square on my way to the streetcar stop on Canal. The resident artists are already set up for the day on the slate walkway, their easels easily visible, their work propped against the wrought-iron fence.

"Excuse me," a man says, interrupting my thoughts. "Are you setting up here?"

I turn to see a man—late twenties, I guess—holding an easel. His fingers and shirt are stained with paint, but he's clean-shaven and sports a boyish haircut. His eyes, a patina green, mesmerize me to the point that I lose my voice.

"I'm not an artist," I finally say.

"Everyone's an artist," he replies.

"That's true. But I'm not setting up here," I add, gesturing to his easel. "Please."

I step back as he sets the easel down and begins pulling his paintings for sale from a large portfolio sleeve. They're the most beautiful I've ever seen and genuinely New Orleans. One is a courtyard, eerily foggy. Another is Royal Street, the pink and greens so vibrant, so true to life.

"They're stunning," I tell him.

"Thanks." He bows his head, as if suddenly shy. "But it's just a hobby. Extra income. I'm in my last year of law school at Loyola."

I continue to look at his paintings as he sets them out. And the last one stuns me. It's of a man under a green umbrella tent, holding his small daughter's hand. In her other hand is an orange—partially unpeeled. It's titled *Sunday Morning at the French Market.*

"I want this one," I say. "I have to have it. How much?"

He studies me and smiles. "It's yours. Take it."

"I can't, not without paying you something for it."

"Well, what's that in your hand?" he asks.

I look down at the paper bag from Café Du Monde, the two beignets I had planned to take to my father's tomb. "Leftovers," I say. "From breakfast."

He rubs his belly. "It just so happens I didn't eat breakfast. Even swap?"

"I kind of promised them to someone else," I tell him.

He winces. "Your boyfriend?"

"I don't have a boyfriend."

He pretends to wipe a bead of sweat from his forehead in mock relief. "Well, if that's the case, then, hi, I'm Julian," he says, his voice buoyant as he holds out his hand.

I grin when I hear my father's uncommon first name and accept his handshake, telling him I'm Ruby. He smiles back, earnestly. And we look into each other's eyes longer, deeper than most people do when they first meet.

"Julian," I finally say, still holding his hand. "Well, if that's the case, then these are for you after all." I hand him the bag.

"Are you sure?" he asks.

I study him and his painting of the father and daughter and the orange.

"I guess there's no way to be sure," I say. "But I've got a good feeling about it."

Dear Jenny,

My dear sister, I can't write fast enough, afraid one of the nurses will discover this pen and yank the lifeline from my hand. The pen belongs to Claudia, the only decent person working here, and I wouldn't want her to lose her job for being so careless with her belongings. It's not like I could harm myself or others with a pen, or MacGyver my escape using one. Or maybe I could . . .

Right now, it doesn't matter. I am writing again. In addition to the pen, I also stole two sheets of paper from Claudia's yellow steno pad, and have folded them in such a way to resemble a journal, securing the binding with a piece of string I pulled from the rug in the group therapy room. It will have to do.

If Claudia ever finds out what I did, I will just tell her why. I did it for her. The only way for me to think well—thanks to the medications they give me—is to write. And I have to think this out clearly and carefully, have to plan how and when and where all of this will happen. Because Dr. Berger must be stopped. In addition to Claudia, I am certain he is sleeping with two other nurses at this facility. I can tell, just by the way they try so hard not to look at him, the way he strokes their fingers when they hand him a file. He's going to hurt them, all of them, especially Claudia. I can tell by the way she follows him with her eyes, even long after he's left the room, that she's in over her head. I sense she's never been in love before. He is her first. And the first, well, we know all too well it can be devastating beyond repair. That is why I can no longer sit idly by. I cannot let her relinquish her life to him. I cannot let her become yet another foolish statistic.

I've decided to help her.

About the author

About the book

Insights,
Interviews
& More . . .

Meet Amy Gail Hansen

Melissa Citarelli

Born in the Chicago suburbs, Amy Gail Hansen spent her early childhood near New Orleans. She holds a BA in English from Carthage College in Kenosha, Wisconsin. A former English teacher, she works as a freelance writer and journalist in suburban Chicago, where she lives with her husband and three children. *The Butterfly Sister* is her debut novel.

About the book

FOR ME, STORY IDEAS have always come unexpectedly and organically from real life experiences, and the origin of *The Butterfly Sister* is no exception.

In 2004 my husband and I went on our honeymoon to Italy. Moments before I checked my luggage, I realized the tag on my suitcase bore someone else's name and address. That's because I'd lent it five years prior to a college acquaintance and hadn't used it since. Removing her leather tag at the last minute and replacing it with one of those flimsy paper ones the airlines give out, I thought, *What if my bag had gotten lost? Would it have gone to her instead of me? And isn't that a good idea for a story?*

Once home from my trip, I hung the tag off the ironwork base of my bedside lamp as a reminder of my *great story idea*. It sat there two years collecting dust before another layer of the story revealed itself to me at a local writers' group meeting. I went only once to this particular group—it wasn't a good fit— but the single experience provided me with my story's setting. That night a woman read a heartfelt poem about her alma mater, Wells College, a women's college that had recently adopted coeducation. It had been a decade or more since the woman graduated, but she was obviously devastated by the change. She cried when she read the poem. Her passion on the subject enchanted me and later, on my drive home, I decided to set my "suitcase story" at a women's college on the brink of going co-ed. And suddenly, but slowly, the story unfolded like petals of a flower.

As I considered women's colleges and ▶

the reasons why girls attend them, I reflected on my own school experiences. Although I was an excellent student—I graduated magna cum laude—there was one thing that sometimes distracted me from my studies: boys. Romantic relationships, whether full-fledged or fleeting, often occupied my mind instead of schoolwork. I suppose that's true for most heterosexual young women, but I wondered if students at an all-female institution had an advantage in this regard. With boys out of the academic equation, could they be more serious? More studious? More successful? Of course, my novel took a different route—because I love irony. It would be ironic for a girl to date her male professor at a women's college, a place where the opposite sex was not supposed to infiltrate her studies. Thus, Mark Suter was born.

Despite having these story elements sketched, I still didn't start writing the novel. So what did it? What tipped me off the edge of the blank page? What bridged the gap between thinking about writing a book and actually doing it? Two things: a book club and my son, Andrew. In early fall 2006, two good friends and I started a book club. Our first book pick was a popular title at the time because a movie version of the novel had just been released. It was a good book and a good read, but I remember reading the last page and thinking, *I could have written this book.* I know that sounds pompous, but I meant it in a very pragmatic way. Up to that point, I had not produced a full-length novel—only short stories—but I realized, after reading this particular book, that I was capable of the feat. I also remember looking at my son, Andrew, who was nine months old then, and imagining him a grown man one day. "My mom always talked about writing a novel, but she never did it," I pictured him saying. Those two things—knowing I could produce a readable story and not wanting to someday disappoint my son—made me finally sit down and start writing this novel.

Five years, two more kids, and countless drafts later, I completed the version of the novel with which I landed an agent, Elisabeth Weed of Weed Literary, who sold the book to Carrie Feron, my editor at William Morrow. Under the guidance and keen eye of both of these women, I pushed the plot and characters of this book to a level I didn't think possible when I started writing it.

Looking back, I marvel that all of this—a published novel and the promise of a career writing fiction—started with a little luggage tag and a big imagination. ᖇᐣ

Author Q & A

Many writers do not successfully publish their first attempt at a novel. Is The Butterfly Sister *your first novel, or is that tucked away in a desk drawer somewhere?*

It's both. At its core, *The Butterfly Sister* is the book I started writing in the fall of 2006, but it's also a very different book, thanks to many drafts and revisions. I still have the very first version I finished in the spring of 2008. It's a bloated manuscript of 480 pages (gulp), but I'll never part with it. To me, it represents a very important stage of my novel-writing experience. At the time, I naïvely thought it was close to perfect and primed for publishing. I even embarrassingly pitched it to literary agents. It wasn't a bad book, but it wasn't my best work. Generally your first attempt at something never is. That's one of the biggest lessons I learned from the process: that good writing requires revision. Seldom does one get it right on the first try.

How much did the book change during the revision process?

A lot. It went from third person to first, names were changed, characters were killed off, and plot lines were cut and twisted. Yet oddly, the main story about a girl who returns to her alma mater to uncover what happened to a missing classmate and, at the same time, rectify her own past remained. And I'm happy to say the very first scene I ever wrote—when Ruby discusses her thesis in Mark's office— is still in the book, even if the details have been modified.

What inspired you to become an author?

My first inspiration to write came from my mother, Gail, an amazingly creative woman and phenomenal storyteller. When she was a child, she wrote a series of stories for kids about a girl named Carol, and she shared these stories with me at a young age. I was mesmerized, not only by the storylines and her illustrations, but by the simple fact that she created them, that they came from her. A supportive and truly dedicated mother, she encouraged me to create as well, and I produced my own set of stories about two girls named Nan and Jan. I know my stories were not as good as hers, but she never let me know it. She praised my efforts, and the seed of creativity was planted. ▶

5

Author Q & A *(continued)*

Much of the story takes place at Tarble, a fictitious private women's college. Did you attend a similar type of school?

No, I never went to an all-girl school. But I always wanted to. As a child, I daydreamed of going off to a private girls' boarding school. It just sounded old-fashioned and proper, a place where I could read and ride horses and do crafts. I did, however, graduate from Carthage College, a private liberal arts school boasting an absolutely gorgeous campus on the shore of Lake Michigan in Kenosha, Wisconsin. Obviously, I based Tarble College on my alma mater. The only all-girl dorm on campus, where I lived my first two years of school, is named Tarble Hall. I considered setting my book in other locales, but I kept coming back to what I knew. I also wanted to pay homage to Carthage, since I went there on a four-year, full-tuition, room-and-board scholarship. I feel forever in debt to the school for the opportunities it gifted me, both academically and socially. Carthage is where I became the person I am today, where I fell in love with literature and creative writing, so I saw it only fitting to place my story at a school both physically and philosophically similar to Carthage.

How much of the novel is autobiographical?

Bits and pieces. I think all fiction is inherently autobiographical, because an author's thoughts and word choices derive from their unique set of life experiences. But I don't think you should put too much of yourself into a work of fiction—it weighs the story down—so I did it in subtle ways, in regards to setting and minor details. For example, I lived in New Orleans for many years as a child and think of it as my second home to Chicago. I hope my love for the Crescent City is apparent in the chapters set there. I also worked as a journalist for a Chicago suburban newspaper and even wrote obituaries for a time (eerily, I got the obit gig a few weeks after I gave the same job to my heroine). I was an English major at Carthage and am a fan of Virginia Woolf, Charlotte Perkins Gilman, and Sylvia Plath. On a sadder note, I also experienced the death of a loved one, my brother, Brian, when I was just sixteen years old. I think these personal details add texture and color to the story, but the rest is all thanks to my vivid imagination.

Was The Butterfly Sister *the original title?*

It was the title of the book when I secured agent representation, and when my agent sold the book to William Morrow, but it was not the original title of the work. It started out as *In Medias Res*, which is a Latin literary term meaning "in the middle of things." Deciding the title sounded too academic and perhaps too foreign, I later used the English translation of the title, but ultimately that was too boring and no longer relevant as the story evolved. *The Butterfly Sister* came to me from a purely business standpoint. I spent a lot of time thinking about titles, which titles worked and which didn't and why. Knowing that women were my target audience for the novel, and how much butterflies and sisterhood seemed to permeate the book and film market, I came up with *The Butterfly Sister* because in the end, it sounded like a book I'd like to read. Fortunately, it also worked with the plot and even influenced it.

Do you plan to write a sequel to The Butterfly Sister*?*

Probably not, because I have lived with these characters far too long. I am currently at work on a second novel, which shares themes with *The Butterfly Sister* but is a very different story. The major difference is that book two's heroine is a good ten years older than Ruby, which reflects my maturity. I essentially created Ruby in my twenties, and now that I am in my thirties, I am writing characters in that demographic. I imagine my characters will always age with me.

What is your best advice for writers who want to publish a novel?

Be patient and be persistent. There are a few exceptions, but most writers did not get where they are overnight. You should write because you want to, because you have to, because if you don't, you'll cease being you. Writing should be like breathing or eating. You should do it every day because it is part of your existence, not because you want to get published. There was a time when all I thought about was getting published, and that was when my writing was its worst. It was contrived. Conversely, my writing improved when I stopped worrying about publication, when I wrote solely to please myself. I wrote the best story I could because I wrote it out of a true desire to create, an innate passion for the art of crafting a story. ᐛ

Reading Group Discussion Questions

1. At the beginning of the novel, Ruby says, "My past was never more than one thought, one breath, one heartbeat away." Later, Professor Barnard calls the past "nature's most underestimated ghost." What role does the past play in the story's plot and the characters' motivation? To what extent does a person's past define who he or she is at any given moment? How does the past dictate the future?

2. Fathers are almost nonexistent in the story, since both Ruby and Beth's dads are deceased. Furthermore, Virginia Barnard's father is portrayed in a negative light. Think about the role a father plays in a child's life, especially in regards to girls. How could a woman's relationship with her father impact her relationships with men?

3. What circumstances could have caused Ruby to fall so quickly and deeply in love with Mark Suter? Do you feel you would have welcomed or resisted his advances?

4. How does the death of Ruby's father impact her characterization? Can the loss of a loved one change who we are? Is the effect always bad, or can it be good? Are those changes irreversible?

5. Ruby's thesis rests on the assertion that madness and creativity are linked. Reflect on creative people. Is there a connection between the two?

6. Ruby's thesis revolves around the Virginia Woolf quote: "A woman must have money and a room of her own if she is to write fiction." What do you think Woolf meant by this? Do her words still hold weight today?

7. Just like many intelligent and successful women, Ruby and Beth are seduced by Mark, thus making an essentially poor decision. Discuss how love can open the door for smart women to make stupid choices when it comes to a partner.

8. After Mark breaks up with Ruby, she tries to take her own life. What part, if any, did he play in her suicide attempt? In your opinion, did she really want to die, or did she just feel like she didn't want to live? Is there a difference?

9. Tarble, a fictitious all-female college in the Midwest, serves as the story's setting. In what ways does this backdrop supplement the novel's plot and themes? How might the educational experience at an all-girl college differ from a co-ed school? Is there still a need for women's colleges today?

10. Feminine depression is a major theme of the story. Is depression the same for both men and women? How might the depression experience be different for a woman versus a man?

11. At Tarble, Tia Clark and the other student protesters carry signs with the phrase *silence is consent.* Is being quiet synonymous with approval? When is it best to speak up, and when is it better to say nothing? ▶

12. Despite what later transpires, Professor Virginia Barnard proves to be an effective mentor for Ruby during her weekend at Tarble. Reflect on your past school experiences. Which teachers made the biggest impact on your academic, social, and emotional growth? How much of a difference can a teacher make on a student, both positively and negatively?

13. While chatting with Ruby, Professor Barnard says "knowledge is power," a quote attributed to English philosopher and author Sir Francis Bacon. Is knowledge power? How does what we know impact what we do?

14. In the cabin, Professor Barnard wants to punish Mark Suter for crimes of the heart. Should he be punished? And if so, how? Do you have any sympathy for him?

15. The relationships between women— mothers and daughters, sisters, and friends—is a recurring theme of the novel. What role does female bonding play in a woman's life?

16. At the end of the novel, Ruby reconsiders the meaning of the term *butterfly sister*. Reflecting on your own life, who might you refer to as a *butterfly sister*? ∞

Don't miss the next book by your favorite author. Sign up now for AuthorTracker by visiting www.AuthorTracker.com.